ROGUE CALAMITY

HAREM SPACE FANTASY ADVENTURE

KIRK MASON

Need to reach me? Email me at: Kirkmasonbooks@gmail.com

PROLOGUE I

"You're finally going to tell me?" Behind the bar, the ginger barmaid gasped, clapping her hands together. It caused her buxom cleavage to jiggle—no mean feat, considering how tight it was tied behind the lines of string.

Violet then passed me another beer from the rack, and twirled her finger around one of her pigtails. The other lay across her shoulder.

"I'm just letting you know," I smiled at her, already knowing the effect the tale was going to have. "I would have done things *very* differently had it happened now."

"Oh Harlen, you were just a kid, you've grown into a," she darted her eyes across my shoulders, "*strong, tall* man since then. I'm not gonna hold anything against ya that you did when you were young, and besides," she leaned over the bar, biting her lower lip. "I'll be right here when the story's over."

Gazing at her cleavage spilling towards me, despite its restraints, I said, "Good, 'cause this is opening up an old wound." Then I took a thoughtful sip of beer.

"Maybe I'll need to tend to it, like I do your other

wounds." She put her finger under my chin, lifting my head to gaze at those bright blue eyes, full of adoration for me.

I don't know why I resisted telling her for so long. She was already dripping for me, and she hadn't even heard it yet.

"Maybe you will."

* * *

"It was nearly ten years ago."

"I can't do it, Harlen!" Savannah frowned, then quickly straightened her face. Her arm hovered over the plain white table, trembling with determination.

I wanted to grab the levitating ornament and throw it against the blank, white, windowless wall, but the golden metal ball would probably just bounce off the metal and land on the bed.

I leaned forward, making two fists. "You're doing it!"

My eyes darted between the floating golden orb and Savannah. Her teeth grit in a *frankly* adorable snarl. A single bead of sweat dripped down her flawless skin before catching in a loose lock of dirty blonde hair, which was tied back in a loose ponytail. The curtains fell to frame her face. Another strand caught in the side of her trembling lip.

Savannah gasped and sat back against her chair, sighing. The ball fell to the table, making a crack sound, then rolled before I picked it up.

She gave off a cute little groan, her nose twitching. "I can't do it. I'm not as devoted as you." *I bit my tongue.* "Show me again, Harlen. I need to see how you do it."

I shook my head. "We don't have to."

But she crossed her arms. "Do it! Please."

With my mind, the golden ornament lifted several

inches from the table. I moved it left, and then I moved it right.

Her mouth formed a perfect o. Like that kid in that movie we had snuck out to watch. In the film, the kid looked at a wooden horse her father had carved, modeled after the one he had comically fallen off herding cattle. It made us laugh—I actually saw her laugh, before the doctrine dug its claws into her.

Every time I tried to breach the subject, Savannah waxed lyrical of how much she wanted it. The excitement had flared through her like lightning at the thought of her hair and eyes changing color, and what it signified.

Why didn't I feel the same? When was I so *gifted* as she said?

She broke my train of thought. "Why can't I do it like that? I've expelled all love and thoughts from myself. I am at peace. I only have a love for Gia!"

My hand fell, the ornament with it.

Savannah got up from the chair and threw herself onto the bed, slamming her face into her pillow. Draped in the plain initiating robes that fell around her body, she looked like a bundle of blankets—the faint shape of her body betraying the material.

"Just... stop stressing about it. It doesn't matter. You know that everyone else must be on your level," I said.

"But it's not good enough!" her muffled voice screamed through the pillows.

My hand raised to touch her. *Where? Her hair? Too personal. Her shoulder?* I reached out and patted her there. Her shoulder untensed at my touch, the fabric of her shirt was soft, her body warm. *Why was it forbidden?*

She sighed and sat up. Her auburn eyes, the dirty blonde hair—it was the only bit of color in this room.

Above her, a pure white shelf ran across the wall. A few books lay neatly there, all presents from me—each one given in secret, she had only recently presented them.

There was a strange limbo between seventeen and eighteen when we could do what we wanted—it was something to do with making the vow for ascension all the more powerful—the knowledge of what one is giving up. Personally, I thought the Head Master was just lenient. He wasn't a bad man. I think he just wanted us to have a bit of fun before we never had it again.

Even bad places have good men.

"Hey," I said simply.

Savannah darted her entire focus to me. My heart swelled, trying to break out of my chest.

"Yeah, Harlen?"

"We're ascending tomorrow. You've passed every test with flying colors." *Color. Ha. Funny word, seeing as Savannah's about to be without any, both inside and out.* "And we're doing it together. We've waited years for this! We got put into the same classes all the way, and we passed everything together! What's more, I'm sure you were the first in your class to work out the levitation. I've read the books, they say that people should only *now* be figuring it out. Some people can't even do it before ascension. You did years ago!"

I didn't mention that she had not progressed much further than that.

Savannah's lips broke into a smile. She inched towards me, only slightly. I recognized that move. She was about to wrap her arms around me into a hug.

But her lips straightened. She sat up straight and smoothed the plain straw-like fabric of her blouse, revealing the shape of her figure again.

The door caught my attention. Its blank rectangular nothingness seemed interesting to me.

Savannah said, more stoically, "We did it. With Gia's Love, we will ascend together."

"Together." The word escaped from me.

I closed my eyes to take a moment to absorb everything.

Ascension with Savannah. Somehow, being with her made it sound good. Even if the rest of the class was there.

"Let's try again." She got up from the bed, leaving me sinking into the mattress. The awful, decade-old springs submerged me to the base of the bed, where the frame dug into my thighs.

My eyes opened to focus on the door again. I remembered seeing a kid's bedroom in a movie—he had a poster on the wall. Savannah had no such thing. We were not permitted, *her* least of all. I suppose I could have gotten away with it. I didn't though, as some kind of solidarity with my friend. I had only convinced her that books were ok because it's a form of study.

What did the masters do with all our personal possessions when they took them? Did they burn them in a fire? It hardly seemed like the Masters to be surrounding a blaze, sparks and destruction reflecting in their cold, dead eyes.

Maybe they donated them to the poor, those who lived below Gia's gargantuan windowless tower.

I doubted it. Gia's Love doesn't extend out those walls.

"Hello? Earth-2 to Harlen, shall we do this?"

"Sure, hold your horses."

"What's a horse?" She slapped her hand over her mouth. "Not that I want to know."

Those movies were all I could think about—I sighed, blissfully remembering the bright lights of the screen like we were there. The cowboys, the space battles. Why couldn't *that* be my life?

"Remember that old film we saw? The thing he rode on?"

"Oh, yeah. The flesh bike," Savannah nodded sagely, her long eyelashes flickering.

I smirked. Savannah looked like a cute cartoon character when she did that. Her head shook and she scowled at me. "Stop trying to distract me! Let's do it."

"Ok, one more time."

The door flung open with such force it slammed against the back of my chair. I leaped up and faced the door, hands together in front of me in the correct pose, back straight, standing to attention—no expression across my face. Even though Savannah stood behind me, I knew she did the same.

The room went cold.

Ruby Knight, the Deputy Master, entered, the door closed behind her.

"One more time at what, *children*?"

Her silver-white hair perfectly framed her face, not a strand out of place, and her pinprick pupils stared deep into me, the silvery-white sea surrounding them like a focus around the dot, squeezing it to scan me for evidence of emotion.

I could imagine *her* before a blaze of fire, laughing maniacally.

Except she didn't laugh. She didn't smile. She was the perfect Subject of Gia.

When the beautiful demon of a woman looked at me, I felt an ant—insignificant, about to be crushed.

I resented that.

"Nothing, *Deputy* Master."

"I was talking to my daughter." Her words were cold and dead, but I could taste the venom. It was a rare gift she had.

"We were practicing!" Savana squeaked in a high pitch cry.

"Again."

Savannah coughed, then said, "We were practicing." This time, nothing—no emotion.

Ruby Knight didn't speak, instead boring her eyes into me.

I stared right back into the void of her gaze, all manner of expletives running through my mind. I hoped she could read it.

Her eyes widened a fraction for a split second. “With each other? Despite it being forbidden to share Gia’s Gift with one another?"

"Sorry, Mother," Savannah blurted out.

"It was my idea," I said, pursing my lips. "I convinced her.”

"Oh, I don't doubt that." Ruby stood beside me. I breathed in. If she weren’t so inarguably beautiful, it would have been easier to be unaffected by her. I had no trouble with the Head Master—a lenient old man.

"Show me," she demanded.

"Mother?"

"Not you. Harlen first."

Thinking that the quicker we got this over with, the faster Ruby would leave us, I spun around and grabbed the white plastic chair. It screeched against the floor, and I sat down and looked at her, waiting for her instruction.

But Ruby was peering across at the books on the shelf. Savannah was trembling.

"Do it." Ruby said, still inspecting the books.

I raised my hand. The golden ornament raised slightly

above the floor, hovering shakily. I shook my hand, to pretend I struggled.

Now Ruby faced us. "I've seen what you can do, Harlen. Now do it properly."

I wish I'd never shown my inert abilities to her mother during our mandated private practice sessions. I didn't know then that I possessed more power than others.

The orb levitated high up from the table. I moved it back and forth, fantasizing about flinging it through Ruby's neck. I'd have loved to, but Savannah would never forgive me.

"Happy?" I snapped.

"Excuse me?" *Flat tone, angry words.*

I shrugged. "Are you happy? I did what you asked."

"Why would that make me happy?"

"You tell me." I stared at her the whole time, the ornament never levitating.

How did she turn out this way? How could a woman so beautiful act like such a monster?

"Take over," she said.

"What?"

"Savannah, take over from him."

Savannah was slouched, fidgeting with her hands. She lifted one, her face scrunching.

"You look like you're trying to suppress a bowel movement. It's no wonder you cannot do it. You are full of emotion."

Savannah straightened her face, going bright red in the cheeks. I held the orb up for her until Ruby snapped at me.

"Arm down, Harlen."

I begrudgingly obeyed.

For a brief moment, Savannah kept the ornament up. Beads of sweat dripped down her temple. Her eyes stared into mine before going wide and rolling back in her head, until only the whites were visible. Her arm shook, and the ornament crashed down onto the table, rolled onto the floor, where it crashed.

She froze, breath rasping.

Her mother bent down to pick up the pieces, placing them on the table.

"If it were up to me, one wouldn't pass with such a poor performance."

Savannah looked down at the thing on the table, eyes going catatonically still.

Ruby walked over to the books on her shelf, taking *Star Crimes: The Adventure* and staring at it. Her billowing robes were almost comical, the way they flared and spread out all over the room, dominating the atmosphere. "If it were up to me. childish books would not be allowed."

"It's not childish," I glared at her. "It's just entertainment. There's nothing wrong with a bit of fun."

"*And* if it were up to me, bad influences would be cast out, no matter how much of their talent exists, despite their insolence."

In a flash, she dropped the book to the bed and thrust her face a few inches from mine.

How did she move so fast?

Pores dripped out speckles of sweat like a toxin. Her eyes, like a lizard, darted back and forth across my face.

I merely froze. Ruby couldn't break me.

But maybe she should?

Maybe she wasn't the problem.

I was.

I closed my eyes, took a deep breath, then smirked.

She took a deep breath too.

I looked her right in the eyes and laughed maniacally from deep in my stomach.

"You should see the look on your face. You look like you're about to pop." I doubled over, acting like I was laughing so hard it hurt.

Ruby ruffled her shirt back down the same way Savannah did, making nauseous butterflies fly up my stomach.

I doubled down on laughing to hide it.

Ruby stepped beside her daughter. "See. He is not like us. Whatever freak nature helps him excel is unnatural, not of Gia. That's why he's able to do it and yet act so insolent. So garish. So..."

My voice went high. "Fun? You need to lighten up."

"What do you think of that, Daughter?"

Savannah glared at me. I gave her a subtle nod. *It's ok, save yourself.*

"I don't think anything. He is as he chooses to be. That is none of my concern." She held her head high.

Silence filled the void. My stomach hardened. Just because I wanted it to happen, didn't mean it wasn't a knife to the back.

Ruby ushered me toward the door. "Harlen, come. Savannah needs time to meditate. She's had enough distractions for today."

She looked at her daughter blankly, and Savannah looked back, putting her hands together in the customary way, and bowed. "Mother."

I was almost proud of her.

"Daughter." She bowed, and then left the room. I followed, not looking at Savannah.

We were like two ants entering the long white hallway. It was featureless except for the pale blue light running a little below the middle, never breaking, never-ending. The light became a black pinprick before the hallway turned, not bright enough to overpower the vast span of the tower.

Savannah's door shut, and the edges disappeared.

"Walk with me," Ruby said.

"Why?" I blurted out. *To be taken to an alleyway and shot?*

She raised her eyebrows momentarily but quickly walked away. Before I knew it, I was gormlessly watching her disappear down the hall.

I followed behind her, but I didn't put my hands together in the customary way. Instead, I just walked like a normal person, like those I had seen all those times I snuck out.

"Where are we going?" I called, catching up to her.

"To your room," she replied.

Her long legs swiftly strode down the hall. I tried to picture what she looked like underneath that ridiculous robe, but I couldn't get a hint of her features.

Never stopped me imagining.

"Why?"

"I don't wish for you to bother her anymore. She needs to focus. She will be taking my role someday, and she cannot do it with you here."

I paused for a moment wondering why she was being honest with me. "I agree," I finally said.

She did not hesitate in her response. "I think perhaps for the first time since you reached adulthood."

Our footsteps echoed in the hallway, cascading into delays of taps.

I said nothing. She broke the silence. "So you won't be down there tonight to receive Gia's Love."

"I won't."

After an eternity, we reached my room. The lines

appeared in the blank wall, forming a door, which opened. Ruby motioned for me to go before her.

My shoulders went tight at the idea of her seeing the mess of my room. A past worry. Irrelevant now. Then my heart raced at the thought of being alone in a room with such a beautiful woman.

But that all shattered when she entered, glanced at the box on my bed I had prepared for my exit, and said, "We should not have taken you in."

"Will that be all?" I blinked at her. I wasn't going to give her the satisfaction, even if she wouldn't show it. *Tell her to fuck off. Do it.*

"Goodbye, Harlen Gray."

"Yeah, see ya."

She left as silently as she had stood outside her daughter's door listening to our conversation.

Crashing onto the bed, I closed my eyes and breathed deeply to release all that pent-up tension. It would've gone over time, but like a toxin, I wanted it rid from me fast.

I dug into the box, looking for it with desperate speed. I saw the black string, slithering out like a snake between a page of the book I had shoved it in.

I shook my head. *No. Screw my parent's wishes. They left a five-year-old kid on his own. They don't get a say.*

Instead, I got up from the bed, and crouched to open the drawer beneath, taking out the immaculately folded robe. I wiped the dust off it, unfolded it, and slipped it on with some effort.

It was too big. It went right over my eyes.

PROLOGUE II

The elevator had the same white walls and pale blue light as the hallways above, like a belt across its lower middle.

My head stayed down, as the plummeting box encasing us rumbled silently, a faint humming betraying the hidden electronics that sent the box down below. The masters would have us believe that Gia's love powers it. Bullshit, obviously—Gia didn't exist.

If she did, she wouldn't have created us with all these emotions, these *needs*, just to have to strive to hide them away, to pretend they don't exist. That is cruel, that is unjust.

That isn't love.

The elevator stopped, and the door appeared and opened. We began to funnel through it like the last grains of sand in an hourglass.

Looking up, the gargantuan temple seemed to go deeper down than even the height of the tower. The light only illuminated so far before turning to black. My vision began to distort and double with dizziness, so I looked back down—all the better to hide my face.

A faint hum in the air sang among the deep blue,

smooth stone-like walls, and it smelt of chalky rock and... a wet, warm kind of smell. Not unpleasant, but strange all the same. Occasionally, there were little rumbles, seeming to come from everywhere. Maybe it was the trains.

The Head Master's elderly voice stole our attention. "Initiates, line up."

I shuffled between my peers, difficult due to my head being down, and accidentally stepped on a few toes before getting into position. Their owners didn't respond.

"Initiates."

The low, neutral voice of the Head Master spoke from up top a wooden stage, out of place amongst the warm stone of the cave.

I could feel the heat through my shoes.

"Today begins the sacred day when you will cast aside the last, gleaming bits of flawed human emotion to accept Gia's Love."

The floor rumbled angrily, causing butterflies to throw up inside me.

"If you have been training every day, as instructed, you will find this process no more bothersome than the touch of a feather."

There were a few gulps, and no floor grumble this time.

"If you have not, it will be... a shock." his elderly voice, stern with its lack of emotion, drove the warning home. "But first, an example of Gia's Gift. As is customary, each student will come to the podium and display their talent." He motioned for the first student from the line to approach. He broke ranks from the line and climbed up the steps onto the stage, then greeted the Head Master with a bow.

The Head Master held out an ornament identical to the one Savannah and I practiced with.

"Begin."

I lifted my head higher for a better look, but darted it back as Ruby Knight's venomous gaze beamed in my general direction.

"Please return to your space."

After his return to the line, the next initiate went. She lifted the ornament no higher than Savannah had done in her room. I didn't need to see them all to know it would be the same for them.

When the initiate next to me left an empty space, a cold fright ran through me, like a blanket being hastily yanked away during the night.

She walked perfectly, back straight, head held high. When she turned from the steps, strands of her dirty blonde hair visibly escaped from her hood—flying across from her panicked breath. Her chest rapidly rose and fell. *Relax girl. You got this.*

“Begin,” the Headmaster said.

She did it.

Savannah returned. I kept my head down. There wasn't any particular reason to hide from her. She expected me to be here.

It wasn’t her I hid from.

"Next initiate."

I didn't move. Instead, I took a long, deep breath of the warm air, then I ripped the hood off. "Nah."

I grinned at the Masters, but mostly at Ruby. Her eyelids flared a microscopic amount. Around me, the other initiates turned in their hoods but quickly returned to staring ahead.

"Initiate. It is time," the Head Master said.

"Nope. Don't feel like it. Sounds like shit." I pulled off my robe with some effort, then dropped it. The heavy fabric landing on the ground echoed up the great tall ceiling.

"Initiate," the Head Master said, still no emotion. "This is not the time."

"Nah, I'm not doing it. It's all just bullshit, isn't it." I laughed, a hearty, childish laugh. "Training all this time just to have some stupid white hair. I'm not even twenty, and you want me to look ancient just so I can make some dumb ornament float, what, a little bit higher? Fuck this." I raised my middle finger at Ruby Knight. "And fuck you most of all, you stuck up bitch."

There was the smallest grab at my shirt, between the tips of two fingers. "Harlen, what are you doing?" Savannah whispered in a short breath.

"What I have to," I whispered back, and stormed away from the line towards the elevator.

My robe was left clumped in a pile on the ground.

A rumble again. Perfect timing. Some of the students gasped. I headed towards the elevator. Strutting in the most unholy way I could, whistling a song I heard in a movie.

"*Don't go.*"

I snapped back around. "Huh?"

It was unnerving, to be stared at wordlessly by a bunch of hooded people.

Savannah's lips peared from her hood. Plump and full, but closed, unreacting.

Ruby cocked her head. "Yes, Harlen? Weren't you leaving?"

My eyebrows furrowed. "Who said that?" *It didn't sound like Savannah, and I hardly had made other friends. Maybe it was her mother, joining in on the ruse.*

But Ruby said, "Nobody spoke. We were waiting for you to leave, so we can continue the initiation."

Awkward.

I headed right back to the elevator, a bead of sweat dripping down my neck and seeping into my clothes.

I thought that I could get new clothes. I could wear whatever I wanted.

Once I got money, of course. I'd have to learn about that too.

* * *

I needed something.

I fell down against the wall of the elevator, rested my head against it, and closed my eyes.

I'll bet she'll end up being able to do all kinds of shit. Gia's backflip? Is that a thing? I smirked. *She'll be happier, at least. Or rather, not unhappy. And I'll be able to do what I want.*

I reached my room, and the cracks shunted apart from the doorframe. It opened for me, and the box lay unassuming on my bed where I left it.

My heart entered my throat—a lump I tried to swallow down. For some reason, I half expected it to be gone.

I approached the box. The black string laid amongst all those books. I pulled at it and let the gold pendant spin in the air, untangling itself.

A quarter-circle, an inch in thickness across and a half across the curve. A little gold wire connected to it, shoddily soldered for the string to loop through. The Masters did not allow jewelry, no matter what age we were. Let alone something so lavish, with its strange green markings engraved across the edge.

A memory flashed in my mind. *Hide it, don't let them see.* Mom must have wanted me to keep something of my own that they couldn't take. I had hidden it under my shirt when I arrived, and then under my bed.

I held it to my chest. My parents gave me the pendant before they left me here. I always hated it—a reminder of their rejection. But Savannah had made me swear to never throw it away. She had even said it in a whisper, lest someone invisible in the room could hear. Probably wise. Who knows how often her mother had listened outside the room.

I no longer hated it. It was the only thing in my life that held any meaning.

I slipped it over my neck and got up.

The silver demon of a woman stood in my doorway, causing my stomach to turn. I grabbed the pendant instinctively, equally clutching at my chest, trying to calm my heart from stopping in fright. *How long had she been there? How did she get up here so fast? I* was the only one in the elevator, there had not been enough time for it to return and bring her back up.

"That was... an interesting trick you pulled." Ruby Knight walked over to me and reached for the ring.

I didn't protest, not seeing the harm in it now she couldn't take it from me.

Ruby stared at it like she had done the books in her daughter's room. "An interesting trinket."

"I'm not sure finding things interesting is allowed." I snapped.

Ruby raised her eyebrows, and her lip flickered. But she let go of the pendant, and it fell back to my chest.

I held it, and my mouth ran. "But I'll tell you what's interesting. The way you got here so fast. How did you do it? Levitate yourself like a ghost? Secret elevator? Fuck it. You'll probably make up some lie." I turned around from her. My blood had begun to boil. "Tell me this. We both know this whole Gia thing is stupid. So, for old times sake, after all these years, What's up with Gia's Love? How does it really work?"

"I don't know."

I snapped back around to face her, holding the pendant tighter in my fist. "Excuse me?"

"I know as much as you. I believe in it, and that allows me to do the things I can do."

I squinted at her. "And what exactly can you do? What's the height of your magic powers?"

Ruby took a step over to my bed and sat down, absent-mindedly tipping the box towards her and looking at the books.

"It's not magic—a genie hasn't given me wishes. I believe in Gia's Love, and as long as I've been here, the beliefs have run true. Expelling emotion makes one receive it better. That was always true, until last year, when I saw what you could do. There's something wrong with you."

I blinked at her again.

She stared at me, a beautiful face devoid of emotion. "You fly in the face of everything we believe in."

I held out my hands. "But how can you not know? Don't you have all the books and stuff?"

"Only the Head Master does. He keeps it locked in a dusty crate in his room, old and worn as he is. When he is gone, all the knowledge he possesses will belong to Savannah and me. I'll share it all with her so she doesn't grow up like I did—in ignorance."

"You'll be kind to her now?"

She sighed. The first emotion I'd manage to wring from her. "She was never the problem. You were."

Ruby flicked through my old possessions. *Would she stay in this room after I left? Exploring the things that kept me sane in my youth. Perhaps I had gotten her wrong.*

I knew one thing for sure—Savannah belonged here, and I belonged as far away as possible.

"Harlen." She picked up a dog-eared science-fiction book. I thought she'd ask about it.

"Yes?"

She kept her gaze on the book's cover. "If you don't believe in it, then how do you explain it?"

My legs shook, the floor fell underneath me. *Ignore it. She's just trying to rattle you.*

I grasped for safety by changing the subject. "If I asked you to say 'goodbye' to her, would you?"

"No," Ruby said softly, flicking open a page.

"Thought not. Well, goodbye then."

"Yes, it is rather good, isn't it?" A flicker of a smile. Then, her eyes darted on me, and either through the sheer force of her will or some other kind of power, my legs threatened to buckle. She seemed so powerful sitting there on the chair, like a demon ready to eat me whole.

But instead of that, through her terrifyingly wide grin, she whispered two words.

"Fuck off."

1

Violet Tucker stood behind the counter of her bar, wiping a dirty mug with a dirtier rag. She then hung it on the tray above us when she finished, where it dripped gray water on the counter.

Meanwhile, I swigged a murky brown beer straight from the bottle.

"And then what happened?" her Cairen-charm accent sang in my ears.

I shrugged. "I fucked off."

Downing the last of the bitter-sweet liquid, I slammed the now lighter bottle down on the counter with greater force than intended.

"Another, Harlen?" She gave a sultry smile.

"Please."

"Glass?" She leaned over the bar towards me on her elbows. The drawstrings of her blouse hugged her breasts tightly together, barely able to contain them, as they fell forward towards me. Two red ponytails rested on either side of her neck, trailing down her shoulders beside her breasts.

My mouth went dry, and my pants became tighter.

Fortunately, I sat on the barstool, so my emerging bulge was hidden.

"My eyes are up here, handsome." Violet stroked her finger under my chin, lifting it to stare at her sparkling eyes, reflecting the dusty old chandeliers above us.

"And what if I want to look down there?" I kept eye contact while her cold hand slid into mine—no, it was a beer.

I took a swig and suppressed a burp.

"What if?" She raised her eyebrows, reminding me all too much of Ruby Knight, making me throb to full hardness.

Unlike Ruby, Violet couldn't help but emanate warmth. It practically *oozed* out of her. She was Ruby's polar opposite, with her need to make me feel good about myself—and boy, I did just by her looking at me, with those pouty red lips, flickering eyes, and every glance I stole of that juicy thick behind, unable to hide under the draping dresses she wore. I couldn't help myself from looking.

The bell on the door behind me rang. My ears perked.

Large.

Hulking.

Not human? Must be an ork. He breathed like he just fought in a battle, and was ready to start another.

Violet's eyes followed the ork. She smiled, but not the way she smiles at me—like he's just another customer.

"What can I get you?" she sang.

"Klargen." He grunted, taking a seat on the other end of the bar.

"One Klargen, coming right up."

I grimaced.

Klargen, a drink adored by orks galaxy-wide. It consisted of the blood of whatever herd animal on that planet, mixed with the most potent alcohol available, usually some kind of rubbing alcohol. This meant that no Klargen was the same, and most of them could kill a human or make them seriously ill.

They did say the real Klargen, from the planet Orkulus, *was* drinkable by humans—they never said it tasted nice, at least not to an ork's face. Even the proverbial *they* wouldn't get in a fight with an ork.

There was a cough at the other end of the room, from the only other guy here—a scruffy animal herder that came often.

I returned to my drink, while Violet grabbed some Klargen from the top of the shelf and began pouring in the thick, maroon liquid. She shook it up to dislodge some of the meat chunks, then reached for a utensil to spoon them out.

"Leave them in," the ork grunted, sitting down at the other end of the bar.

I suppressed another gag, and the smell of putrid vinegar swam down the bar.

He inhaled as if savoring a fine wine. The hulking green ork held the glass up against his tusks and took another sniff.

"Is this real Klargen?"

"Only the realest." Violet beamed, throwing the dirty rag over her shoulder and putting her hands on her hips.

He took a sip, puckered his lips in an overly showy way. Outside, the clopping horses and cheerful townsfolk seemed to quiet down too in anticipation. The ork took another sip, then put the glass down.

I breathed a sigh of relief, and took my hand off my gun.

The ork took another deep, long sip that reminded me of myself with a beer after a long hard *five minutes*. He slammed it down, and it splattered all over the bar, resembling a murder scene.

Violet shot me a glance. *This was not the time to worry about spilled Klargen.*

I hadn't had a good fight in a while, though. I had done such a good job of being the muscle of her *fine* establishment. People in the town knew not to mess with her—most people. But, a large planet with a lot of trade meant not everyone who came here was a local. That's why she hired me.

"Fake," snarled the ork.

I shook my head. *Stupid ork—All Klargen was fake. If he wanted the real stuff, he'd have to find a ship somehow and get to Orkulus.* I shuddered at the thought of a cow-sized spider, with its leathery, flesh-like skin.

Of course ork's herded giant freak spiders.

Violet's voice stayed polite. "I assure you, Sir. This is the finest Klargon this side of Caria." *I loved when she got all fancy like that.*

Right on time, the herder at the other end of the bar spoke in his proud Carian drawl, "I farmed that cow myself. It ain't fake."

"Ha! You admit it!" The ork reached for the hammer on his back.

What could he do with it, with the herder on the other side of the room?

I cocked my gun. "You better think twice about that, friend," I took another sip of beer.

The ork's red eyes twinkled. He grinned at me. At least, I think it was a grin. Then he got up, and the floorboards whined under his lumbering towards the herder.

Hand on my pistol, my chair swiveled when I stood up. The farmer stood up too, to meet him eye-to-eye, or rather, *eye-to-chest*. At least the cowboy hat gave him a few extra inches.

"It's damn near real as any cow I ever milked."

"Not real Klargen—fake," the ork spat, reaching for the hammer on his back again. It had a carved hole burnt around the ridges. The same burns my pistols got when I over-exerted them.

The ork hovered his hand above the handle.

I tutted, cocking my gun. "Sign outside says no guns allowed."

"Then how come you've got one?" The ork kept facing the herder, and his fingers closed around the handle.

I slid over a table and grabbed his forearm before he could draw the weapon. If I played my cards right, nobody would get hurt tonight, and Violet wouldn't be stuck cleaning blood off the floor. Maybe I'd be wiping off something else from her lower back.

My fingers didn't even meet halfway around his arm.

He arched his neck towards me and did that horrific half-grin. My eyes watered from the waft of Klargen and who knows what else from his mouth, coating me in a disgusting mist.

With his other arm, he swung slowly.

I lurched my whole body back, falling into the table, the same one I had leaped over moments ago. I kept rolling over it to land on my feet, hoping Violet saw the whole move as purposeful. Now the ork and I had a table between us.

The cow herder said behind the ork, "Now, fellas. There's no need to fight over this."

Little too late, pal.

The ork thrust his elbow back right into the guy's nose, and I winced at the sickening crack. I'd help him set it after I dealt with the ork currently pulling the hammer off his back.

Nobody could outshoot me, at least in this backwater town.

In a flash, I aimed the gun at his hand and fired. A purple laser shot from the gun and hit the spot between his forefinger and thumb.

"Oww!" He inspected his hand, which hung limp, but he shook it out and made a fist. "Gonna need more than that, meatsack."

I adjusted the setting on my gun from *stun* to what I liked to call *very stun.*

"No guns," he snarled.

I should have shot him there and then. But this was no five-man bar chaotic brawl. A one-on-one had certain expectations. I won the shootout, where I had the advantage. He wanted to bring it more to his favor.

It had been a slow day. Likely after this, a little slower. *I could have a bit of fun.*

The ork casually strolled around the table, like a wolf approaching wounded prey.

My fist socked him in the mouth—slamming right between those yellowed tusks, causing a crack, not from his teeth. Red hot pain seared through my saliva-covered knuckles. I fought back a gag.

The ork grinned again. "Heh. That tickled."

My heart raced. "Alright, back to plan A."

While the great lumbering ork began his windup - how did he hit anything when he was so slow? - I grabbed my pistol from the holster and shot him square in the chest. It burnt through the leather of his armor, right onto the green of his pecs.

"Hey, That's not fair." The hair on his chest burned, tiny lines of black smoke billowing out from the hole in his shirt.

A hand on my gun, snatching it. *Fast. Just playing before. Shit.*

His other hand wrapped all the way around my neck and lifted me off the ground.

Violet screamed. The herder nursed his nose. I saw it from all the way up there like I was on a ferris wheel looking down at the town.

"Still wanna say it's a real Klargen?"

"As real as the stank on your breath," I spat.

The point of my boot connected with his stomach. He fell back against the table, loosening his grip on my neck. I slipped out and rolled over the table behind me.

I had another gun on the other hip.

And a perfect target.

Sliding the dial from *stun*, *very stun*, to my new personal favorite, the newly renamed *kill, or stun a bigger thing*. I held down the trigger, the ample purple light charged up.

The anticipated recoil flung my hand back, sending vibrations of pain through it.

The ork fell flat on his back, causing the bar to shake. Glasses on the rack trembled against themselves.

"Should have paid attention to the rules, friend." I strutted over, the spurs of my boots clicking as the wheels clicked against their holsters.

The ork groaned, his thick eyelids glazed over. "I was just messing."

"And I won't set my gun to stun next time."

Or very stun. Or *kill, or stun a bigger thing.* My pistol was beginning to run out of notches.

I crouched over him, leaning over his face. "You know full-well ain't no Klargen real except the one grown on Orkulus. So what's your problem?"

"Bored." He grinned sheepishly.

My eyes watered from the stench of his breath.

How the hell do you grin after getting hit by two shots? Enough to kill a human.

I shook my head. "Go be bored elsewhere."

Before he could get up, I rummaged through his pockets. Shuddering disgust slivered down my spine like a snake when my hand slid over some bones and bits of meat to find a couple of coins.

"Always gonna pay," he hummed.

He must've been concussed.

I put the coins in my pocket and lifted the ork onto his feet. Even though he towered over me, his suddenly diminished IQ made him like a giant teddy bear—a bear about to fall, he stumbled back and forth.

"You ok?" I held my hands up in case he fell on me, but he clambered towards the exit.

"It was fun. We should do this again sometime," the ork grunted, reached for the door, and fell on his back, cracking his head on the floor.

"Oh shit." *I didn't want him dead. That would have been a whole other thing to deal with.*

"S'all good, my friend." He sat up, revealing a crack in the wood, where one could trip over even on a sober day.

I guessed it *was* all good, but the two blood-covered coins I had swiped from his pocket weren't nearly enough to repair the floor.

The cow herder smirked at me. His nose seems to be not as bad as I thought. He grinned through the dried blood staining the cracks of his teeth.

The ork seemed to have regained some of his equilibrium, and pushed open the bar door, swinging it wide open and heading out into the day. The long, wide dirt path welcomed him. He whistled, heading out into the town.

"Got' damn it," Violet complained.

"It's only a crack," I said, as the door swung shut.

"Only a crack? Look at the state of my bar."

I swung around and gawped. The table the ork fell into had split in two, and on the ground, both planks he'd dropped on had broken.

"Looks like it's time for a renovation, Violet."

"You think I can afford that?" She laughed, shaking her head at me. Her breasts jiggled against the tight strings compacting them. My mouth went dry again.

"Not with what you're paying me," I smiled at her.

She put her hands on her hips and shook her head.

Now the dust settled, adrenaline surged through me, making my heart race and my cheeks flush. It had to go somewhere.

I stepped towards Violet, fire in my eyes. "We ain't likely to get many more customers until later tonight. Let's close up."

"Are you injured?" Her tone was gentle.

"Yeah. Got a crick in my back." I stretched.

"Oh, a crick? Is that even a word?" She walked over and placed her hand between my shoulder blades, rubbing back and forth. I closed my eyes and sighed.

CRACK

"Ow!" Pain shot down my spine.

"How's that crick now? Ya dirty boy."

"Still bad." I rubbed my aching back. "I'm getting in the bath."

Violet shook her head at the herder, smiling as if to say, *'can you believe him.'*

Yet, when I left the bar to climb up the stairs to the bathroom, I heard her say, "We're gonna close early. Drink up, please."

2

A dirty window overlooked the town, framing a line of store roofs. Inside, a desolate sink, where a single bar of soap laid.

Violet sometimes allowed ladies of the night to entertain their gentlemen in the bathroom—if she liked the lady and didn't mind the cut of the man.

After scrubbing the bath clean, I turned on the taps, filling it with water. Fragrant bubbles appeared from the bubble bath liquid I swiped from my *other* employer's private store cupboard.

A knock sounded on the door.

"Harlen?" her honeyed Carian accent sang, a little off-key.

"I'm here."

The doorknob shakily turned.

Violet entered quickly and shut the door behind her. Some of the strings of her blouse were looser, her breasts falling out more towards me.

She closed the distance between us silently and began to undo my top button. Given a close up view of her bosom, I gripped the sides of the nailed-down tub, which dug into my legs.

Another button freed, and another, until there were none left to undo.

"Up," she commanded me like when she tended to my wounds—but I didn't have any to tend to today—none on the outside.

Her soft hands stroked across my pecs, drawing a shiver from me.

"So many scars," she said softly.

Her perfume smelt like Violette sweets, after her name. My entire being swam in her scent, floating dreamily.

She touched another scar, lower on my hip.

I smiled. "That was a big one."

Her finger went over the smooth skin, fixed like it never happened, thanks to her skills at patching me up.

"I thought I lost you that time. You can't keep doing this."

"Huh?" I opened my eyes, staring at her matriarchal presence.

She put her cheek on my face. "One of these days, you'll get cut too deep, and I'll be left holding your body. I can't do it again, Harlen."

"I'm not your kid," I said bluntly. A dangerous path, or perhaps, the right one, to shock us out of this dangerous game we were playing.

"Every time I see you come in through those doors after a job gone half-bad, I feel that same hurt, knowing you barely made it back to me."

"What else am I gonna do with myself?" *Crushing honesty, one that could only be had in a tender moment like this. Damn her.*

"Find someone, start a life somewhere."

"It's a big galaxy, and there's a lot of people. I wouldn't know where to start."

Violet unclipped my belt buckle. I throbbed hard against my pants, prominent bulge impossible to hide.

She cooed. "You could go anywhere, be with anyone, instead of wasting your life on this backwater planet looking after some old broad."

"You ain't that old."

"Yet." She smirked. "Up."

I pushed myself up from the tub, now close to overflowing.

Violet reached around me, holding onto my thigh and stroking right up between my legs. She grazed under my balls, making me groan. Her other hand turned the taps off and then returned to me. At my belt, her nails lightly grazed against my hips, digging into my pants, lightly scratching my groin now. She looked up at me with those beautiful blue eyes and bit her lip.

An unsaid word between us then. But I wanted to be sure.

“This is just for tonight,” I said.

"Oh? Is tonight the only night you'll be hurtin?"

"What do you mean?" But I gulped. Violet had yanked my pants and briefs down in one motion.

"My, my," she said, smiling in satisfaction. "I always wondered."

I looked down at the curvy ginger vixen in shock.

“What?” She grinned. “Just curious.”

As her hand slid up my thighs, goosebumps shuddered over my body. She explored further, her fingers slipping over and squeezing my tightened balls. My rod twitched in delight, a single drop sliding down the head.

"Fuck," I grunted.

"Maybe," she purred.

I reached for her shoulder to untangle the strings of her blouse, but she slapped away my hand.

"Where are your manners, young man?"

I laughed. "I ain't used to girls being like this."

She tutted. "*Girls*? Is that how you address *me*?"

"No, Ma'am."

She stood up and pressed her breasts into my chest, stroking up my back. My hardness pushed up against her stomach.

Violet whispered into my ear, her cool breath making me shudder, "Now get into the tub, young man. You're dirty, and you need a bath."

Her body left mine, and she put her hands together, smiling.

I nodded and slid into the tub. Water splashed everywhere, wetting her blouse and dirty apron.

She gently scolded me. "Look what you've done,"

"Sorry, Ma'am."

Violet shook her head, undoing the strings covering her breasts. I reached for myself to appease it, but she grabbed my arm, denying me again—a dangerous game.

"Hands where I can see them," she said, imitating a cowboy.

If Violet needed to play a game to make it ok, I was willing to let her. Another string loosened, and her ample breasts spilled out slightly. And then another, they took up more space, the tight compression alleviated. The faint lines of the string had left marks where they were tied up too tight.

"If you were my woman, I'd make you walk around naked," I said.

"But I ain't your woman. You're my boy, and I'm looking after your wounds. Don't you forget it."

"Yes, Ma'am."

The horizon of her nipple appeared, a chestnut brown. She removed more strings. They hung over her thighs like the fringes of a jacket.

Violet slipped one shoulder off, then the other, the blouse fell to her hips, and she stood there like a goddess, pushing her arms together to squish her freed breasts.

They were perfect—fat and swollen. Drooped slightly from her age, but it made me like them even more. Her thick nipples begged to be sucked on.

"Your face will get stuck like that if you keep gawping," she smiled, cheeks gone a little red, but smiling all the same.

She leaned over the tub, grabbing the sponge. "Arm up."

I lifted it, and she began rubbing soapy suds all over me.

Violet's breasts drooped over the tub, grazing my bare skin. I wanted to reach them, to grab for them, but I knew she'd smack my hand away.

All wrong. Not the way I liked it.

It was right for today.

"I can see you're hurtin'," she said, stroking the sponge down my chest. I gripped the sides of the tub as her wrist grazed against my throbbing. The head poked out from the water. I instinctually thrust my hips forward.

"I'm fine, no bruises." My voice sounded husky.

"You know that's not what I meant. I'd been begging you to tell me that story for a long time. Now you have, I can see why you didn't."

Violet stroked down the hard muscle of my abdomen, this time, no sponge. Her hand wrapped around me, and I cried out in bliss.

"Oh fuck." I trembled. Pleasure shot through my body like lightning.

"I have one question," she said, like what she was doing was no more out of the ordinary than cleaning the countertop.

"Yeah?" She squeezed gently and stroked over me, making me tremble. Her hand grazed over the swollen crown, too sensitive, stuck against the friction of the water, sliding over in jerked motions.

"Why didn't you use your power? Gia's gift? Would've come in handy with that ork, or any other time?"

The pleasure was building. "I can't do it anymore. Only works when you're in the temple." I sucked in a breath. "Fuck, that feels good."

Her other hand reached into the water and stroked over my balls.

I was close.

Violet stroked back and forth, more water splashing over the tub onto her fallen blouse. Her breasts fell straight down, swaying hypnotically.

"Can I?"

"Just this once."

I held one, lifting while pinching her nipple. It hardened to my touch.

"But I thought *they* could do it?" she asked.

I grit my teeth, barely able to answer. "Who?"

"Gia's Subject's."

She pumped faster, making me cry out.

Too much.

"They can. They have to... Fuck. Oh, Violet. I'm close."

She let go, leaving it trembling, slapping in and out of the water. Drips slid from it.

I gripped onto the bathtub, panting.

Violet stood up from the tub. "You got me all wet." She smirked, swiping her ginger hair out of her face and slipping out of her clothes, revealing herself to me.

Even with her legs closed, her trimmed orange pubes showed, glistening wet.

“Am I too hairy for you?” she ran her fingers through her pubes, cooing.

I shook my head. “I love that sexy color.” I grabbed her arm and pulled her towards me, her lips crashing into mine. Our mouths opened, the wetness of her tongue coated mine, her breath fresh and minty.

We parted. I stared into Violet’s beautiful blue eyes.

"I love you.”

She nodded. "I know you do. Not in that way, though." She shook her head. "It doesn't matter."

"I'm sorry," I said, kissing her again.

Her hand slid around me. The break had let me recover some. She broke the kiss and kissed my forehead. Her strokes were slow now, gentle, leading me there.

I reached down her abdomen, slightly chubby from where she had given birth but still impressively toned. I went past it, sliding through her folds, the pubic hair soft against my hand as I found her spot.

"Mmm, there," she said. "I love you too. But not like that. Like a-"

"Don't say it. Not now," I said, stroking faster on her button, coaxing her to go more quickly on me. I was *close* again. "But I love you like that too."

"That's why this is ok. It’s a wound you need healing.” Violet’s legs trembled as she pressed deeper. She closed her eyes and moaned, then said through a hushed breath. “I know it won't heal forever, but it will last at least for now. And then, sweetie, after-"

I stroked faster, slipping through her swollen wet folds into her tightness, which clenched around me, so tight, because she hadn't been with someone in so long? I pushed in, and her swollen folds gripped me, almost strangling my finger.

"And then after?"

"Oh Harlen, *fuck*. It's time to move on."

"What if I don't want to?"

"Then." She squeezed me, stroking over me. "I'll just have to fire you. Not now, I need to get some of that toxin out of you."

"Maybe you should suck it out." I grabbed the back of her neck.

"Maybe I should." she grabbed my wrist and pulled my hand out from inside her, let go of me, and stood up.

My member trembled in pain from being withheld, but this time I didn't care. She turned around, that fat juicy behind bouncing with each step as she strutted away, turning once to grin at me.

"I'll be in your room."

"You dirty whore, I bet you wanted this all along."

Violet put her hand on her mouth in mock shock. "Is that any way to speak to your..." A smile broke across her lips as she caressed her own breast, stroking her nipple between her fingers, licking her lips.

And then she left, leaving the door wide open, her soft footsteps getting quieter.

I climbed out of the tub, dripping water on the creaking wooden floorboards, my rigid rod swinging with every step, ready to dive into whatever hole she presented with me first and not leave until it was done.

No way would I leave. All just talk. I was here for the long haul, especially when I now had her mouth. It was never gonna be just one time.

My bedroom door was slightly ajar. I pushed it open and had to hold onto the door frame to steady myself. My jaw dropped.

Violet lay on her back, her head dangling over the foot of my bed, where I could crouch down and feed it to her. Her legs spread out, and one hand stroked between those sparkling ginger pubes while the other pinched at her nipple, teasing and pulling at it.

"Don't you think it's time you made *me* something to eat?" she licked her full, red lips.

I approached her, bent down, and slipped myself into her upside-down mouth. She swallowed the head, her tongue sliding over it, sending sparks of pleasure all over my body.

Violet was not a timid woman. She slurped and licked in the noisiest, wettest way she could.

I trembled, my legs buckling, ramming deeper into her throat. She gagged but didn't tap out, so I began fucking her mouth while her upside-down tongue lapped at me. My hand stroked down her stomach towards her cunt, and I hooked my fingers inside it, pumping two digits in and out of her slick, gripping wetness. Glistening sultriness flowed from her, making her trimmed pubes sparkle even more. Violet cried out, groaning against the gagging.

I thrust my hips deeper into her mouth, wrapping my hand around the back of her neck and pulling it into me against the side of the bed, her legs raised to help her. I grabbed her thick thigh and lifted it up while slamming my hips forward, the base meeting her lips.

I stayed there, fully submerged. "Oh fuck." I cried out.

She licked and devoured me, her tongue sending juicy sparks of pleasure through my body.

"You first," I said through gritted teeth, and pumped my two fingers into her so fast they were a blur. My palm kept slapping her gem, which swelled out of her folds, hardened and ready to burst.

That sound she made shook me to my core. Like the chokes a person makes when fatally wounded and choking their last breaths. Creating life and leaving it, so similar in sound. But we weren't creating life this time. We were creating selfish, needy pleasure.

And she got her fill of it from my hand alone.

So why was my mind elsewhere, in such a horrible place? Shouldn't I just be in the moment?

Get yourself back in it.

She squirted all over my hands, soaking her thighs and my bed. I thrust into her mouth, grabbing the back of her neck and pulling her into me even though I was already submerged down her throat. Her tongue was sliding over the base of the shaft.

"Take it." I kept pumping at her through her orgasm. I wanted to extend it for her, to make it last as long as possible, thanking her for everything she had done for me.

I sunk my hand in and kept it there, her swollen cave constricted around my fingers, and my vision became nothing but light. My whole body is filled with it.

My head fell onto her stomach, and I grabbed her hips for dear life as I throbbed painfully. An orgasm so powerful it hurt, and yet in that pain, more pleasure than I had felt in years.

It shot down her throat.

She swallowed it all, her throat constricting around me and lengthening my orgasm, much like I had done for her. I cried out, holding her thighs, inches from her gorgeous smelling cunt.

I was spent, but I kept thrusting forward from minor aftershocks of my orgasm while I licked at her swollen bead, tasting her juice that had spread all over her groin.

I pulled out of her mouth, and she gagged a little, then slid her hands over my sensitive hardness. I groaned.

Violet gave it a kiss, then a suck, cleaning off the last of my release. Then she tapped my shoulder, indicating for me to move.

I said nothing, falling down the side of the bed, still twitching.

Violet got down on her floor and wrapped her arms around my shoulders in a tight embrace. Her pillowy breasts comforted my cheek. My arms went limp.

Her lips pressed against my forehead, leaving a long, wet kiss there that I frowned and wiped off.

"Good boy, that wasn't so bad, was it?"

She got up, those thick bouncy cheeks the last thing I saw, jiggling as it left me. I stood up, went to the door to shut it behind her, and collapsed onto my bed, instantly falling asleep.

3

Where did you go?

I tossed in my bed, sheets clinging to my sweat-soaked body, drifting halfway in that awful space between sleep and wake.

Echoed all around me, another voice coming from everywhere. *Hide this, don't let them see it.*

"Mom?" A bubbling pit of anger festered in my stomach.

Dad's voice came next. *Son, do as your mother says, don't make a fuss.*

In my half-dream state, I made a fist. If he were in the room, I'd slam it into his jaw.

SQUARK

A bird outside tapped on my window, waking me. I opened my eyes, squinting against the blinding sunlight shining through the window.

Grumbling, I lifted my head to grab the warm, sweaty pillow, and threw it at the window. The hinges shook, the raven squawked, and the windows bellowed in the wind. The damn thing's wings flung dust from the air into the open window. Rage filled me—the sort of anger that can only come from being woken prematurely.

The raven landed on the window sill and squawked again.

Knowing when I was beat, I pulled my sheets off with a sigh.

My nakedness brought my head into my hands as Violet's sweet, honey voice echoed, *Harlen, I need to suck out the toxin.*

I hit myself in the head with the side of my fist. "Get it together, asshole," I muttered. "If you act normal, she will, and you can go right back to the way things were." *Or I could fuck her again. Maybe bend her over the bar and take her from behind.*

I sprung to hardness at the thought of her doubled over, that thick butt presenting itself to me. I'd spread her cheeks and dive into her slick, hairy slit.

Nope. Not today. I was gonna get out of the house. If there was ever a thing to get me soft, it was today's destination. Long overdue—my pockets were empty.

But first, I had to find my clothes.

I strutted naked to the door, listening for anyone in the hallway. It would be bad enough to give them an eyeful of my bare, scarred-up body, but with the current raging monster I was sporting? They'd probably spread rumors around town about how much of a pervert I was.

Not far from the truth.

From downstairs, patrons muffled cheers and heated, jovial discussions vibrated through the walls. It seemed like yesterday's quietness was being made up for today, and in the morning, no less.

No. Lunchtime, judging by the sun's position. I had slept like a log.

When I was sure the halls were empty, I popped open the door, and stopped when my bare feet kicked the pile of clothes on the ground.

Not a pile, an immaculately folded square. My boots sat beside it, neatly laced. I smiled, grabbed the clothes, and pulled them in. Taking a whiff, the musky odor told me they needed cleaning, but so did all my clothes. It didn't matter. Dirty clothes were better suited for today. Perhaps Felice Volt wouldn't put his arm around me if he could smell me first.

Whatever, I had only been lazing about in them drinking beer.

Once dressed, I still felt naked, so I knelt at the bedside cabinet and pulled out my pendant, slipping it around my neck.

Stepping down the stairs made the floorboards creak, which made me wince, but that didn't matter, what with how loud the patrons were.

I entered the bar and said, "Mornin' Violet."

Violet rushed back and forth across the bar, wearing that dirty barmaids dress she wore yesterday, her breasts tied behind lines of string like they had committed a crime.

"Good afternoon," she corrected me. "Sleep well?"

"Like a baby." I walked behind the bar, putting my hand on her hip when she got in my way of the drawer. Violet's sweet subdued perfume, likely left over from yesterday, drifted up my nostrils, making me sigh with comfort.

"Can I help you, young man?" She smiled at me. One ginger pigtail lay on her breast while the other fell down the side of her shoulder. I fixed it for her, and she shook her head. "Hands to yourself."

"Yes, Ma'am." I let go of her and scolded myself internally. *That is not acting normal.*

"I'm heading out," I said, finally finding what I needed in the dusty drawer—goggles and a bandana. A tiny crack ran through one of the goggle's eyeglasses, but it was only superficial.

"Where you off to?"

"Got a job." I lied. *But I'd get one.*

"Harlen, no." Worry drew across her face as she handed another customer a beer glass, taking his coin and putting it in the cash machine, which clunked satisfactorily when she closed it. "Look at how busy we are. I can pay you just fine."

"It's not for me, Violet." *Why did I say that? I don't need her thinking she's a charity.*

Right on time, a yell sounded across the bar. Both Violet and I turned our heads to the source of the commotion. An oldboy in a hat far too big for him rubbed his knee. "Got' damn it! Who put this dent here."

May as well be honest.

I shrugged to Violet. "The place is in dire need of fixing up. You can't deny that."

She crossed her arms over her breasts, *no mean feat*, and ignored a customer about to give her some coin. "Nuh-uh! I refuse! You can't!"

I tied the bandana around my neck. "It's not up to you."

Violet's lips pursed tight, but she said nothing.

She knew she had no argument. She could pretend all she wanted—she wasn't my mother.

I made my way towards the door, pushing through the wave of people. Most of them were locals, and there wasn't an ork insight, so there probably wouldn't be any trouble. They all respected Violet and knew not to get on my wrong side.

"Be careful ok!" she yelled.

"I'll be careful." I waved goodbye.

The doors flung open, and the goggles were over my eyes just in time for a blast of sand to get me in the face. I spat it out and raised the bandana over my mouth and nose.

Sand, so much sand. It's a pity we couldn't eat it, then we'd all be millionaires, *'An live off the fatta the lan'* or whatever that character said in the book I read as a kid.

The long, dusty dirt path had rows of stores on either side, with apartments above each one. Apart from a few houses on the outskirts, most folk here lived on top of their businesses, no sense in doing otherwise, and when business slowed, they could hardly afford to be elsewhere.

Business was often slow. That's when Violet couldn't afford me, and I could pursue other jobs. When it was busy? She needed me most.

Apart from the regulars, most folk were from all around the planet, trading cattle and whatnot. Them's the folk that caused the most trouble, because they thought they could get away with it and slink back home to be the good guy again.

Today though? I needed to be as far from her as possible.

Fuck this dusty planet. How'd I ever end up here?

I felt a tug at the knee of my pants.

"Harlem, look what I got!" Big eyes blinked from behind oversized goggles—one of the local street kids.

I bent right down to get on his level.

"What you got there, pard'ner?" I asked.

He held up a toy truck. It was entirely out of place in the grassy desert of Caria. Had it been real-sized, sand would suck right up into the joints and parts, and it'd be rendered useless. Hell, the same thing would happen to the toy.

"Try not to play with it on the sand too much, yeah?" I then explained why, and the cute kid looked at me with those innocent eyes fogging up in the glasses. He took a second to pull them out to release some steam and then rubbed sand from his eye.

"I won't!" he grinned.

Something struck me.

"Say, where'd you get that anyway?"

Toys like that weren't natural on this planet. Kids usually played with small wooden carts or horses. Not a straight-up automobile truck, made of plastic or whatever it was.

"Traded it for some of mom's crops," he bounced on the heels of his feet.

"With who?"

He pointed in the direction of a familiar man sitting against the wall of the robot shop, taking a bite out of a hand-sized breet—A vegetable not dissimilar to a beet, hence the name, except more suited to grow in the hot climate of Ciara.

"Run along," I said to the kid, standing to my full height.

I headed over to Bobby, who was clearly eating his first decent meal in weeks.

"I thought your type didn't go for food like that," I said.

Bobby crunched down on the breet, the juices squeezed out from his teeth and dribbled down his chin.

"I'm goin' clean, Harlen," he beamed. "I ain't used for a day."

Tomorrow will be rough for him. I'd seen it before. Cane addicts *thought* they could get clean, but the moment they stopped, their bodies scrambled for anything it could get. Usually, food, seeing as they'd been so starved of it. Cane was unlike any drug I'd read about. It didn't react the same way others did. It was probably because it *did* have some sustenance in it, meaning people could take it and maintain a somewhat healthy weight.

That's its selling point—they act like it's good for you.

Nothing good about what happens when you stop taking it. Or when you're lying on your deathbed, a few decades early, insides all crystallized from the synthesized elements your body couldn't process.

Bobby grinned at me, his teeth sparkling white between the staining of the breet—another element that made people think it was good. Who wouldn't want to have *literally* sparkling whites in a place like this?

"What's made you go clean?" I asked.

He poked at the wall of his brother's store. "Jack's making me. Says if I wanna live with him, I can't be addicted to that crap. But I don't get it. I feel great. It ain't crap."

"You won't be feeling fine in a minute."

He waved my hand away. "You don't believe in that. That's just rumors by the crop farmers, scared they'll run out of business. Look at all this red stuff on my hands. Cane don't give me that. Bet my teeth are starting to go red with it too. Cane don't give me that either."

Cane gives you a lot you can't see.

"Anyway." I shook my head. "Where'd you get a toy like that, the one you gave to the kid over there."

"Some guy." Bobby froze up.

"You fancy giving me a bit more than that?"

"The same guy I always get it from." His big eyes went shifty.

Why's he so alert?

"Bobby. What guy? Name?" My voice hardened.

"Sure!" He took another big bite of the breet and said something utterly unintelligible through his gross chewing sounds.

"Bobby, what the hell are you trying to say!"

He swallowed, the lump visibly traveling down his neck, his eyes darted to the ground, face turning flush.

I waited, until finally, he said, "I got it from some other guy. He said he worked for Felice. "

"When?"

"Not long ago."

"Thought you went clean? Forget that. Did he come here?"

"Nah, I was out by the hills, at my usual spot where I sleep."

So the guy didn't want to be seen. Why'd he given Bobby the truck then?

"When?"

"An hour ago."

Something wasn't adding up. I studied Bobby, trying to figure out what. He seemed to be his regular ol' high self.

"Bobby, did you take Cane?"

He nodded, taking another huge bite of the breet.

If he had taken Cane, why was he eating? He should've been beyond satisfied, yet he snacked on that breet like there was no tomorrow.

"Bobby, don't get anything from that guy anymore, yeah? Go to your regular guy. There's something off about this stuff."

"What could be off about it? I feel great!" He flashed a breet-stained grin, but his teeth sparkled through the red. Even in his eyes, sparkling tears brimmed his eyelids, highlighting the bloodshot whites. When did he last blink?

"I'm gonna go see your brother," I said.

"See ya, Harlen!"

"Stay safe, Bobby."

Shaking my head, I stepped around the side of the shop and onto the wooden steps, letting myself into the store. The smell of oil and coal perforated the room. Robots lined the walls, hanging off a little hole at the top of their head, where they were slotted onto nails like a clothes rack. Bobby's twin sat behind a counter, squinting through glasses with multiple magnifiers lens aimed at a bronze robot head. Sparks flew from the tips of his tool as he worked.

"How's business, Jack?"

"Crap," he grumbled without looking up.

I always appreciated his honesty.

"And Bobby?"

"Crap." He glanced at me. "What can I do for you, Harlen?"

"I'm looking for a bot."

"Ha! Like hell you are."

"It's no surprise business is crap if that's the way you speak to your customers."

Jack leaned back against his chair, scratching his whiskery white beard, the many lenses on his glasses aimed at me. The giant eye, magnified and terrifying, had me visibly taken aback. He took it off and put it on the counter.

"Sorry. It's been tough." He sighed, rubbing the bridge of his nose.

"Been tough for us all."

Jack ran his hand over his face. "And now, with Bobby here, I gotta feed the both of us. With what? Nobody can afford to buy a bot. Anyone that can doesn't come here. They go to Blanchet's, over on the other side of the planet."

"Well, about that."

He looked up. "Don't you give me that hope."

When did he last sleep? It looked like whatever energy Bobby took from that new Cane was getting sapped out of Jack.

"I'm going for a job, a good one. It's been a long time since I saw Felice. He should have them lined up for me."

"What do you need?" he said, shaking his head at me.

I didn't want to waste his time, but I didn't want to put in all that work if I wasn't going to get it.

"You got Guard Bot's, right?" I asked.

"Fastest shots in Caria, except perhaps you."

"What about Cleaners?"

"Got those too."

"Both?"

"Yea, I got Guard and Cleaners. Didn't ya hear me?"

"No, both. Can you get one that does both?"

"Now why the damn would you want to do a thing like that?" Jack lifted an eyebrow. "You don't give a pristine Guard the demeaning job of cleanin', and likewise—a bot that cleans can't shoot, every bot has its place in the world."

Whether the fumes had finally got to his brain, or if he just saw these bots as his children, I didn't care, long as he'd take a second to look past it and see my point.

"Hey, why don't we take one of them Guards out, see how good it is." I said.

Jack groaned and stepped off his chair, mumbling to himself as he wiped his hands on his coal-stained brown apron. Then, walking with a limp, he lifted one of the robots off from the rack with some effort - I tried to help, but he brushed me away - and put it down and reached behind its neck.

The robot's eyes dimly lit up. The voice was fuzzy at first, like an untuned radio.

"**Schchchhhh,** hello!"

"Come with us, robot," Jack grumbled.

"My name is robot number 2!"

The bot was eerily chipper, while completely accentless and genderless.

"Of course it is. I named ya." Jack said with a roll of his

eyes that told me he heard that phrase often.

Jack stepped out of the shop. The robot followed him. Pumps and gears shifted while air constantly blew out of its many vents. Some of it got on me when it walked past, but it was just air, so I didn't mind. I'd probably mind a lot more when it was sand.

We went around the other side of the store, avoiding his brother. Was Jack embarrassed about him insisting on laying outside in the sun for all to see? *Not my family, not my problem.*

Behind the store, a target sat a few yards away, overlooking the mountains.

Jack stood with his hands loosely shoved in the pockets of his apron. "Robot."

"Yes?"

He pointed at the target. "Hit the-"

PING

Before he could even finish the sentence, the robot's arm flung up terrifyingly fast, and a little dot appeared right in the middle of the target, where the bullet pierced it.

"Holy shit," I said with genuine surprise.

"Yeah," Jack dusted off his hands, standing taller. "Pretty fast, huh?"

“And you don't have to buy bullets?”

“Nope! He filters out the iron from the sand he collects and blows out the rest from his vent.”

I whistled to show I was impressed. Of course, I already knew how Jack’s robots worked. He’d shown me when I was younger. I think he explained it to anyone who came to buy. Not that many did. He probably just liked talking about it.

"How much for one?" I asked.

"For you? Forty."

I pursed my lips, nodding as if thinking about it. "Felice

has paid me that before. I'll get more than that this time, for sure."

"If you ain't dead first, I've seen you hobbling down that street full of holes to get patched up. What if you don't come back?'

"Then you'll be in exactly the position you were before, and frankly, it won't be my problem—I'll be dead. Besides, it ain't like you've got to hold it for me in case you sell out."

He grunted. "Fair enough. You want one when you get back then?"

"Yeah. I gotta question, though."

"Oh?"

"What about when it ain't shooting?"

"What do you mean?" He frowned, like the robot would never be doing anything *but* shooting.

"When it ain't shootin', what's it doing?"

"I guess it's just standing there." He shrugged, then he wagged his finger at me. "Oh, you sly dog, I see what you're doing."

I laughed, holding my hands up. "Why can't it be cleaning? If I'm buying two of these, I could buy one cleaning and one shooting. Or I could have two that do both. If it filters out iron from sand to make bullets, it can do more of that when it's cleaning."

He shook his head at me. "You've got no respect for the sanctity of robots."

"Just makes sense to me."

"Yeah, whatever. C'mon robot. Back on the rack, we'll see how good Harlen makes on his promise first."

"I always make good on my promises."

But Jack had already hobbled towards his desolate store. He entered to a ringing bell and slammed the door behind him.

Returning to the street, I Intended to head to the stables, but got distracted by Bobby, who had just finished his breet and thrown the stem on the ground beside him.

"See ya, Harlen!" He yelled enthusiastically, about five times as bug-eyed as before.

"Don't you wanna put some goggles on?" I asked, concerned for the old junkie. "You'll end up blinding yourself."

"I can't feel it!" He grinned, eyes wide, body rocking back and forth erratically.

I marched back to the store entrance and pushed the door open.

"What!" Jack yelled at me, having just got comfortable again in his seat behind the counter.

"Jack, your brother ain't right, might wanna check on him."

He mumbled something along the lines of *'nothing ain't right in this world,'* hopping off his chair behind the counter and headed towards the doorway.

I got out of his way and went toward the stables, not wanting to be involved in whatever family drama was about to happen with the old twins. Besides, I was no doctor. I couldn't do anything for him.

Their voices got quieter as I walked away.

"What's up, you alright?"

"Never better, brother!"

"Yeah, you're alright. Can you go behind the store or something? You're freaking out the customers."

"You ain't got no customers!" Bobby's hysterical laughter turned into a violent cough.

I shook my head, trying not to laugh. He wasn't wrong about that, but Jack would have a thrilled one when I got back.

4

The smell of hay and horse shit enveloped me.

"How's she doing?" I patted Daisy's scaled body, and she huffed in response, blinking her triple-layered eyelid, shaking her head. Her long lizard-like tongue sliding out to lick off the mushy feed that had spilled down her chest.

"Been doing just fine, Mr. Harlen," the stable boy tipped his hat.

I flicked him a silver, which he caught in one hand.

"See that, Mr. Harlen! Caught it in one this time."

I winked at him. "It's a lot cooler if you act like it isn't cool—act like it happens all the time."

“Gotcha, Mr. Harlen!"

One foot in the stirrup, I lifted myself onto Daisy in one mighty heave of my upper body. Her scales were cool against my legs. I patted her neck, and she neighed.

"You've rested enough ain't ya. I should've taken you out more."

"I've been making sure she's been getting out!" the stable hand said as Daisy clopped us out of the stable. "Have fun, Mr. Harlen!"

I whistled the call I had conditioned into Daisy, and she leaped into speed.

Bobby waved rapidly at me as I rode past. I didn't know if a trick of the light or the way Daisy lurched forward, but his eyes looked like they were about to pop out. But Daisy's hard-scaled hooves flung us along on the sandy path, leaving the town behind us.

And I could put it out of my mind, for now.

Ahead, mountain ranges emerged from the ground, covered in patches of green grass amongst the dried, dead stuff that posed frequent fire hazards. The mists never kept it alive for long, nor did the cold stone protruding from the sand. The mountain points were surrounded by a ring of clouds like a crown. A few of them had two.

They weren't my destination.

The Carian dirt paths got harder against Daisy's feet. She neighed out some air, blinking her triple eyelids to wet her eyeballs.

"Yeah, that's it, girl. Nice being out?"

She puffed in agreement. I gently kicked the side of my spurs against her thighs to make her speed up. It was good to see how fast she could go. She hadn't been out since our last excursion.

Wolf Water lay beyond the horizon. It was the closest city to Hot Sands.

Felice Volt lived there in his lavish house filled with cool springs and fountains. Meanwhile, the rest of the world sipped on the spit of the world, fighting over what water remained because it was more precious than diamonds.

Sure, he gave some back, sending water to farmers who

needed it, paying all of his workers handsomely, that sort of thing, but he gave something else to Caria too. A gift nobody asked for, and we were all better off without.

One of these days, he's gonna go too far, and some other lord or lady will put a hit on him. I'd take it without a second thought.

I pulled on Daisy's reins as we approached the pressure rocket's crossing. A simple wooden gate before a black dirt path where the rocket's incredible velocity had scoured the land—a ring around the world. Miles crossed in seconds, silently. A super-powered one-man train without a track.

A few cattle bones lay across the path. They didn't bother to gate up the trail, so If a cow got in the way of a pressure rocket, there wouldn't be much left to bring back home.

I blinked, and the pressure rocket flew past. Daisy reared in surprise, so I patted her side.

"Easy girl."

The gate swung upwards, controlled by a wire from afar, and we stepped across the path, dodging a bit of sparked sand on the ground we crossed.

After riding for an hour, we turned around the familiar pile of boulders a few clicks from Wolf Water.

Daisy began to pick up speed, sensing we weren't far from rest and water.

* * *

Wolf Water.

A town more populated than Hot Sands, with more families and houses to home them. It was a farcical name. Most of the water poured into Felice's fountains. Maybe the town should be renamed *Wolf's* Water.

At the back of the town, the manor overlooked it like a castle.

He wasn't ever appointed Mayor. Nobody voted for him, and as such, he wasn't going anywhere. Just as well—there would likely be far worse than him to take his place—a necessary evil. But if what I saw of Bobby was anything to go by, Felice had gone a little eviler since we last met.

Daisy clopped across the sand path, neighing and shaking her head like she sensed my unrest.

"Almost there, girl," I said, patting the side of her neck.

There were piles of people sitting between the cracks of stores and whatever they could rest in a spot of shade.

Each one of them a *Bobby*, each one with a family. Huffing Cane, snorting it, or injecting it. However they wanted to take it. It's all the same poison.

But these guys all seem rather chilled out. They weren't buzzing off their tits or chewing on real food. They were sustained, body temperatures cooler, allowing them to relax in the blazing sun. They'd live longer than a person going hungry on nothing.

Without Cane, I doubt this town would be thriving.

It didn't make it ok.

It was what it was.

So what was that other stuff?

After dropping off Daisy at the stable, I approached the gates, two guards on either side, baking in the heat of the sun. The iron gates to the green grassy courtyard wide open like always.

"Who's that?" one asked, swiping a rag across his sweaty brow.

I pulled my goggles up over my head and the bandana down for him to see.

"Freddie, look, it's Harlen."

“No kidding? We ain't seen you here for months.”

"Yea, been a while," *Small talk bullshit.* "How's the kid?"

"He’s five now! No, six."

I whistled. "They grow up fast. Felice in?"

"Felice is in."

"I'm heading in then. See ya."

"See ya, Harlen," said the guard I knew but forgot the name of.

The gravel path was uneven against my feet after riding for so long, but I adjusted fast, walking towards the front door.

The many windows of the manor shined like jewels against the sun. Cleaned and polished daily.

I stepped into the house, scraping the dirt off my feet on the mat. Statues, trophies, and artwork adorned every spare bit of space. Every surface a dark varnished wood. I looked away from it.

"Don't worry about that," a matronly maid sang, seeing my wiping my feet on the mat. "He's upstairs in his office."

I didn't recognize this one. "Ma'am." I nodded, heading to the stairs.

I pulled the bandana down my neck and took the goggles off.

"Felice? You up here?" I yelled, not wanting to catch a horrific sight of him with his pants down or something. Just for myself, I mumbled, “*You bastard.*”

"Harlen, my boy? Is that you? I'd recognize that voice anywhere."

His voice reminded me of those pickled breets he loved to wolf down.

I gripped tighter on the carved varnished banister, reaching to the top of the stairs. Golden framed paintings adorned the hallway, jewel-encrusted plates with pictures of wars fought long in the past hung next to them, and sparkling chandeliers hung overhead, with each christal piece polished within an inch of its life.

I patted the pendant under my shirt to check it wasn't above it. Felice wouldn't let me out of here alive if he saw it, just to put it in a glass case, another one of his prized jewels.

In the doorway, His rear end stuck out in oversized striped dress pants.

"Been a while, Felice," I said.

"Far too long. I was about to send someone for you."

Not long enough.

"Yeah? Got a job for me?"

I strolled slowly, wishing we could just have the conversation across the hallway. He was certainly loud enough for it.

"Oh, my boy. I've always got a job for you."

"Anything to do with a truck?"

"What's that, my boy?"

"Nothin', I got something to ask you, though."

He got up from the floor, his bulging circular body coming into view of the doorframe. "Ah, there he is," he said, putting on the thumb ring he had retrieved from the floor.

A round boulder of a man, with two oddly slender sticks for arms and legs. I imagined if one pushed him over, he'd start rolling and never stop until he hit Hot Sands, where the wooden houses would be no match for his velocity. Hell, if he went on for long enough, he'd probably outrace the pressure rockets.

Felice smirked at me. "It's great to see you, son."

He held his arms out, nearly spanning the width of the room before drawing me into his embrace, the smell of spoiled *who-knows-what* escaping from his mouth. His warm and disgustingly sweaty body enwrapped me, wet patches under his armpits pressing against my shoulders.

My eyes started watering. I patted Felice's back, laughing to stop myself from gagging. "It's good to see you too, Felice. Got a drink?"

I needed it to hold my nose in and hide from his foul smell.

Why does he smell so bad if he's the one with all the water?

"For you? Only the best!" Felice walked over to the cabinet, where he pulled out a delicately carved glass canter.

"Speaking of the best, that Cane you been making seems a lot better than the old stuff."

Felice threw the glass against the wall. It shattered into a thousand pieces. He turned on me, skin turning breet red. I stared blankly.

"That is not my product!" Felice stormed past me, his shoulder knocking mine as he gripped onto the frame of the door and yelled, "Maurine! Come and clean this shit up!"

"Coming, Mr. Volt!" she sang from downstairs.

"Now!" he growled, spittle dripping down his double-chin, his mustache shimmering with sweat.

Some landed on my cheek. I fought down a gag.

"You came at the right time, Harlen," he said, calming down.

"I'm glad. I need a big job. The biggest job you have."

"Ha, that ain't the biggest job I have."

"What's the biggest?"

Maurine skipped in with a dustpan and brush to sweep up the broken glass, but Felice snapped at her, "Maurine, get the fuck out! Close the door behind you."

"Yes, Mr. Volt," she chimed, speedily walking out the door fast as her feet could carry her, yanking the door behind her but stopping just before it closed to prevent a slam.

Felice grabbed a bottle of whiskey and poured a glass, handing it to me. I ignored the sweat marks from his thumb on the ridge, turning the glass to bring an untouched part to my lips. The unfathomably expensive whiskey, imported from the other side of the planet, swam down me, its harsh warmth making him more tolerable already.

He poured another glass for himself and said, "I need you to go to Padrorix-"

I held my hands up. "I ain't got a ship."

"*And* then, I need you to find a way into the forest pit king's castle."

I took another deep gulp, his voice becoming distant and dulled to the sweet lullaby of taste on my tongue.

"And steal his coin. He has more than he knows what to do with." Felice swirled his whiskey for some reason, then took a huge gulp, slamming it down on the ornate metal desk, where it spilled everywhere. "You're not familiar with him, are you?"

"I know he lives in a forest."

Felice shook his head, wiping his greasy hair away from a sweat-beaded forehead, then he filled my glass.

"He bleeds his planet dry. Those trees are like steel, worth more than any other kind of lumber in the galaxy." Felice tapped his metal desk. "This is a gift from him."

I blinked. I'd heard about it but never seen it, or, never had it pointed out to me. *Why tell me now?*

"As such, it's become a hot commodity around the galaxy. Imagine a material like steel but organically grown. It can be molded and set into whatever shape you like, then once the wood starts to dry out—bam!" He slammed his fist against the table, shaking everything on it. "Harder than my dick for that foxy maid."

"So, why would I wanna steal from this guy? He must be powerful?"

"Because, ma' son, he's pure evil. Bleeds his planet and keeps it all to himself. So I figure if he ain't sharing it, I should have some of it."

"Shouldn't his people have it?"

His laughter was like a barking dog. "And do what with it? They'll always be in his grasp, whether they've got coins or not."

I frowned, seeing the holes in his logic, and wondering if the only reason he looked after this side of Caria was that he had no other way of maintaining power.

The golden-brown liquid in my glass had stilled. "So you got a ship now?"

He laughed. "No, I ain't got a ship."

Choosing not to wipe the spit off my face, I took another sip of the whiskey, then said, "So why are we having this conversation?"

"You're Harlen Gray. You always find a way."

"Not this time. And besides, ain't you got enough? You seem to be living comfortably." I gestured around the lavish room.

He slammed the glass down again. It would've irritated me if I hadn't already gone whiskey-numb.

"More?"

"Please." Felice poured whiskey into my outstretched glass, then I said, "Anyway, I can't do it. I don't have a ship."

"Then we've got nothing left to say on the matter."

His clock ticked the silence away. I took another sip.

He slurped his like a dog on the side of a river, and said, "Anyway, that's the biggest job I have."

"How about the second biggest?"

He chuckled. "You don't want to go there."

It was all a ruse. He mentions the impossible job, so this one would seem less so.

"Try me," I said.

"This new Cane you've heard about. It's not from me."

"Cane's not something I want to get involved with."

"I'll give you fifty."

"For what? You ain't told me what it is yet."

Felice shrugged. "I need a sample."

"That's all?"

He barked laughter again.

I took a sip of whiskey. And then another, much bigger one, becoming numb to it. There wasn't much stronger around, and yet I'd need it if I had to spend a moment longer with Felice.

"It's guarded—heavily. My men can't get in there."

Felice's men were primarily rent-a-soldiers—family men. I doubted they wanted to try.

"So you want me to sneak in, get a sample, and get out?"

"And maybe kill them all?" he said, sickly sweet.

"Why do you want a sample anyway? So you can make some of your own?"

"Ha! No. If I sold that stuff, I wouldn't have any customers left. It kills you. I don't know why they're selling it. What's the point of making something if it kills your only customers."

I clenched my fist. *His* stuff killed customers too, just more slowly.

"How long does it take to kill?"

"A day or so."

"So you want to make an antidote? How long will that take?"

"A day or so." He flared his dirty yellow grin.

I doubted he knew how long it would take to make a cure. How would he do it when he hadn't seen the product? He wasn't a scientist. And hell, I had just led him into that question.

But

It was my only hope. Hot Sands was my home—my responsibility. That meant saving any druggy waste of space that lived there too. If I didn't, I was no better than Felice.

"If I do this, I want an antidote as soon as possible. I ain't leaving until I get it."

He gasped, then clapped his hands together giddily. "All the more time to put you under my wing. You know I need somebody to take all this over when I'm done. Have I ever told you how you remind me of me when I was a boy? When I..."

Every time I came here, he ended with *'have I ever told you...'*

I dreaded the thought of my future as a round, mean, lonely mayor lord, fucking the housemaids. No wonder I hadn't come back in so long.

"...so I leaped over the table." His mustache flicked whiskey on his lap from his animated acting of the tale.

I stood up, cutting him short. "I got a friend back home that's taken this stuff. Where's the hideout?"

5

In the center of town, the rocket attendant yanked my belt so tight it strangled my neck. *Fucking pressure rockets*, why did the hideout have to be so far away? I shouldn't have had those whiskeys.

Some kids stood around the ship, pointing and oohing. *Hadn't they ever seen a rocket before?*

“Now what you wanna do," the slack-jawed attendant said. "Is turn the rocket around to exactly the opposite direction, then move it left 3 degrees. You wanna end up slightly left of the town—not inside the town. See, we don't usually do this, but Felice demanded it."

The brass rocket smelt like sweat, and the seat cushions collapsed to nothing under my weight. The hard metal underneath hurt my ass, and the viewing glass was stained from years of use with what I hoped was just condensation.

“How do I start it?”

“Press this button.” He tapped outside the ship where I couldn't see. The tapping vibrating through the ship’s inside made me feel like an animal in a zoo exhibit getting annoyed by some kid.

I frowned. "But it's on the outside of the ship. How am I gonna press it and get my arm inside?"

"Quickly." The attendant gave a shit-eating grin, then inspected my seatbelt again, and was visibly satisfied it still cut into my neck.

An awful lot of safety measures when there'd be none on my way back.

He stood up straight and pulled at his suspenders. "Goggles on tight? I don't need to tell you what happened to the last guy not wearing his."

I made sure mine were secure, then frowned. "Hey, what if they got a crack in them?"

The attendant peered over my goggles, getting up close so I could see the shaved speckles of his beard. He tapped my eyeglass, making me blink.

"Hmm. Should probably be fine," he said, shrugging like it wasn't my entire life on the line.

Before I could respond, he shut the door, leaving me alone in the claustrophobic nightmare of a shuttle, surrounded by the odd brass walls and glass.

"Hey, wait. Probably?"

His mouth kept moving, but I heard nothing. He pointed to his ear to show he couldn't hear me too and shrugged, laughing as he leaned forward and pressed a button on the outside of the ship.

At least the glass was secure.

My head slammed into the worn cushion, hitting the hard metal behind it. Everything outside became long and distorted. My mouth filled with air, the bandana doing nothing. I quickly shut it and held back the whiskey sloshing around my stomach like Violet churning the dirty washing.

The rocket stopped. My body lurched forward, my

adam's-apple slammed against the seatbelt, reminding me all too much of the ork's hand on my neck. Acid tickled the back of my throat while blood rushed to my head, turning me blind. My vision brought back a searing headache. I groaned, unclipped the seatbelt, and pushed the door open to a burning sun. Stumbling out of the rocket, leaving on it for a second before standing up straight, I shook my knees awake, then looked around my surroundings.

Ahead of me, there was a single mountain with those clouds around it like a crown. Black smoke broke the ring, permeating the edges with its toxins.

The attendant had programmed the pressure rocket to stop outside of its usual parameters. At least, he said he programmed it. I had watched dubiously when they turned the ship in the direction of the mountain and hoped I wouldn't end up a stain on the rocks. The bastard probably just guessed the direction and power needed.

"Thanks, Felice," I said to nobody, swallowing down the acid that had spiraled up my stomach.

Walking to the rocket's point, I pushed it a hundred and eighty, finding it scarily light. Then, guessing three degrees and going a little further out than that, I drew a line in the sand until satisfied it was deep enough to stay.

I wiped the sweat from my brow, sighed, and began my trek to the mountain.

It was astonishingly high, the clouds seeming to get bigger too. I wasn't sure what I would find or if I would be found first, was it close enough for the sound of the rocket to have carried? Both guns on my hips were set past the silly named notches. No time for games now. If I shot someone today, I didn't want them getting back up.

Closer to the mountain, I stumbled across a few horse tracks, where I tried to walk inside them. Any close inspection would've had me found, as would the trail leading right to the pressure rocket, but I wanted to hide my presence as much as possible.

My nose twitched at something peculiar in the air. The black smoke from the side of the mountain. It smelt like manure, mixed with oil.

They couldn't actually be inside the mountain? I guess they didn't care about superstition.

I turned back to look at the ship, in the middle of the desert, the opposite of subtle. Why did Felice put me right at this spot? I could hardly take over from him as his prodigal son if I died. Probably just liked the idea of it, much like he liked the idea of getting whatever's in this new drug, so he could profit from it himself. No—he wanted the antidote. Like he said, a dead customer can't pay.

I needed that antidote too, and I needed those bots.

Most of all, I needed shade from the burning red sun and to not feel my boots digging in the sand, socks filling with it no matter how I stepped. And how sweat-drenched into everything I wore, rendering me a musky mess the moment I put any clothes on.

My eyes watered. It was the putrid stench that had tickled my nostrils earlier, coming from whatever they were cooking inside. The source of all that black smoke on the side of the mountain and the modified Cane.

Broken dirt and yellow grass began to break up the sand. Unnaturally broken pieces of boulder marred my path, making the journey difficult. The rocks appeared splintered from digging, their surfaces scratched by whatever device crushed and dragged them here. There were so many of them.

How deep did they dig?

The sun finally escaped from the morning horizon. A

great red ball floating above that endless sand, making me appreciate the brown, barely alive grass back home at Hot Sands. Here, there wasn't a town or village in sight. No one to hear the drilling. No one to smell that putrid smoking billowing into the sky like an active volcano. What I wouldn't give for some whiskey to mask the scent. Felice's body odor was a field of flowers in comparison.

My eyes caught some Karlindar on the ground, a plant customary to put inside your bandana to mask bad scents. I crouched down to grasp some, and it crumbled in my hand, black and dead. Whatever the hell these guys were making, it wasn't Cane.

I found it odd that there was no path. *How did they get all their stuff here? Not by road.*

I couldn't go knocking on the front door, so I began my trek up the mountain path, being careful not to slip on loose rocks, of which there were many. Vibration rumbled beneath me. The pulses were intermittent—every few seconds.

After half an hour of trekking, with sweat clinging my bandana to my mouth and my hair stuck flat to my head like glue, I made it to the top of the mountain. It wasn't far from the smoke funnel, where I could lean over and plan my attack.

Back home, the steam lake baths had my name on them.

I pinched my nose over my bandana to shield myself from yet another gag-inducing smell, peering over the cliff's edge.

A long open duct escaped from the cliff, pouring sludge into a lake I couldn't see before, which shared the same brown color. The thick sludge almost looked like it could be stood on. I didn't feel like testing the theory.

And then I saw it.

A white shuttle ship, big enough for about one person, parked before the river. Memories flashed of being young, over a decade ago, thinking they looked like military vessels ready to go to war, the way rows of them were lined up outside the tower.

My eyes widened, and I hid back behind the lip of the cliff. My heart fought against the constraints of my body, racing. *Having an attack?* I breathed deep, slowly in and out. *A hallucination brought on by my ingesting the fumes of whatever was coming out of that pipe?* I gripped the edge of the cliff, trembling fingers pulling myself over it, just an inch, so I could see.

Why were they here? Were they connected with the drug?

They're here for you, I thought.

Nonsense. If they were, they wouldn't be on the far side of the planet. There's no way for them to know I'm here—a coincidence.

It's a small galaxy, after all.

My heart began to slow back down, I peered back over the lip.

Directly below me, a young skinny guy in blue overalls stood on a platform, leaning back on the handrail. *Probably got told he'd have a cushy guard duty, standing outside in the middle of the desert where there wasn't a soul to be seen.*

I set my gun to stun and began climbing down the mountain. Stepping sideways, my heart raced when I slid down some loose rocks, sending them tumbling over the edge.

I froze. But the guard merely coughed.

I continued my descent until finally, I got to the foot of the hill and tried to mentally put aside the white ship that caused anxiety to surge through me like a toxin.

I'd need Violet to suck it out later.

* * *

At the foot of the hill, I crept towards the underside of the pipe.

It seemed sturdy enough. It survived this long despite the cracks weeping liquid and the empty bolthole billowing sludge like a sausage pushed through a grinder. Holding my breath, I walked under the pipe, keeping my head down so that I wouldn't get it in the eye. I didn't feel much like going blind today. No amount of coin was worth that. If there was, I doubt Felice could pay it.

The Forest Pit King, maybe.

Free from under the pipe, I aimed the pistol, cocked it, and fired at the man, hitting him square in the head. His head slumped to rest on his neck, and he sagged where he leaned, having not made a sound.

But when I climbed up the railings, it shook violently. Bolts loosened and rattled with each step. The guard railing shook too when I grabbed it. Was it a sloppily completed job or wear from repeated use? How long had they been here?

Not my problem. Eyes on the prize.

The man I stunned was snoozing, a snot bubble billowing out of his nose, growing and shrinking with his breaths. I ripped open his overalls, glad he wore pants and a shirt underneath. The guy must've been burning to a crisp wearing all those layers beneath the red sun.

Once the overalls were on, some lettering under the breast caught my eye. Turning my head and the logo, I read the name, *The Hardest Wood, ltd*. It sounded like a name for a building company. Was it a front for the whole thing?

And what was one of Gia's ships doing here? That white,

unnaturally smooth thing stuck in my mind. The 'calming' blue light around the middle stuck out like a sore thumb in the desert.

So does my pressure rocket.

I lifted the guy on my shoulder and carried him down the railings. Each step clanged, no matter how softly I treaded, but I hoped that it was nothing they weren't used to. Everybody needs to take a leak now and again.

But every guard needs to switch shifts.

Once he was wedged safely between a few boulders, I climbed back up the platform, patting my overalls to check my spare gun was hidden securely underneath it. I took a deep, disgusting-tasting breath and found myself oddly calm.

6

My descent into the dark, dreary cave.

Liquid dripping off of thin pipes everywhere, splashing onto metal railings cascaded at odd intervals. My steps rang on the metal. My spurs jingled. Dim orange lights lit my way, barely adequate. Their reflections in the metal were an eerie mirror.

Metal.

Was it metal? Veins ran through the length—Pradorix wood. The only other of its kind had been a gift from The Forest Pit King to Felice. Was this from him too? Perhaps the answers lay below.

Below me were the lids of giant drums, connected to humming machinery. Was that where they made the drug?

I crept further into the metal maze, pathways splitting in many directions, but all heading down, following the pipes that lead up to the sludge duct.

Down and down I went. The stairs zigzagged, the lights dimmed to just the essential orange bulbs giving off enough of a glow to barely light the way. My cold breath escaped from me in clouds. Instincts screaming for me to get out kept shuddering up my spine like millions of tiny little spiders.

If they weren't from here, they didn't know the stories. You don't dig deep into mountains. It's not done, story or not.

Eventually, I made it to a cross-section. I could go down, or across to overlook what looked to be the lab. Two men stood there, talking just loud enough for me to hear.

I crept across the walkway.

The white-robed figure paced with his hands in *that* position. A deep-buried instinct told me to stand up straight, put my hands together and drop all expression. I ignored it, studying him closer.

There was something different about his attire—metal pauldrons across his shoulders, ornated in a royal, medieval-looking crest. It wouldn't have protected much—probably ornamental. The effect was apparent. I could not simply think of him as a monk, but a knight—a peculiar word, the sameness of it to a person's name I once knew spurred prickly feelings in me I pushed deep down.

"It will not be necessary," the Subject - or Knight - of Gia said.

I didn't miss that cold lack of emotion. So unnatural, it sent a chill down my spine. Humans were meant to feel, to love, and even to hate. To deny us that was to deny us our humanity.

"Are you sure?" The other man, in the same uniform as me, asked. "One dose, and it alleviates the effects."

"We are not interested in a cure."

"I see. Well, I thought you could have it anyway, if you're buying some."

"If I were you, I wouldn't waste my time on such things."

"With all due respect, it's not up to you—and besides, What about the people of this planet?" The man in the overalls, was also not of this world, that was for sure. His accent had an exoticism to it I couldn't place. If he wasn't from Earth-2, nor here, he must've come with the wood from Pradorix.

"Unnecessary." The Knight of Gia said. "Is the product ready for purchase?"

"It works, yeah."

I felt the platform shake too late, and the mouth of a gun shoved into my back.

"Who are you?" Another hard prod, this one nailing me in the kidney. "And how did you find us?" *Same Pradorix accent.*

I lifted my hands up. "I just started working here."

"Turn around."

I did so slowly, while hiding my gun behind my back.

He had a worried snarl across his face, similar to that of a cornered wolf. I guessed because he didn't expect anyone to be here, and now he had found me, he didn't know what to do with me.

"I just started today," I repeated.

"Not with that accent," he sneered.

Got' damn it, had it grown on me that much?

"Sure I have." I tried to speak with his accent, but sure as hell, I was a Carian more than I had ever been of Earth-2.

The guard straightened up, keeping the gun pointed squarely at the chest, *the money shot.* If he was a trained man, I would have felt safer. His shaking hand told me he wasn't. Someone so obviously unused to holding a gun would possess an unpredictable trigger finger. He might kill me and not even mean to. My heart raced, but I stared blankly at the man, measuring my blinking.

He shook the gun with emphasis. "Then what are you

doing here? Shouldn't you be at your post? And what did you do with Oren?"

Somehow, I doubted his gun was as sophisticated as mine. Probably used real bullets. No stun setting there. One shot, and I'd be a goner.

"Now, let's solve this amicably." I tried to keep my voice quiet, calming.

Judging from the way his hand shook, they hadn't expected anyone to find them here, nor to find anyone.

"You can't trick me." He yelled down to the lab below. "Intruder!"

So I drew, aiming square in the chest. Shock drew across his face amongst the tiny purple photon blast. I hoped it would be dim enough so that anyone down there thought it a trick of the light. That would still be eye-catching, but at least it wasn't loud like a regular gun.

He fell down onto the railing, crashing on his back, shaking the platform violently.

My stomach did a backflip. The rails were put up poorly here, just like outside. Was nothing here sturdy? Was *The Hardest Wood* just a front name? Now wasn't the time to figure it out.

The platform shook underneath me as I leaped over the guy and ran to find some new cover, but I was grabbed by something and pulled over the railing. Falling to my imminent death before I could even get hold of what had happened.

I was always gonna die on the job. I'd made peace with it years ago, didn't make it any less crap.

I jerked to a halt. My face, and body, levitated inches from the grated floor. My body rotated in the air so they could get a good look at me.

"Who are you?" Gia Prick asked.

I shrugged. "It's my first day." Then I aimed my gun at him.

"That will not work here," he said.

I tested my finger, it moved. The Gia Knight was probably only focusing on the barrel, putting a shield over it, so no bullet could shoot. It's what I would've done, if I thought it was a regular gun. This was not. I bet photon light was an entirely different matter to manipulate.

"Intriguing. Not Padoraxian. Not Carian either." He walked over and crouched down next to me.

I saw sand had stained the perfect white of the foot of his robe.

My gun still pointed squarely at the Knight with the empty white eyes, his pupils turning into pinpricks, betraying his lack of emotion.

He then said, "You *are* intriguing."

We had to be roughly the same age, and although his skin was a lot smoother, unweathered, his hair and eyes now white, I knew his face.

He had been in the temple that day. I shared classes with him all my life. The overly eager one. Got every question right —hand always raised, way too keen to be the Head Master's pet.

Ignored, obviously—the Head Master had no need of such a thing, choosing instead to focus on my rebellious questioning, to stamp out my flames.

Look at him now, some kind of Knight. Hadn't done badly for himself.

"Percival, was it?"

His eyes widened, betraying the years of schooling his emotions. "Who are you?" he demanded.

Was that all it took to break his stoicism facade? He was never very good at it. This was my only chance. He let his guard down, scouring his memory for recognition of my now battle-worn features.

I squeezed the trigger.

My blaster's photons were mainly made of light and some other techno crap I should have probably learned the names of. These guns were impossibly rare, especially in a place like this. He must have expected a pea-shooter.

The light went right through the layer of his pristine white robe and sent him to the ground. My body met the grated floor cheek first, rewarding me with a dull pain that had me blinking, my eyelashes tickling against the grate.

If I had time, I would have set it to be more powerful. That trick wouldn't work twice, and who knew what sort of armor he had underneath that robe.

Grumbling, I pushed myself up, pointing the gun at the scientist.

"Now, let's not do anything hasty," I said.

He threw his hands up. "Nope! Nothing hasty here!"

My shoulders slacked slightly. "Finally, somebody reasonable. Now. About that antidote. I need a couple."

He shook in fright. The glint of his wedding band sparkled against the amber light. "There's some on the desk just there. Don't hurt me."

My ears tickled.

More of them downstairs, a commotion.

"What is that?" I demanded.

"I'm sorry. Don't hurt me!" He shielded his torso with crossed arms.

I grunted, losing my patience. "I won't hurt you. Just tell me what that is."

I ran to the desk, scanning the contents—pens, a toy truck, more stacks of paper than I had time to look at, and finally, a couple of vials. I pocketed them.

I turned my attention back to the man. "How do they take it?"

He cried, shaking his arms. "Don't!"

Why did he react that way? Did he think I'd shoot him? May as well use it.

I fired a warning shot. It ricocheted off practically everything before settling in the cave wall. I didn't wince even though the thought of it hitting me made my heart stop. The last thing I needed was to be paralyzed and at the mercy of whatever was grumbling downstairs. It didn't sound natural, not like any beast or human I had ever heard in my life.

Was it... no. Just a kids' story—a superstition.

"How do you take it!" I yelled at the scientist.

"Drink it," he stammered. "Oh god, please don't hurt me." He faced a huge oil drum, cowering against it, hiding his face.

Downstairs, cracking like a thousand whips, yet heavy grumbling, whirling steam engine roars, all coming from the mouth of something. I couldn't explain how I knew the sounds were *alive*.

The floorboards whined underneath me. The stairs clanged and crashed. Whatever it was, it ran—on multiple feet. Two? Four? Two sets of four. Three sets. More than that, much more.

Oh no.

They crashed into the wall, deep dark black bodies under the dim orange lights. There were hints of their shining reflection, they were made of smoke, but then my brain decided flesh. Scales, and then fur. Back to smoke.

"Don't hurt me." The man trembled more violently.

I grabbed him. "C'mon." I pulled at him, trying to get him to run, but he was paralyzed with fear, legs turned to stone. "Now that is neither fight *nor* flight," I said, slapping him in the face. "Snap out of it right now, or they're gonna hurt you." I managed to get his legs working, but I suddenly stopped frozen, not of my own volition.

The pile of white robes on the ground groaned, its hand raised.

"Intriguing. What a peculiar gun that is."

The Gia Knight must not have realized what was behind him. Behind him, black eyes shone.

The white robes disappeared under darkness, as it trampled him back to the ground and engulfed him.

"Now!" I pulled at the scientist, and we ran together, our boots smashing into the stairs like thunder. Stress-led sweat filled my nostrils.

Up and up, they went forever. Turn and up, turn and up. I didn't dare look back. By the sounds of their screeching roars, I feared that I would see them. Were there this many before? I became a singular focus—escape. *Don't get caught. There are worse things than being eaten alive.* I didn't want to find out. The man next to me clearly had an inkling.

We must've been in the middle of the cave. The beasts slammed into every corner, shaking the foundations. Pradorix Wood was strong, but whoever had set this up was no foreman. Images flooded my mind of Its sheer weight decapitating whatever limb it fell on. If we had the misfortune of it being only an arm or leg, we'd lay half-dead and helpless, at their mercy.

I would've preferred Klargites.

A hundred Klargites.

No, *more.* They all had the head of Ruby Knight, snarling *that* grin. That horrific, inhumane smirk with fangs dripping black toxin as they inched closer, sharp toxic breath on my skin, slowly scraping at the top layer of flesh stroking at my exposed shins with pointed pincer feet. Razer feet to draw blood as they got closer up my legs. It tickled, before it became agony.

"Fuck off," the spider Ruby's whispered, cascading into infinity as they all said it at chaotic intervals, a volume beyond what my ears could handle.

The grins grew wider. They were all around me, flaring their bodies, raised on hind legs to present the horror beneath them.

* * *

I slapped myself in the face with the side of my gun, panting with relief that my legs were still working. My mind had been infected, but I had shaken free while still running.

The beasts were directly below us, a single perilous staircase below. They weren't *that* close before—they must've been gaining on us. Maybe I slowed after all. Maybe they were faster. Maybe running was hopeless, and I should just stop and give in to it all.

Above us, the glow of orange lights broke up the darkness like stars in the night sky. How long had we been running for? Were we close?

"I can't," the man moaned. My hand still gripped onto his shoulder, I was yanking at him, but he was slowing, drenched in sweat that made my grip slip.

"Now, you better run. Your wife is waiting for you back home."

I didn't care what this man did, how many people died because of it. Nobody deserves what these beasts would do if they caught us. But the faster I got, the slower he did.

"I'm letting go now. You're gonna keep running, ok? Just keep running up those stairs, and you'll be fine."

I let go of him and took the steps many at a time. His

screams only made me go faster. I didn't have a choice, I told myself. I did what I could.

The stairs ended. My legs were a searing burn that threatened to crumble beneath me, and my lungs burned from sucking in air so fast.

The door.

The door was right *there*. So close, just like they were.

I ran, following the open sludge pipe to my left, and slammed right into the door, shaking at the handle—locked. The man from the walkway had locked it.

They jumped at me. Dark shapes my mind refused to recognize.

I leaped the fence, my foot propelling me up above it. Something grabbed my wrist. It was everything I had ever felt in my life, every wrong thing. Slimy and yet scraping, searing burn and yet, cold, so cold. A light touch, cutting through my wrist.

But then I landed in the disgusting sludge.

It was a natural, single sensation, one all-around every inch of my body. The bandana did nothing to keep it off my lips, but I didn't care. I could wash it off later. It was only a physical sensation. Only a disgusting taste.

My salvation.

Even unfathomable hell beasts will shriek away from jumping into sludge. Not me though, I needed the bath.

I swam, in the direction of the flow, until I suddenly came free and fell. I couldn't see. The sludge covered my goggles. But the wind around me told me that I was about to die. My head spun, throwing my balance off weight. I hugged my body to protect my organs.

No.

Winded from my body hitting the water, I submerged

into the sludge lake. I gathered my wits and swam what I hoped was in the opposite direction I had fallen.

My scrambled brain had done a number on my sense of direction. I could only assume that was the way I had come, but what if I was wrong? What if I was swimming to the base? If it wasn't deep, I'd be ok. If it was... well, there were worse things than death.

I pushed myself out of the water, wiped the goggles of sludge so I could see, and swam to the edge, pulling myself up onto it and laying on my back to catch my breath.

The bandana peeled off me, then the googles. I wiped my face with my hand, but that only spread the sludgy chunks around my face. My stomach finally gave, releasing what little contents it had onto the ground. Mostly whiskey. Burning, expensive whiskey.

I laughed, but that just made me gag more.

I was safe.

They were trapped behind that locked door. Whatever was in that pipe, they wouldn't go near it. I didn't blame them.

Roaring thuds made me sit up alert and see dents in the door. Another appeared, followed by shrieks of unfathomable rage. I got up. Sickness spilled from my throat, causing me to stumble. My stomach constricted and gave in, but I wouldn't.

My aching legs kept running.

My rocket was pushed up against the rocks where the door guy lay, the rocket was likely moved there by the man that discovered me.

The door guy was still passed out, snoozing.

I'm sorry. I need to survive.

I grabbed the stupidly light rocket, pushed it, pushing and pushing while I lifted the lid.

A thundering crash behind me caught my attention. The cave door flew open off its hinges, sliding down the mountain, followed by that shriek again, this time ear piercing. I kept my resolve and pushed the rocket. It was so light it kept going faster from me, escaping from my tips, the only blessing.

Red spots of blinding sunlight filled my vision, but I saw *it*. The line I had made in the sand. I just had to push the rocket and climb in.

I snatched open the door, my hand slipped, and it slammed shut again against the force of the air. On my second try, I kept it open and jumped, pulling myself into the rocket, slamming my tailbone on the metal. The ship shook back and forth from the force of my weight. If it flipped or kept spinning, then I was gonna spend my last waking moments in a god damn upside-down pressure rocket. It was the least of my worries, considering what would happen next, but the thought still spurred me on. It was an easier one to manage than the horror.

I thrust my body to the right to counteract its rocking, it seemed to correct itself and keep going, but its speed slowed to a crawl. Then, I blindly slapped around for the button. Fright surging up like electric shock at my hand being exposed, could they bite it off. Did they even have teeth?

If the ship had to have gone too far from the line I had drawn, I had no way of knowing. All my senses were scrambled. All of them were alert and overly stimulated.

I slammed the button, then pulled my hand back in quickly.

Everything went black. A human handprint slapped on the glass, its owner unseen against the smoke.

7

My head slammed back into the headboard, rewarding me with a searing headache. The interior of the rocket became a blur, just like the outside.

The rocket stopped dead in its tracks like it had been stopped by the Gia Knight. Not having had time to put on my seat belt. I launched from my chair like I was a rocker myself. My body's velocity pushed the glass door up, because I hadn't known how to secure the safety, and I fell face flat into the desert.

There were screams all around me. My vision went back.

Oh no.

But It was just the sounds of kids screaming because a man covered in sludge had just flown into the air and landed face down in the middle of their street, having ejected from a pressure rocket.

I was safe. I made it.

The sun, high up in the sky, beamed down on me. Once the dramatic screams died down, they were replaced with grunting snickering of a couple of orks standing outside a bar.

My thoughts went hurriedly to the beasts in the cave. *they wouldn't come here. They don't travel from the nest for long. That's what the tales say.*

I was safe.

I was...

I patted my pocket.

Oh no.

Shakily, I sat up in the middle of the street, pulling the vails out, and found them entirely intact. I grasped them in my hand, holding them to my chest like they were more precious than gold.

I was safe, and I had the antidote to show for it.

Fuck.

Those beasts.

I threw up.

Then, I pushed it to the back of my mind. The only thing I could do now was pretend it hadn't happened. Find a nice, deep compartment, amongst all the others, and slot it in. Tie it up like a bow. Forget circumstances. Forget ifs and buts. Just lock it up and forget about it—they didn't exist, not underneath the planet like it was just a thin blanket for them. I would have to keep believing that.

I climbed up from the ground. My stumbling legs felt like they had two sets of knees, the Harlen-shaped sludge angel in the ground and the rocket where it crashed.

It's not like I was going to get a parking ticket.

* * *

I limped towards the guard.

The guard put his hand up. "Whoa, you can't come in here like that!"

"Are you gonna stop me?" I asked, shambling forward.

He got out of the way. Touching me wasn't worth whatever Felice paid him.

Each step dripped more sludge onto the expensive fancy carpet Felice imported from another planet. Part of me was going to enjoy this.

"Evenin', Maurine."

"Hello, Mr- oh god." She held her hand over her mouth and ran screaming when the repugnant smell wafted up her nostrils.

"Felice! I'm coming up, Felice!" I hollered.

"My boy! You're back!"

I grinned. *Let's see him hug me now*. I flicked my hand, spraying the foul chunky liquid everywhere. I would've felt bad for Maurine cleaning it up, but it was worth it for Felice's reaction. And besides, after what I had seen, there were worse things than cleaning up a bit of sludge.

"Oh, I'm comin'!" I yelled, halfway between laughing and throwing up again.

At the foot of the stairs, Felice Volt stood just behind his doorway. The man took up more space than it should fit, and it gave me a memory I thought I forgot, of being young, no more than three, and trying to push a big circle into a tiny square hole.

"My boy?" His tone was drenched in worry, obviously not for me but the cleanliness of his house. "How did you do?"

"Drink," I said bluntly.

"Harlen?"

"Drink!" I spat, heading towards him.

He jumped out of the way and rushed to his liquor cabinet, pouring me a healthy glass of scotch from a decanter.

Felice winced, holding his arm out as far as he could to keep his body from me. I took the glass and slammed back the liquid—precious burning relief. Then I looked at my other hand. I was holding my gun. I had been holding it the entire time, in the rocket, on the walk here.

I pointed it at him.

"Double," I said bluntly.

"Now, wait just a-" I tried to cock the gun, but its parts were caked with sludge. The click was less than satisfactory, more like a little thud. I doubted the gun worked.

Sludge splattered everywhere when I put the gun on the desk. I sighed and realized I was still wearing the overalls.

"Does this mean anything to you?" I pointed to the company name on the badge.

He shook his head, his cheeks flapping. "No, not a clue."

I grabbed the gun by its barrel. "I can still throw this pretty hard."

"I mean it, nothing!"

I groaned and sat down on his chair.

I knew I wasn't really being an asshole to him, but whatever poor soul had to clean this up after me, probably Maurine. But the expression on his face was just too damn satisfying. He looked like he was trying to hold in a fart from his mouth.

His eyes darted to the ground, and he fiddled with his hands. "I erm, did you get it?"

I took one of the antidotes from the overalls pocket and put it on the desk. The other I kept hidden.

"I got the antidote. Didn't get a sample of the drug. But believe me, you don't want it."

"That isn't what I paid you for. I wanted a sample."

"You said you wanted to make an antidote, and I got you the antidote. The place is clear of men now anyway, so you're welcome to go and get it."

He clapped his hands together. "My boy! I-"

"It's clear of men—but there's something else down there."

His upper lip twitched. "Something else? Pray tell what, my boy?" His voice quivered.

Was he as clueless as I had believed? I didn't know if he had genuinely known if they were real and they were down there. I didn't care. I just wanted my coin and to get out of there.

"Double."

"Right..." he wobbled over to his safe. "No peeking," he said, grinning at me with those wet eyes.

I shook my head and looked away as he clicked the dial, again, and then again, until it was open. He put coin after coin into a little brown bag, which he then tied tight.

Felice shakily held his arm out at an even greater length now, not wanting me to touch him. I snatched the bag and put it on the desk, downed the last of the scotch, and got up.

Then I looked down at my attire and laughed. "Why am I still wearing this? Covered in god knows what, carrying whatever diseases, and I'm still wearing it! Can you believe that?"

"No." He chuckled in a way that said absolutely nothing was funny.

"I'm still wearing it." I shook my head in laughter, then slipped it off and stepped out of it, leaving it on his floor. It slapped wetly on the ground.

Thankfully, my other gun was completely clean in its holster.

"Oops, can't forget this," I grabbed my gun and the coins. "Nice doing business with ya, Felice."

I didn't bother counting it. I could tell from the weight it was enough to get the two robots I needed, and more.

* * *

In the stable, the stable hands gave me a wide berth.

I apologized to Daisy. "I'm sorry, girl, I know it stinks."

Even without the overalls on, sludge still caked my hair and shoes. Daisy was not having any of it. Every time I patted her, I just got more of it on her.

"Now listen. We are gonna get home, and then that nice stable boy you like is gonna clean you right off, so the sooner I get on top of you, and we're out of this forsaken place, we'll be back at that *other* forsaken place, and you'll be able to get cleaned. Would you like that? A bath?"

She partially understood the sentiment and settled down, stopping bouncing on her front legs to let me climb atop her. I flicked a few coin policies at the stable hand, thanking him. He held his nose and was clearly grateful for my leaving. He yelled to the other stable hands, "Wowwee! What a stank!"

Daisy clopped out of the stable.

A bath certainly would be nice—a real one, from the springs.

8

Daisy galloped with all her might, sending sand flying in every direction like sparks from a welder.

With no goggles nor bandana, I had to keep my mouth shut and squint like my life depended on it. Every time a particularly nasty waft of sand blew in my face, I turned my head sideways. If I had time, I would've showered and brought some goggles, but a man's life was on the line. Thankfully, Daisy knew that the quicker we got home, the faster I'd be off her back. I decided that the next time I saw her, I'd get her some of her favorite treats to make up for the sludge I was dripping down her back.

We flew past the boulders I always used to mark my position to Wolf Water, past the marks in the sand the pressure rockets made—thankfully, the gate was open, and I didn't have to wait.

Hot Sands appeared in the distance in record time.

"Not far off now, girl."

Hopefully, Bobby hadn't dropped dead by then. I had as much death today as I could handle.

* * *

Daisy slowed on the dead grass walkway that split Hot Sands. I waved at some ladies, whose grins quickly fell flat. They covered their mouths with the front of their dresses.

"That bad, huh?" I chuckled.

Baking in the desert heat, the smell wasn't getting any less repugnant, but I was almost used to it. When I got to the stables, I stepped off Daisy, slapped her on the ass so she'd go in of her own volition - didn't need much convincing - and made a beeline for Jack's shop.

"Harlen!" a young voice called.

Rage bubbled inside me. "Got' damn it won't you leave me be for one second!"

The little kid's eyes went wide with fright behind his oversized goggles, quickly dissipating my anger.

"I'm sorry, kid. I'm just grouchy 'cause I had a hard day."

He just looked at me, then sniffed, immediately burst into tears, and ran away from me.

Something caught my eye.

"Wait, kid," I called, heading after him.

He stopped in his tracks, pinching his nose and making a big show of it. "I don't wanna. You smell bad!"

"Just a sec' kid, what's it say on your truck?" I bent my knees to get on his level.

He hugged the truck close like I was gonna snatch it. "I don't know. I can't read."

"Just... face it towards me. I don't wanna take it."

He held it out. I mouthed the name of the company. The same one on the overalls. *The Hardest Wood.*

Why? They were in the middle of nowhere. What possible reason did they have to hide behind a name like that? They even made weird merchandise to further stress the point that they were nothing more than a construction company.

I didn't know what to make of it, but I still had something else to deal with, so I said bye to the kid and ran across the road to Jack's shop, skidding to a halt at the alleyway when I spotted a body laying there.

"Bobby." I shook him, hoping to hell he wasn't dead.

He sniffed. "What's that smell?"

His eyes bulged out of their sockets. The blood veins were thick, pushing out against his eyes like they were laid on top of them. Twitching. Pumping something.

I grabbed the vial from my pocket and undid the lid, holding it over his mouth.

"Drink this."

"What..." He was dazed, acting sluggish and tired, yet if you looked at his eyes, you'd think he was about to fly off into space.

"Drink it now, you druggy fuck!" I shook him harder. "It's gonna get you high, real high. Higher than you've ever been before!"

"Well, alright then." He took the vial from me and knocked it back, then blinked, smacking his lips together at the peculiar taste.

Nothing happened for a while, I thought it might've been something else, some other actual drug, and I had just sent Bobby speeding off towards his death.

He blinked again, and his eyes started to go back to a regular size, the veins disappearing into the whites. Then, after a moment, he passed out, slumping down on the floor.

Was he dead? My heart stopped.

Bobby started snoring.

I fell back against the other shop wall, relieved—also,

disappointed, I wanted to ask him some more questions—about the man that gave him the drug, for starters.

The bell to Jack's store chimed, his hobbled groans alerting me he was headed my way.

"Now, what the hell is that smell? Saw you run in the alleyway, Harlen."

"Oh, it's nothing," I smirked to myself. "Your brother's fine, by the way."

"Of course he's fine!" Jack rubbed his eyes, smearing more coal on his face. "He's sleeping, just like he was before you got here."

I shook my head, laughing. Then, I couldn't stop.

"You're one strange man, Harlen." Jack looked at me like he thought I was crazy.

After the day I had and the shit I'd seen, maybe he was right.

"Yeah, yeah, and you're the most regular guy this side of Caria." I waved him off. "Now, you got those robots for me?"

"I got 'em both, damn crime against nature if you ask me, making a cleaning guard bot be-"

I held my hand up. "Robots ain't natural, neither is this coin I'm about to give you, so I suggest you shut your mouth and take it."

He shut his mouth, shrugging. "Sorry, Harlen, I was just sayin'."

I sighed, leaning against the wall of the other store to take a breather. Bobby snored loudly in the background.

"I'm sorry, Jack, it's been a long day. Why don't you show me these bots?" I shoved myself to stand at my full height.

He nodded, then limped in the direction of his store. I went to follow, but he held his hand up. "Nope, you wait outside."

I chucked. "Fair enough."

With great clunky noises, the first robot appeared out the doors, and then the second. The bronze rigid things stood before me, almost to attention in a way that reminded me all too much of my past.

"So, eighty was it?" I said, stepping past the robots. Jack sniffed but was polite enough to not mention the smell again.

I pulled the bag out of my pocket and handed him the coin pieces. "Oh, and can you take a look at this?" I fished the sludge-soaked gun from the holster.

He leaned in, stroking his chin, while his nose flickered at the stench. "Is this that fancy gun of yours? I mean, maybe? Robots are one thing. I just hook up the AI chip and let it do its thing."

"Might wanna be a bit quieter about that Jack, rest of the town knows how easy it is, they might start trying it themselves."

"Heh, yeah. Well, anyway, I'll take a look at it. No promises." He took the gun between the tips of his two fingers and hobbled back into his store, leaving me alone with my new robots.

"Hello?" I tested.

The lights of their eyes glowed a dim teal hue.

"**Sccchhh**, hello, I am number 05."

"Hello, I am number 06."

"Go to Hot's Colds, over there." I point. "Tell Violet the barmaid that you are at her service for protection and cleaning duties. Do whatever she says."

They clunked and tooted, vents blowing cold air in my eyes, making me blink. The robots turned in the direction of her bar and began walking.

I followed close behind, wanting to see her reaction to them first. Something told me she'd be annoyed with how noisy they walked. Or what bad conversational partners they'd be. But when she saw them working tirelessly to keep her place clean, I thought she'd change her mind.

Eventually, the bots reached the shop, while I rested against the door listening from the outside.

"Damn it, why did you let your 'bots in here?" Her Carien twang yelled, making me twitch *down there.*

I smirked. In the bar, the robots said the line I had given them.

"This some kind of game he's playing, give me a robot so I gotta pay for it? He knows I can't afford it."

That was my cue. I pushed open the doors to the bar. It had died down since I was last here, there were just a few lone drunks on the far ends of the room.

"I got them," I proclaimed.

Violet put her hands on her hips, her nose scrunched at the foul odor permeating her nostrils. She waved her hand in front of her face. "What in hell is that stench?" Her eyebrows rose as she realized it was me. "I should be relieved you ain't injured, but this ain't much better."

"Yeah, I'm gonna head to the baths in a sec."

The bots stood in the middle of the bar, doing nothing, looking kind of menacing but also useless, like statues.

"What do they do?" She eyed the robots distrustingly.

I had to admit they looked strange, standing in the middle of the bar, devoid of life. It looked like they were incapable of doing all the things I was sold on. The rigid bronze things just stood there.

"Whatever you want."

Violet twitched her eyebrows, grinning cheekily. "*Whatever* I want?"

I said nothing, strolling over to her, muscles aching from today's excursions. With one hand, I grabbed her arm, my other slid between her legs, holding her mound over her skirt, cupping it completely.

Her smile faded to a look of forlorn submission.

"You got me for that now. You belong to me. I got the bots to clean and protect you. Now I can spend less time here and more time *here.*"

I cupped her tighter, pushing against her hole through the folds.

It might not have been strictly true that that was the reason, but it was a good enough reason for now. "*And,* I don't care who knows it. I want them to know it. You belong to *me.*"

She nodded in agreement. "Ok. Fine. But not with that stench."

We both smirked.

I let go of Violet and waved the words away. "Yeah, yeah, I'm gonna have a bath. And then we'll see."

"We'll see." She smiled, getting closer to one of the bots and poking him in the chest.

That reminds me. "Oh, bots."

"Yes?" they buzzed.

"She's your master now, do whatever she says, protect her, keep the place clean."

The bots sprung to life, the metal tubes under their wrists extending and vacuuming dust around the bar.

Satisfied, I made my way to the stairs, rubbing my aching back.

There was a gasp behind me from one of the patrons. "What is that?"

Another cackled, "It's aliens from space!"

"Don't be stupid. Aliens don't exist."

I groaned. "What now?" Grunting and slouching my shoulders, I dragged myself back around to look at the door.

A looming shadow began to permeate the floor of the bar. I looked at Violet, but she was as confused as I was.

"Stay here," I warned her, hand reaching for my missing gun first, then the one I still had.

I stepped outside and looked for cover, only finding the bench in front of the bar. It would be useless from an air attack.

A great shadow blocked out the sun, the edges were blindingly brighter by comparison, like they were on fire with the blazing sunlight. I shielded my eyes, then they adjusted. I saw it for what it was.

The white ship.

It's him.

The Gia Knight had escaped.

Of course he had. After I stunned him, he would've shielded himself.

A man who had trained himself not to feel emotions attacked by those hell beasts' terrifying power. Could he shield himself from *that*? Did he have to feel it all while protected from their physical attacks? I could only imagine what horror escaped from the cave, crazed and vengeance-obsessed.

The ship fell unnaturally fast, then crashed onto the ground, spitting dirt and sand everywhere. It hit shop windows like thousands of tiny bullets.

I would only have one shot—one chance to get him off guard. After that? The town would be at his mercy. Maybe even the planet.

The door's frame appeared on the smooth white surface, shunting down to the ground in a slow mechanical hum, and the end of his pristine robes appeared.

Shoot him, do it now.

9

How were the robes clean when they were so dirty before? How mad could he have been if he had stopped to tidy himself up?

The Gia Knight walked down the steps, his, no, *her* body coming into view. It was another Subject of Gia. This one bore no armor around her shoulders. I supposed I couldn't call her a knight. She put her hands together and strolled towards me.

"Harlen?"

Wait.

My knees threatened to buckle. I couldn't sit down on the other side of the bench, so I leaned on it, but it would not avail the knot in my stomach.

"Is that you?" she asked.

I breathed in, but the breath would not go out. *Why would she be here?*

"You must come with me." She paused and sniffed. "What is that odor?"

I gripped my gun tighter, I knew I wouldn't use it, but its presence comforted me.

"Erm, sludge." I coughed from awkwardness.

"I see."

Her oversized robes seemed to billow like a flag in a nonexistent wind. It was awkward. Well, for me. She just stood there, studying me with that blank Gia stare. I noted her changed hair. Silvery white. Her eyes, white and emotionless. even her lips seemed even fuller, but her nose was still perfectly cute.

"What are you doing here?" I asked.

"I came here for you."

The words I should have wanted to hear felt so confusing coming from Savanna's lips. I had so many questions. Why did she want me? How did she find me? Why now after all these years?

"Why?" I blurted.

"You need to come back to Earth-2. It has been decreed." She sounded less human than the robots in the bar.

"Decreed by who?"

"The Head Master."

I wasn't going anywhere, but I wasn't about to send Savannah away, either.

"Well, I gotta take a bath. Why don't you wait in your ship for me."

A few kids from the street had come to marvel at the strange white pointed orb of a ship sitting right in the middle of the road, while adults eyed it distrustingly. Jack looked more like the kids, eyes wide in wonder.

Savannah nodded. "That is wise."

"Your ship's gonna be alright like that?"

With a wave of her hand, the door closed, and the frame disappeared, earning an *'ooooh'* from the kids.

"It will be impenetrable," she said, returning her hands together.

She wasn't *Savannah.* It may have been her body and her name, but this was someone else.

The bar doors squeaked open, and Violet peered out from the store. "Harlen, what's all this?"

Great.

Violet crossed her arms when she saw Savannah. "What are *they* doing here?" Her voice shook in that familiar off-key worry.

"They're here for me, apparently," I said.

She nodded. "Right on time too."

I was taken aback. "Excuse me?"

"Thought you were off on an adventure."

That isn't what I said to her in the bar.

Savannah studied us, saying nothing while holding her hands in the religious pose.

"I mean, kind of," I said. "But not with *them*."

Then Violet yelled, "How rude of me!" She uncrossed her arms, and then broke the distance between her and Savannah, holding one out to the stoic monk.

"Hello, my name is Violet. It's so nice to meet you."

Savannah looked at the hand, clearly baffled by the polite gesture, before unclasping her hands to offer one to Violet, who took it warmly in both of hers.

"Savannah."

Violet's eyebrows shot to the sky. "*Oh*, Savannah? How lovely to meet you. You didn't mention she was so beautiful, Harlen."

What is happening? I need to take control of this madness.

"Listen, ladies. This is all well and good. But I think everyone can agree I need to go and take a bath."

There couldn't have been a worse time for me to be covered in this whatever-the-hell-it-was.

Violet put her hands together in an almost mock way of

Savannah, but I could tell it was her trying to make her feel welcome. "I'll keep Savannah entertained."

I could hardly argue with that, but who knew what they'd talk about? My shoulders slumped, the adrenaline rush from before starting to subside. "Sounds good to me. I'll be upstairs."

Violet took Savannah by the hand. "Come with me, *darlin'*. Do you want a drink?"

"Water will suffice," Savannah's cold voice replied.

"Oh, *pish*, you don't come all this way from Earth-2 to drink water. I've got a beer with your name on it."

Violet practically yanked Savannah into the bar, leaving me standing there, still gripping my pistol. I looked at its lazer setting—the strongest, and was glad I had the forethought not to use it.

Then I headed in. Violet seated Savannah on one of the bar stools, where her billowing robe went tight against her buttcheeks. The curved crevice made my eyes go wide with awe.

"I'll be back soon," I announced.

"Not too soon, I hope—us girls have got some chatting to do, oh don't look at me like that. I won't divulge anything you wouldn't want me to." Violet winked at me.

I was relieved, if not entirely convinced, but if Violet thought she could convince this stoic monk girl to break all her oaths for me, she was welcome to try, something told me she'd do anything she could to send me on my way. At least Savannah could hear about all my daring deeds. However, judging by her persona, she'd probably consider it the exploits of lesser people. Savannah didn't even consider that the middle of the street wasn't a good place to park her ship. She was not the woman I remembered.

Climbing the steps and running the bath took ages. Downstairs, Violet howled with laughter. At least *she* was having a good time. I tore off my clothes and left it all in a pile, wondering what Savannah was making of all this.

The warm water eased my aching muscles. I closed my eyes, letting the water get into my pores. Submerging myself, I looked up at the world above me. I could just stay down in the water forever. I wouldn't have to deal with any of it. But when I emerged, it was all waiting for me downstairs. And the longer I stayed up here, the worse it would get.

After leaving the bath, I brushed my teeth within an inch of their life, gargling the toothpaste water. I pushed my hair behind my ears to let it dry, and walked back to my room naked, leaving wet footprints on the dusty floor while Violet howled downstairs, "No way, Harlen did that?"

At least they were getting along.

The violent vacuum sound of the robots flared up.

"Not now, robot. Can't you see we're having a conversation?"

"Yes, Ma'am. I will continue after," it said.

Violet finally had someone who would do what she wanted and not argue back. Two of them, in fact.

Once in my room and dressed, I left my gun holder and gun on the bedside cabinet. I then found my other pair of shoes—the ones without any spurs, and made my way downstairs.

Violet howled. "Ha! I can't believe he did that."

Seems like Savannah is the one surprising Violet.

I stepped into the bar, head held high.

"It is true. He did that." Savannah sipped on a still nearly full beer. I looked to see if she was affected, wondering how a woman in her twenties would react to her very first beer.

Upon seeing me, she jumped off her stool. Her robes billowed everywhere, a patron sitting at the table brushed her ridiculously long sleeve out of the way, but she didn't notice.

"We are ready to return to Earth-2 now," she spoke bluntly, but assuredly, as if it was to be expected.

I shook my head. "I ain't going there."

Violet scowled at me.

I ignored her and exited the bar.

Sand blew past the white ship. From far away, a crow squawked. I put my new, clean bandana on. I would have to live with some sand getting in my eyes, but it wouldn't be bad on the short walk.

Savannah appeared beside me, making me jump.

She came right up to my ears, just a little shorter than me. Her hair perfectly framed her face, not a strand out of place. And she wore no perfume but didn't smell of anything either. Perhaps she could just *Gia* the perspiration off her own body.

"You look different," I remarked.

We stood on the wooden platform to the bar, overlooking the long dirt road, which her ship was slap-bang in the middle of.

"So do you."

I scratched the back of my neck. "Yeah, the sun will do that to you." *And all the knife and bullet wounds. It's a marvel I'm still alive to tell the tale.*

"So we are going back to Earth-2 now?"

"No. Weren't you listening? I ain't going back there."

I started walking. Behind Hot's Colds was the long trailing path that eventually led to one of the sparse forests. At least we called it a forest, but it was more a collection of trees covering up the lake.

"Listen, darlin'" *Why did I call her that?* "I've had a long hard day, and all I've been thinking of is those steam baths. Now, the one I had upstairs got me clean for sure, but it did nothing to relax me. So either you're coming, or you're not, but I promise you, the last place I'm going is inside that ship of yours."

She said nothing, walking swiftly along to follow my long strides.

"Well then, we can take the ship. There is no need for us to walk."

"Like I said, I ain't getting in that ship."

"I see."

We strolled in silence across the weathered dirt path that weaved in and out of a few trees. With any luck, we'd be alone, and I could relax without whoever it was gawking at the strange white monk in my company.

The grassy knolls began to get a little greener.

The silence wasn't awkward. If anything, it seemed to permeate an understanding between us. That if she wasnt getting what she wanted from me, she would have to find new ground.

I still felt I should break the silence. "So, that your first beer?" I asked.

"It was."

"How was it?"

She took a moment to ponder her answer. The sand shuffling between the dirt was the only sound besides my heavy breathing.

"Interesting."

"Oh, I bet it was. And what about Violet?"

She didn't hesitate to answer. "Interesting."

"Yeah, that's one word for her."

"Did you two have sex?"

I coughed, choking on my own spit, laughing nervously. "You just said that, didn't you?"

But she stood there, hands together. That great billowing robe must've been making her sweat, but her skin was smooth, not shiny like my arms, glistening with it.

"Aren't you hot in all that?" I said.

"No. I can repel the heat."

I stopped to muse on the insinuation such words carried. Did she repel the color from her hair? Did she ever need to shower?

"Makes sense. Let's carry on. We're almost there."

"Did you have sex with Violet?" The way she repeated the question unnerved me. She had no shame, no caring of others feelings.

"Kind of," I admitted. "Why do you want to know?"

"I find it interesting."

"I bet you do, yer dirty pervert."

"What does that mean?"

I closed my eyes in exasperation. "It's like talking to a robot."

It wasn't her fault. Besides, wasn't this precisely what I wanted when I left?

"I see."

So she took that literally? Why did I feel like everything I said was getting stored and used as a reference point for a later conversation?

After far too long, we approached the trees. I was eager to see where the new scenery would lead our conversation. What the relaxation of the baths would do to her temperament.

"It's just through here," I said, pointing out the obvious.

"I see."

Part of me wanted to grab her by the shoulders and

shake her to see if anything of Savannah was still in there. But after a decade, *I* was hardly the person I was back then. It was silly to assume she would be, even without all that Gia crap.

I rubbed my eyes, which seared with tiredness. How many hours had I built up from my journey to the other side of the planet? *Hadn't I gained some?* Even so, what I went through was enough to exhaust anyone.

"Why are we going here and not back to Earth-2 like you are required?" she asked.

A stroke of something came to me. I wouldn't call it brilliance, more bargaining.

"Hey, remember how, before we ascended, we were allowed to have whatever things we wanted, to make the ascension all the more powerful because we were leaving it all behind."

She nodded. "Yes?"

"Well, how can you know it's right for me to go back to Earth-2, to that tower, if you don't know what it is I'm leaving behind?"

She paused for a second. "It's an interesting proposition."

Interesting—interesting just meant whatever word she wasn't allowed to use. She *was* there—deep, deep down, hidden. Waiting for me to pull her out?

No. It wasn't my responsibility to do that. It wasn't my right. And if I did, would Savannah have some kind of crazy breakdown? It wasn't fair of me to do that.

We approached the great baths, and I made a note to keep my mouth shut for the time being.

The baths were a huge freshwater lake, the bed of which was stone. This meant that it took months to catch up to the heat of the summer sun. During certain times of the year, the baths were a middling temperature, perfect for lazing in.

Around us, trees gave us privacy. If anyone were to approach, we'd hear them before they saw us.

Slinking my belt off and throwing it to the ground, I began unbuttoning my shirt.

"What are you doing?" she asked, eyes wide in alarm.

10

I smiled. "Yeah, fair enough. Like I said. It's been a long day. I forgot myself."

Without speaking, she pulled up her robe. Her pants were a kind of thin knitted material that was fitted impossibly perfectly to her body. She raised the robe over her thighs. The line of her thighs curved perfectly over her mound. I filled with blood at the sight of her thigh gap and put my hand in my pocket to hide it. Now she had started, she didn't seem to care that I was watching. Maybe she didn't even recognize that she was a sexual being—I sure did.

The thin, knitted material hugged her perfectly everywhere. The fabric hugged the shape of her breasts completely—they were thick and full, and I could actually see the faint hint of her nipples pushing against the grey-white cloth.

A line of buttons started between her legs, going up her stomach to her neck, suggesting to me how easily it could be ripped apart to reveal *everything*.

That wasn't something *they* thought about. That was the way *my* mind worked.

I undid my pants and slipped them off, throwing caution of my hardness to the wind. Taking my shirt and pendant off, I left it on the pile of clothes and then jumped right in. Water splashed all over Savannah's bodysuit, revealing the silhouette of her nipples, they hardened into the fabric.

She merely looked down at it with interest. Standing there, tall and slender and thick in all the right places, Savannah looked fit, her stomach toned and flat but the silhouette broken by her ample bosom. There seemed to be no support in her catsuit, but her breasts stayed up like she was a carved statue, so thick and full. They almost hypnotized me, but I managed to tear myself away to look at her in the face.

"So, you're getting in?" I asked.

Savannah pulled her shoes off, and something about seeing her bare feet was far too intimate for me to handle. My hardness must've been making my head feel lighter. I couldn't concentrate on anything but her.

She dipped a toe into the water first to test it. Once satisfied it was a warm, comforting temperature, she slipped in with all the grace of an elegant swan.

I was under the water, so she couldn't see my scars, which I wanted to hide from her for some reason. It was like I didn't want the Savannah of old to be worried about my many scars and wounds. Or worse, I'd find out this new Savannah didn't give a damn about it, which was much more likely. That would cut too deep.

"*Ahh*." I groaned in relaxation, the warmth finally relaxing some of my pent-up stress, the tenseness in all my muscles, except for one one, alleviated.

She mimicked me, leaning against the pool's edge and resting her head back.

"Nice, right?" I asked.

"It is ni-interesting. Yes."

I let out a little laugh. "So, how come you don't have armor?"

"Armor... on my shoulders?" She turned to me. My eyes darted to her lips, which pursed open slightly. A perfect peach color. She wore no lipstick or makeup. She didn't need to. Her skin was flawless, with no eyebags like Violet and I. An untouched sort of beauty that was as rare as water on Caria.

It enamored me, but I couldn't ignore the words that came from those lips I stared at. "When did you see the Knight of Gia?"

"Today—on the other side of the planet. You didn't know he was here? I thought at first you were him."

I neglected to give her the details, partly for her sake, primarily for mine. I didn't want to relive it.

Then I realized something. "Wait, so they're actually called Gia Knights? That was just the name I guessed for them. How come they have the same name as you?"

"They are named after my mother. They are hers."

"She's still around then." I pushed whatever feelings I had about that deep down and asked Savannah, "How come you aren't one? Savannah Knight the Knight—has a ring to it."

"I cannot be both a Knight and Deputy Master. She says it would get in the way of my duties."

She breathed in deeply. Her heaving breasts escaped from the water's surface. Her nipples were hardened now. *From the water or something else?*

Now it was my turn to be short. "I see."

So she's Deputy Master now. That could only mean her mother had taken the role of Grand Master.

"There weren't any *'Knights'* around when I was there," I said.

"Things have changed since then."

"Is that why they want me back?"

"Yes. It is not right for a chosen Subject of Gia to leave," she said. "That is the new belief."

I snorted. "New belief. That isn't how these things used to work."

"I only follow what is right as decreed by the Head Master. That is the way it has always been. As the Head Master did before her, he was more lenient. More accepting. Things... toys, books, these are not allowed now, even before ascension."

"And yet, here you are, divulging in the acts of sinners, despite the Head Master's wishes—as the Deputy Master no less."

"I did what I had to do to ensure your arrival. It is what the Head Master would have wanted, I am sure. When she told me she would be sending a task force to retrieve you, I told her that you would more willingly come with me. It is... unfortunate I was wrong about that."

"Couldn't you have just forced me with your magic Gia powers?"

She looked at me. Even without any expression, I could tell what I said had been deeply offensive to her. Now *there* was a thread to pull on. But that way led even more disdain —or perhaps, unearthed thoughts, even if she didn't know they were buried.

Screw it.

"So your mom didn't want you coming?" I asked.

Her lips pursed into a straight line, no easy feat due to their plumpness.

She was beautiful.

"She did not."

"Hmm." I closed my eyes and interlocked my fingers on my chest.

The warm water splashed around her changing position. Was she facing me? I opened them to see her big glowing, white eyes, close enough for me to see my own reflection.

"What?" she asked, even though she was the one staring at me.

"It's just funny. You assumed I hadn't changed at all."

"You are clearly still stubborn."

"And you're eager to please *her*."

"That is cruel."

She returned to rest on her back, deep breathing. The sounds were like a calming symphony. Even though she was cross, just hearing that sound, the same breathing you'd hear sleeping next to the soft sighing snores of a woman.

"Does that bother you?" I asked.

"It does not. It was merely an observation." She was curt again.

I had clearly struck a nerve. The same I tried to soothe way back when were now to be poked and prodded at.

"What will you do if I don't come?" I asked.

"I don't foresee that."

"Oh, your kind has *that* power too?"

She crossed her arms. "Do you have any of yours left?"

She was actually getting annoyed. It tickled me.

"Wouldn't you know that already?"

"I asked you a question." Savannah stared dead ahead to the other side of the lake.

"I asked you one first."

That back and forth was just like when we were kids.

We looked each other dead in the eyes, and a smirk drew across my face. I began to laugh. She, however, did not. But I saw it, a tiny little flicker. I'd need more than that to break her.

I stretched, showing my hard-earned muscles and a bullet wound that had been particularly bloody—obtained when my old mentor and I went on a bounty hunt across the plant.

"What is that?" she asked, poking the mark.

"It's from work." I casually replied.

"What do you do for work?"

"Whatever I'm paid for."

I wanted to shake her, to look deep into her eyes and say *look, it's me. Let's just throw away the pretence and kiss.* But I knew I was at fault too. Neither of us knew how to act with each other.

She wasn't who she was. I wasn't who I was.

And I was no longer eager to make her laugh. Why should I, when this was who she was? It didn't stop me lusting after her though.

Her wet kitted catsuit hugged her cleavage so tight it was like she wore nothing. Above the water level, it stuck to her body from being wet. Was it wool? Shrinking in the water?

Her fucking nipples. If I tried, I bet I could suck on them even over the material.

"You can't stop looking at my body," she remarked, her voice devoid of emotion.

I didn't look away. "I can't," I admitted. "Does that bother you?"

"It's interesting."

I inched closer to her. My thigh rubbed against hers.

"Interesting how?" I pressed.

"I..." she stopped. Her cheeks turned a little rosy. *Finally, some color.* "It's interesting—like what you did with Violet. I'm not exposed to such things. It's not allowed. So I'd like to hear about it."

"What me and Violet did was a little... advanced. It might make your head explode."

Did I hear people approaching in the distance? Or was it paranoia that this moment could be ruined.

"I'm not going to do it. I just want to hear about it."

"You *want*? Isn't that a sin?"

"I..." she trailed off again. Crossing her arms, then uncrossing them to try and get out of the pool, but I grabbed her arm, and she made no resistance.

"Where are you going?"

Our eyes locked.

My heart fought to beat out of my chest. I felt it all the way down to my groin, a lustful need, more than just lust. I needed to have her. There could be no other option.

"I don't know," her soft voice barely escaped from her lips.

"Good." I pulled her close.

She came all this way for *me*. I could help her, starting with a kiss, and then quickly more.

I let go of her arm and touched her cheek. She stared up at me with those glowing white eyes. Was there a hint of auburn in them? Just a tiny, little flicker—an imperfection in the flawless white.

The trees brushed open behind us. A couple, merrily chatting and laughing, entered the baths and then went far from us to give us privacy. I frowned. We needed more than that.

Savannah inched away, as if the interruption reminded

her of her principles. She crossed her arms and breathed heavily.

"The bath is nice," she said. "We do not have baths like this. Just showers."

I said nothing.

The couple chatted while we laid there without speaking a word.

It wasn't an awkward silence. Although there was much to work through, Rome wasn't built in a day.

The fact she wasn't storming off, branding me a traitor to Gia, was enough.

For now.

11

"What shall we do now?" Savannah asked, then took in a sharp intake of breath.

I measured my breathing, making sure it was slow to give off an impression of being relaxed. "We could get a drink at the bar?"

She sat up straight. "More beer?"

"Got a taste for it?"

Her nose scrunched up in remembrance. "No, it was distasteful. And yet it made me feel *warm*—not in the way the sun does, on the inside."

Savannah climbed out of the pool, kneeling over the edge to get out and giving me a full view of her behind. Her wet attire hugged her completely, including the curves of her cameltoe.

My lips went dry.

When I climbed out, my shape and hardness were apparent in my briefs. It swung from my movements.

We stood there, and her eyes caught it immediately, flaring wide momentarily. The couple across the pool laughed again. I had half a mind to grab Savannah and have my way with her regardless of them being there, but what I wanted to do to her was beyond what should be witnessed by others. If I kissed her, I wouldn't be able to stop until I had mounted her.

Instead, I grabbed my pants and stepped into them, then did my shirt up. Savannah slipped her shoes on. The warm evening air was already starting to dry our clothes. The sun began to disappear under the horizon, its orange hue wishing us goodbye.

"Shall we go?" I asked, offering her my arm.

She frowned at it. "What do I do?"

"Take it in your hand."

Gingerly, her dainty fingers slipped over my arm, naturally fitting there, and we left the pool.

Her robe remained forgotten on the ground.

We walked back up the dirt path in silence. Though there was more to talk about, and I had more to ask Savannah, I didn't feel like it. I just wanted to be with her. There was all the time in the world to sort out everything else.

There wasn't this desperate need to get in her pants I thought I should feel. Even though I wanted it badly, I knew the time would come, and before then, I could enjoy her company. It would make it all the sweeter when we did finally tear each other's clothes off.

I had many funny stories to tell her, and I couldn't wait to see her reactions—to see if I could break the cold, stony mask she wore.

"What else can we do on this planet?" she asked.

"We can ride horses. Have you ever been on a horse?"

"Horse?" Her eyebrows furrowed.

"You used to call them flesh bikes. It always made me laugh."

I expected her to smirk. Instead, her face straightened, and she let go of my arm, walking freely.

"I was foolish. I shouldn't have owned any of those books. Mother was right."

"Your mother-" I began, the rage fueling my words, but I quickly calmed myself and said instead, "how did you get on when I left?"

"*Get on*?" She said each word like they were new.

"With *her*, with everything. How did it go when I left?"

“Well. It went well." She placed her hands together.

"Is that all you're going to give me?" *Why was I so curt? To draw it out of her?*

"I am the Deputy Master, Harlen."

And she was meeting me there. Well, she started it.

"Yeah, that's pretty well."

We walked in silence. The sexual tension was gone. We were back to hiding behind our walls—and building them higher than ever.

Stars in the sky sparkled on our walk towards the approaching town.

"There are other things you could try, you know," I said.

"What?"

"Other than beer. There's whiskey, wine, Klargen?" I said the last word with greater inflection to let her know it was a joke.

"What's Klargen?"

"Don't worry about it." *Baited.*

"No, tell me." She pinched at my shirt, just the tips of her fingers, pulling at me like she did when we were kids.

"Well..." I explained how it was made, the blood of whatever herd animal, the most potent alcohol available, usually fatal to humans. I left out the part about what animal the real stuff was made from.

Disgust trickled across her face, making her nose twitch. It pleased me more than anything to see such a visceral emotion from her. "Who would drink such a thing?"

We reached the front of the bar, about to push open the doors.

A deep yell snarled across the highway, “Harlen!"

I quickly went into a battle pose, reaching for my guns, making sure the notch was in the right place.

The ork i had tangled with earlier lumbered down the walkway towards the bar.

"Stand behi-" I began to say, but when I glanced at Savannah, she merely stood there, not moving.

She stared at me, her face devoid of emotion. "What?"

The ork reached for his hammer. "It's time for round two."

"The hammer shoots photons, not regular bullets. They're made of light or something, not physical matter," I quickly explained to Savannah.

"I understand." She nodded calmly while the ork pulled his gun out and shot at us.

Blinding purple energy beams stopped dead before they could harm us, they floated in the air, giving the impression time stopped. Savannah's trembling hands were outstretched, breaking the illusion. Her eyes flickered wide in surprise, but she held the beam steady, her hands shaking slightly.

I cocked my gun and fired at him, but he was quick, too quick. He jumped out of the way behind a shop wall, my lazer leaving a black mark in the wall. His hammer was hanging over the edge.

Savannah discarded the floating light like it was nothing but a bit of dust, waving it away to dissipate into the dirt.

"What?" she asked, because I was staring at her, blinking

at how quickly she had leaped into action, seemingly from a state of obliviousness.

"Nothing." Many feelings rose in me I couldn't reasonably assess, though excitement was one of them. I aimed at the ork behind the wall and fired. It hit his hammer and ricocheted into the dirt.

"Hah, now we're talking, an even match," he yelled.

"I beat him last time," I told Savannah.

"Clearly."

"Is that sarcasm?" I said, grabbing her arm and pulling her behind a bench for cover.

"I wouldn't know how to do that." She was blinking rapidly, regaining her composure. *Had that one blast taken all of her power?*

"'Reckon you can do it again?"

"Once more, then I'll need a rest. Physical objects are easier."

A shadow loomed over us. Reminding me once again that orks were quicker than they looked.

"Ain't falling for that again." The ork spat.

The great hammer slammed down. I pushed Savannah out of the way. We flung in opposite directions, rolling across the sand and flicking it in the air. The hammer hit the bench shattering the wood, splintering it like it would our bones if I gave him a chance to strike again.

She thrust out her hand, and the ork flung backward, landing in the dirt with a grunting thud. I leaped over the remains of the bench and aimed right at his head.

And then he was dead—headless in the dirt, replaced by blood splatter.

If I were a fool, or rather, if Violet were watching, I would have spun my gun when I turned back to the bar, but

I knew it would have made Savannah's eyes roll if she was capable of such an emotion. I just put it in the holster.

The bar doors opened, steam shooting from the robots as they stepped outside, closely followed by Violet, who put her hands on her hips to survey the scene.

"A lot of good these bots are. Took them that long to hobble out of here. I wanted to push them," she said, shaking her head and tutting.

Was that really all she had to say? No 'how are you Harlen, are you safe?'

"They're not gonna be leaving your store, Violet. They're to protect you, not whoever's outside."

Savannah was still on the ground, so I hurried over and grabbed her arm to lift her up. Violet did the same to her other arm.

"How about that drink?" I said, grinning at Savannah.

She nodded. "I will have a drink."

It seemed no matter how I pushed her, she dug firmly into her roots.

We stepped into the bar, and the few patrons inside cheered at our efforts.

"Never did like that ork," a mustached one said.

"C'mon Savannah, let's go sit at the bar." My hand reached towards her but retreated when I realized what I was doing.

At the bar, Violet put both of her hands on the counter top.

"So what brings you to this neck of the galaxy, Savannah?"

I sipped my beer, watching the interaction with interest. Had the women not spoken of that already when I was bathing? Surely they'd not spent the whole time talking about me?

"I came for Harlen."

Violet clicked her tongue. "I know he's handsome, but all that for a little 'ol him?"

"Nothing little about me." I bounced my eyebrows with a grin.

"I know," they both said in unison.

I took another sip of unusually refreshing beer, taking the comment in my stride. Violet licked her lips, looking from me to Savannah.

Surely not? I wouldn't say no, but it was a little fast for Savannah since she was so inexperienced. She took another long sip of her beer—gaining the courage? I grabbed her hand and held it while Violet strolled off to let us have our words.

"What does she think we will do?" she asked.

"Nothing you aren't ready for," I said. "At least, for now."

"She is very beautiful. Objectively, of course. And it would be very interesting. But I am so..." A flash of horror appeared on her face, so I gripped her hand tighter. "And it's forbidden! Why are we having this conversation?" She crossed her arms, leaving my touch.

I shrugged. "I always get this way after a fight, don't you?"

"I do not fight."

"That your first time?"

"Yes."

"Didn't seem like it. Seemed like you had been preparing your whole life."

Perhaps in a way, she was.

She took another long, thoughtful sip, and Violet returned from serving the customers.

"So, when you leaving on your grand adventure?" she chimed, eyes darting between Savannah and me.

"Grand adventure?" Savanna asked.

"Harlen's been preparing for it," Violet explained.

"So we are going back to Earth-2." Savannah took another thoughtful sip of beer.

"I told you, I'm not going." I hit my fist on the table so hard that our glasses rattled.

This whole thing again. How many times did I need to say it?

"Then where were you planning to go?"

"Padrorix," I lied. "There's a job there."

Violet clapped her hands together, cackling. "You can go in her ship."

Savannah stared at me. "This is not agreed."

"You said you wanted to see what I got up to, so why don't we go do that. Then maybe I'll think about going to Earth-2."

"You are lying," she said bluntly, even more blunt than her usual affixation.

"How can you tell?"

"Mo-" She hesitated for a split second. "I can just tell."

I looked at Violet, who raised her eyebrows at me, and took both our glasses.

"Another?" she asked.

"It is late," Savannah said.

I realized how much my eyes hurt from the tiredness. My bones ached. Each movement felt strained and slow, Like I had to pick each one deliberately.

I stretched and yawned. "That it is."

Savannah stepped off her chair. "I will sleep in my shuttle."

She was already at the doors when I became annoyed, though I wasn't quite sure why. I yelled, "Why don't you move it out of the middle of the road while you're at it?"

She turned. I thought she would be rude to me, but instead, she just said, "I will."

When she pushed through the door, my cock twitched at the sight of her, her cheeks gently bouncing with each step.

"Boy, you really messed that one up." Violet tutted.

I groaned. "Don't start with me. What was I supposed to say? She wants me to join her freaky cult."

"I don't know. Moving stuff with your hands sounds fun."

"I can already do things with my hands," I said, grabbing her hand and pulling her in, then holding the back of her neck and dragging her mouth onto mine.

A patreon coughed from awkwardness, but I didn't care.

"And what do you think you're gonna be doing with them tonight?" she asked against my lips, not caring either.

I could *feel* the submission in her voice. She'd had a taste of me, and she wasn't ready to give it up just yet.

"Whatever I want—close up. *Now*."

Violet grabbed my wrist, pulling it off her. She strolled to the bell of the bar, ringing it loud and clear. "Y'all best be drinking up."

What few patrons were left in the bar grumbled. I grabbed a glass from the table and smashed it on the ground. "Now!"

They quickly got up, bringing coins to the counter to pay for their drinks, tipping their hats at Violet and eyeing me judgmentally. A robot shuffled over to clean up the smashed glass.

"Sometimes you've gotta be the bad guy." I smirked at Violet.

As she leaned over the counter, her lips brushed against my ear, her cleavage directly below me, material covering it begging to be ripped open. "And you've been very bad."

I grabbed her cheeks and neck, squeezing tight. "Nope. We're not doing it that way."

12

When the last of the patrons left, Violet and I eagerly ran upstairs.

We tripped over ourselves, crashing into my door. My lips touched hers, Violet's hand slid over my pants and stroked me, and we fell on the bed.

"You gonna take me like I'm that pretty thing in that ship?"

I tore open my belt clasp, then grabbed her thighs and flipped her over so she was on her knees. "Nope, I'm gonna use you like the dirty slut you are."

I lifted her many-layered skirt and slid her panties down. Her thick behind presented to me, revealing her orange hair covered slit. Stroking over her trimmed pubes, I found her swollen spot and pressed on it, bringing her to wetness.

She moaned in delight, gripping the bed sheets tightly. Her womanly scent filled the room, sending me into a frenzy. I mounted behind her, grasping myself in my hand and sliding it back and forth across her glistening slit.

"Oh, don't stop," she begged.

I gripped her hip in one hand, pulling her onto me, and

I thrust inside her slit, submerging into her warm, wet, gripping folds.

"This is the last time," she cried, a desperate attempt to add some extra naughtiness to the situation as if there needed to be any more.

I grabbed both her forearms and lifted her up, pushing her fat cheeks to swallow me. I wrapped my arms around her midsection, tearing at her cleavage, slipping my hand in and pinching her nipple. Ramming into her, Violet soaked and clenched around me.

"Yeah? I don't think so. I think this belongs to me now," I growled against her ear.

Her curvy milf body was mine to use whenever I wanted. She knew it. I knew it.

She groaned through her words, confirming it, "I didn't say it don't. But it's still the last time."

My thrusts got faster. I wouldn't last long, and I didn't care. This wasn't for Violet. This was for me and *my* release. She could come later by her hand if she wanted it.

I fell over her, and we crashed on the bed. I vertically thrust down into her slick wetness. Her cheeks clapped loudly against my groin and thighs.

"I can have you whenever I want," I spat.

She screamed. "You can. This is yours. It belongs to you."

Was she close? She was wet and tight enough, her muscles constricting around me, that multi-textured cave of hers eager to bring me to climax.

"But you're still going. Oh god, I can't take it anymore. I'm so close."

Then she looked out towards the window, and sighed. "You need to get off this stupid planet."

My body froze, fully submerged in her. Her folds

clenched around me when I said, "And what about you? I can't just leave you here."

We turned on our sides now, our bodies moving in a matched rhythm. Violet's backward thrusts met mine, dancing against them like waves of water on the shore.

"My place is here, not out there."

I slid my hand between her legs. She spread them for me, and I rubbed her swollen bead rapidly. She cried out in her release while squirting over my hand. Then she slipped off me, pushing me on my back and climbing on top of me. She slid over me with impossibly pleasurable ease. Her cheeks quickly bounced up and down, sliding right up to the glans and thrusting down over it.

We stared into each other's eyes intensely.

"You're my thick little housewife, aren't you? You'll be waiting right here for me when I return." I grabbed a fistful of her hair, forcing her to arch.

"Uh-huh." She cried through the painful pleasure, bouncing faster on me. I tore her dress apart and pinched her nipples. "And you can tell me all about it. Such a good boy, getting that money and robots for me, so I'd be safe."

"I look after my women."

"I know you do." She lets out a sound somewhere between a laugh and a moan. "All this time, I thought I was looking after you."

"We were looking after each other."

I flipped her on her back and lifted her legs high, gripping her ankles and slamming through her. She was soaked in wetness that dripped down my thighs.

And then I pulled out.

Miraculously climbing over her, my head disappeared between her lips. My muscle throbbed, twitching in release. Her eyes went wide when my offering filled her mouth, her tongue lapping it up. I groaned until she sucked me dry.

Then I collapsed. Violet wrapped her arms around me and put her head on my scarred chest.

"That wasn't such a bad goodbye present, was it?" she asked.

"Not bad. Next time though," I slipped my hand onto Violet's slit, cupping her entirely. "I'm finishing here, and I don't care what happens."

After an eternity of a moment, she got up, pulling her dress together. She smiled at me, half of regret and sadness, because we both knew we had no idea if there would be a next time.

"So what now?" she asked, holding her dress together, barely able to cover her cleavage with the torn cloth.

"You know what." I held my hand out for her to take, which she did, her cleavage fell a bit, but I went back to look at those blue eyes of hers, at those lips. She licked them. They went shiny from my come that had remained in her mouth. A bit of it dripped from the corner of her lips. She licked it off, leaving slick, shiny wetness from her spit.

"Now that's an image I'll treasure forever," I said.

Her hand left mine.

I might have to.

* * *

Violet left me alone in the room.

I got dressed, gave myself a cursory sniff, and decided I was acceptable.

When I passed her door, I hesitated for a second, and then went downstairs.

I took one last look at the bar, its dustiness the robots

hadn't even begun to tackle. It's broken floorboards that somehow I knew Violet wouldn't bother to get fixed. And now those noisy robots stood in either corner, ready to protect her in my absence.

It was time for me to leave.

* * *

Outside, infinite stars stared down at the town, all seeming to be pointing at Savannah's strange white ship.

I didn't know where to knock. There was no obvious place, so I guessed where I saw the door fall from and tapped my knuckles against it. After a brief moment, the door appeared and a platform slid down onto the sandy dirt.

Savannah's head poked out. "Yes?"

"We need to talk."

"Then you should come in."

"I should."

She disappeared inside.

I stepped up onto the ship, taking a deep breath to guard against what I thought would be overwhelming. And it was, in a way, but Savannah standing there expectantly, crossing her arms under her breasts in that skin-tight knitted bodysuit, was pretty distracting. Besides, much as the ship was recognizable as any room in the tower, with its dim blue light surrounding it. The strangeness of it bewildered me. Where was the bed? The chair? The controls? It was just an empty white room.

"What did you want to talk about?" Savannah asked.

"I'd say we should be sitting down, but-"

She waved her hand, and a rectangular crack appeared on the wall. A bed slid out, and she sat down, crossing her legs. Between two buttons, her bodysuit bent open a little at her bare stomach, showing flawlessly smooth, white skin. I took a deep breath to steady myself, thankful I was too spent to get hard again - although it was trying. I smelt that familiar scent of woman. It makes me forget myself, as thoughts flood me of wanting to get closer to its source.

What had she been doing in here?

I sat down beside her, putting my hands together. "So— we have this drug here called Cane..."

I went through it all. When I got to the Gia Knights' fall to the beasts, I expected a reaction from her when I revealed it was Percival, but she just nodded. I left out the part of how the horrid beasts make you live your worst fears, making them out to be not dissimilar from wolves.

"Why are you telling me this?" She asked when I finished.

“Because something is happening on Pradorix, and I need to find out what. Before it decimates my whole planet. I might've stopped them once, but who says they won't try again?"

"You stopped them to save your planet?"

If there was ever a time I wish I could read her, it was then. Was she surprised? Impressed? What?

"Yes," I lied. That hadn't been the reason, but it was at least one now. "This was my first real home after leaving Earth-2. I can't let it fall to ruin."

"It's my order to bring you back to Earth-2. Mother says it's your home, and you can't leave."

I closed my eyes, breathing deeply in exasperation. "Did you not hear what I said?"

Savannah paused. I waited for whatever internal struggle I hoped she was having to be over.

"You need my ship," she said.

"I need your ship."

She stroked her chin. "I must experience what your life is like before I can bring you back to see what it is you are leaving behind."

"It's not something Ruby would like."

"But the old Head Master would have," she said, tapping her fingers against her chin in thought. "My mother would not approve." Her eyes flared briefly, which I took to be her version of excitement.

I grinned. "It's just another day for me—heading out for some crazy job with the promise of a coin and saving the planet in the process."

"Will there be coin involved?"

"That's how I heard about it."

She didn't reply, leaving us in silence. My mind began to weave memories of white rooms and bring back associated feelings I didn't want to deal with.

I broke the silence with a clear of my throat. "Say, how much do you know about The Forest Pit King of Pradorix?"

"Little. I know of him, but there's no reason for me to learn of him at the tower."

"Well, they say he bleeds his planet dry..." I went into an almost identical speech as Felice did. The hairs on the back of my neck stood on end in warning, but I ignored it. "Anyway, none of that is important now. We just have to find out why they were testing out that new drug here. How they were making it and why. But most importantly, we have to stop them."

"Can we not simply go back to the site where you discovered them?"

"No!" I snapped. My vision went blind with rageful fright, then I closed my eyes and saw *them*. I opened my eyes and calmed down, as the room came back into view. "There's too many of them. Even with your powers, it wouldn't be enough."

"I see. I trust you on this."

I was glad she didn't react to my outburst. And those little words, even though they were meant for just this specific thing, still rang through me like a bell.

She trusts me.

Savannah stood up, revealing a spot of dampness at her crotch. Was that there when I arrived? Did my shouting *excite* her? She walked to the front of the ship, waving her hand at the wall. The Viewfinder appeared, showing the long stretch of Hot Sands main road. A chair rose from the floor and some controls across a flat touch screen. She pressed buttons, and the ship vibrated. It was a light, calming shaking, mildly pleasant on my balls.

The road disappeared beneath sight as the ship lifted off.

Just like that.

I wished for one last look at the bar. I thought Violet would be waving out the window at us. But we already said goodbye.

The gravity of the ship stayed the same while the world around us turned. Ships weren't supposed to do this. The ones I had been on only adjusted their gravity when we got out to space—a nauseating experience.

This was just surreal.

Star-filled space filled the screen. We headed away from Caria. Stars began to drift past the ship, darting past while the ones ahead got brighter.

I glanced at Savannah, who pushed a button and sat stoically while the ship lifted off to the great beyond.

We flew through a wispy cloud, the only way I could gain my bearings on where we were in the maze of stars.

There was a bright flash of light from far below the viewscreen as we flew past the gaze of Caria's sun and into the starry abyss.

A shooting star flew past the corner of my vision. Water brimmed in my eyes. I last flew out to space a decade ago, and I'd all but forgotten how marvelous it could be.

"I'll put in the coordinates for Pradorix. The ship should take us there in a day and a half."

"You're not even driving this ship, are you?"

"No, it's an automatic."

I whistled, genuinely impressed. "Not driven by Gia?"

"Don't be silly," she said. "That would be tiring. And I have other things to do during the flight?"

"Oh yeah, like what?"

Savannah turned to me. A strand of her hair caught in the side of her mouth, having escaped from its designated place. She swiped it back, just like she always did *back then*. "My duties."

I leaned back on the single bed. Wondering where I would sleep, before closing my eyes and drifting off against the wall.

Space *was* marvelous, but it had been a long day.

13

“Harlen.”

My eyes seared with the tiredness that comes from short, interrupted sleep. Had it been ten minutes or an hour?

"What is it?" I groaned, rage pitting in me to rival the very fires of whatever hell demon I believed existed that week.

Savannah said nothing, so I opened my eyes and looked at the viewscreen. Two identical white shuttles floated still in the black void. They had an oddly alive quality about them, waiting before us as if annoyed.

To confirm my feelings, a man's voice blared through the speaker, "This is not the direction to Earth-2. Please return to the course."

Savannah calmly said, "We are taking a detour. We will return to Earth-2 in time."

"Those are not your orders."

"How are you aware of my orders? I am the Deputy Head. I order you to return back to Earth-2."

"Our orders come from the Head Master."

"My mother," she said bluntly.

Ignoring that statement, he said, "We have been ordered to bring you back."

So not much had changed. The words of the Deputy Head meant little, a position in keeping and nothing else. If anything, it seemed like she had even less power than her predecessor.

But Savannah seemed determined for that not to be the case. "I am the Deputy Master, and I order you to stand down and leave us be."

Was it a religion or a military?

"As a Gia Knight, our instructions remain to bring you back. Prepare to be boarded."

"My name *is* Savannah *Knight*!" *Exacerbation. Frustration.*

But when I looked at her, she was visibly calm. It was a brief blip.

It was enough for the Knight, as he said, "We have reason to believe you have been compromised. You are acting emotionally. Please prepare to join the ship."

"We are going to have company." She grunted in frustration and pressed a button.

"Does this ship have weapons? Fire a warning shot." I gripped onto the back of her chair.

"Yes—but I don't wish to kill them. They are my people."

"I said a *warning* shot."

"Fine. That is acceptable." She reached for a button and pressed it. A small screen appeared, a touch screen where she stroked her finger across to aim at the pixelated ship on the screen, then beyond it. Thelaser fired harmlessly past the ship, the red light shrinking as it drowned in the great void of space.

If a ship could look unimpressed, the one ahead of us was managing it.

"We have reason to believe you have been compromised," the Knight said.

"Ship, dodge whatever they fire at us," I said.

The ship did not respond, and for a moment, I wondered if they had taken control of it. Was that something they could do? However, when the great flaring red light grew before us, the ship lurched out of the way. We didn't feel the sharp movements, but space spun in random directions through the viewscreen. The ship, with a mind of its own, dodged their blasts.

And I resisted the urge to throw up the already empty contents of my stomach.

"What do we do?" Savannah put her hands on her hips like the issue was a puzzling crossword.

"Fire back?" I suggested, annoyed.

Red lasers flared everywhere across the screen. Our ship seemed perfectly capable of dodging them forever.

"We are not trained for that."

"Are they?"

"I don't think so. Nobody ever challenges us. Why would they when we're peaceful?" Then her eyebrows became two wiggly lines of confusion. I didn't need to point it out for her. It was written all over her face.

I shook my head. "So the moment they figure out that they need to fire where we're going to be, and not where we are, we're screwed."

The ship shook gently. I'd have been forgiven for thinking the hit was harmless. It was more like a vibration than a shake. Like the ship didn't really feel the blast but was electronically reinforcing the idea that it should probably not happen again.

The red lights that flashed inside the ship were another warning sign. I would have at least assumed there would be some kind of *'warning, warning, do not get hit again, stupid.'* thing through the speakers.

"Ship's not very talkative, is it?"

"Why would the ship talk?"

I really needed to teach Savannah about sarcasm.

She was just sitting there, calmly doing nothing. She had leapt into battle before with the ork, so what was stopping her now?

"So are you gonna fire on them or what?"

She turned to look at me. I could recognise the forced blank expression for what it was—the desperate need to show nothing, to hide everything she was feeling. She was in trouble, and I needed to save her.

I leaned over the desk.

"How do I work this thing?" I asked.

"You just put your hand here and fire when they come into view," she said calmly.

On the desk, the radar had a pixelated view of the ships coming across the crosshair. All I had to do was hover my hand over it and wait for them to go into the circle. It was perhaps the simplest controls I had ever seen. In my brief experience of starships, I had seen overly complicated buttons and levers.

I tapped the screen with perhaps more force than necessary, then looked up in the ever-rotating viewscreen to see the laser fire, missing the ship.

Ok, so it wasn't *that* easy.

The ship vibrated again. The red lights continued to flash.

"I guess that means we're screwed."

She nodded. "I believe so."

I stretched my hand. *C'mon, you're the fastest trigger finger on Caria. You can work this thing. You just have to figure it out. Aim for where they're going to be, not where they are.*

The ship began to inch towards the circle, I tapped it, and suddenly, it was gone from the radar. A flash of light in the corner of the viewscreen confirmed the shuttle's destruction.

"Yes!" I grabbed a fistful of air. "That's how you do it."

Our ship slowed, it was still dodging the fires from the other ship, but it didn't need to exert as much speed nor agility now.

"We still have one more." Savannah stared lifelessly out into the viewscreen.

I wanted to reach out to her, to put my hand on her shoulder and tell her it would be ok. Hell, I would skip all that and take her in my arms, kissing her forehead. She'd probably burst into tears, finally releasing all that emotion she had been holding in.

But I had something *slightly* more important to focus on.

"Ok. Last ship," I said with resolve.

"You can do it," she said, looking up at me.

I nodded, then hovered my hand over the screen. The ship flew across it. I fired, but it dodged. It seemed to have figured out my tactic. Every time we fired, it escaped out of the way.

I gulped.

Then the voice blared into the speaker, emotionless as always, "Savannah, this will be reported to the Head Master."

The ship turned and began retreating. I fired, but it had anticipated and dodged to the left.

“Shall we chase after them?” her eyes went wide in fright.

She had had enough excitement for one day, so I said,

"We have other things to do. The sooner we get out of this part of space, the better."

"It will take him some time to get back to Earth-2."

"And then what?"

"Mother will punish him, I assume."

"Savannah..."

I put my hand on her shoulder and squeezed it to comfort her. To my surprise, her hand touched mine.

Worry drew across her face. "Why would they attack us? I am the Deputy Head."

She stood up and fell into my arms. I held her up as her hand rested on my chest, making a weak fist.

"Why would they do that?" she repeated. "It goes against everything."

"Does it?" I couldn't help but say. "Killing can be a cold, emotionless thing. Maybe they thought they were doing you a favor?"

"A favor? To be repaid?"

"That isn't what I meant."

"Maybe it is," she remarked.

Her first tightened against my chest, I rested my head on hers, and she hugged me tight, then I felt her head move against my chest, her soft hair messing up against the friction of our bodies.

She looked up at me, her eyes gleaming with the beginnings of tears. I could do nothing but kiss her. Our lips met with a crash. The entire universe disappeared, becoming nothing but the press of her soft, full lips against mine.

"That isn't allowed," she said when our kiss broke.

"And yet killing is?"

We were just two people standing on a ship in the galaxy. Alone together, neither able to make sense of anything except the need we both had at that moment.

"Why did you leave me there? I always wondered."

My hand slid down her hip, her body shivered, but I wasn't going to touch her intimately yet. Instead, my fingers slid between hers, and she gripped tightly.

"I thought it was the right thing to do. I thought it was what you needed."

She sighed. My heart started racing against our closeness. Only our clothes were in the way. They couldn't hold back the heat of her body. I needed to swim in it.

"It was what you needed, at least. That made it ok."

"Are you saying I did the right thing?"

A tear slid down her cheek, and she blinked. Her breasts heaved with her deep, long breath. I became very aware of them pressing against me. I lurched to hardness, pushing against her mound. I moved it away to not scare her, but she grabbed me tighter.

"It wasn't the wrong thing to do." She seemed forlorn. "Being with you all this time, seeing how you ended up—if this is the path that was meant for you, then it was the right one to take."

She ran her fingers through my hair, her nails softly scratched my scalp, releasing a flood of good feeling in me.

"It would have been interesting to see what you'd look like with white hair, though," she said.

I stroked her hair. "Yours looks beautiful. but you'd look beautiful no matter what color hair or eyes you have."

"Is that what you think?" she asked, eyebrows raised. "I'm beautiful?"

"I always thought it."

Our lips met again. I grabbed her slender waist, my fingers resting just above her ass. Her kiss was innocent, new, but she was eager, opening her mouth to join in with mine. And when my tongue motioned for hers, she joined in. They danced around.

Her body nestled into mine.

Then she let out a soft sigh, and said, not meeting my eyes, "I don't want you to..."

14

"Hmm?" I stopped my advances but kept stroking her hair.

Her mouth was slightly open, and she stared up at me with a kind of wonder. Her eyes seemed bigger, almost glowing, shining with the tears that lingered from before.

"I don't want you to go easy on me, or treat me like I am fragile because I've never done this before."

I cupped her cheek and said, "I'm not going to hurt you. It can be painful the first time."

Her eyebrows furrowed. "But then it will feel good."

"Ssh. There's no rush." I kissed her forehead.

"I want to do what Violet did for you," she said shakily.

"We don't have to talk about her right now."

"But you enjoyed what she did. I want to do that too."

My heart raced. I shouldn't take advantage of this. I should be gentle with Savannah for her first time. I should go easy on her.

But if she wanted it, who was I to stop her?

Savannah ran her fingers up my back and asked, "What was the thing she did that you said was advanced?" She pressed her body closer into mine, knowing the effects her breasts had on me. Her body rubbed against my hardness, which was painfully fighting against the steel of my zipper.

"She put me in her mouth." The memory of her sloppily going to town on me made me think that this might be a mistake. Was Savannah ready for that? Would I even enjoy her amateurish attempt? Was it fair to think that?

"I want to try." She interrupted my thoughts. "It sounds fu-interesting."

"Gia isn't here right now. You can be honest."

"Gia is always here."

"Then why don't we give her a show?"

She gasped, putting her hand on her mouth, although I thought what I said was no less scrupulous than what she had been saying.

I took her wrist and pulled her hand down to my bulge. She grasped it, moaning in a kind of primal satisfaction. I did the same to her, cupping her mound through the thin bodysuit. I had almost no barrier between her.

Her eyes were half-lidded in her lust. "I've done things before... with myself," she admitted, cheeks going red.

Like earlier.

We cupped each other, gently stroking while still standing.

"Let's go to bed," I said.

"Oh, ok." She left my embrace to sit down on the bed, resting on her hands. Her breasts heaved with her breath, nipples hard through the material.

I walked over and stroked her cheek while she grasped my belt buckle.

"I want to try it," she looked at me with big, pleading innocent eyes.

"I'm not going to stop you."

I closed my eyes as Savannah fumbled with my belt

buckle. It fell to the ground, then she grasped the clasp of my jeans, struggling to open it.

I supposed for her, the world must've been ending, and she was finding solace in rebelling in this way. If she always thought of her first time as some kind of perfect love-making event, then she would say *'no, I won't give in to that idea. I want to put it in my mouth.'*

I was hardly going to argue.

My jeans finally fell, and she paused. Staring at *it*.

"Are you ok?" I asked.

"It's a lot bigger than I thought it would be." Her shoulders went tense.

"You don't have to get the whole thing in. Just take the end, the rest you can stroke with your hand."

"I see, thank you."

"Thank you?" I arched my brow.

"For your patience."

I said nothing as her hands wrapped around it, stroking as little sparks of pleasure appeared. I groaned and closed my eyes, then opened them wide as her mouth wrapped around it. I couldn't believe what I saw. Savannah's perfect full lips wrapped around the head.

She removed it from her mouth. "Did I do it right?"

"You need to do a little more than that. Use your tongue." I raked my hand through her pale hair, tipping her head up, forcing her doe-like eyes to stare into mine. "Don't be ladylike. Be messy."

"I see."

Her lips slid over my glans again. This time, her tongue darted out, testing how I tasted. She closed her eyes and moaned a deep appreciative moan while stroking and licking over me.

"I need to sit down," I said as my knees trembled.

The pleasure began to shoot up from deep within me. The soft wet licks and sucks making a fire burn behind my groin. My body blazed with heat and need.

She motioned for me to sit down, and then bent over my lap while sitting next to me, bouncing her head up and down. It was heaven, perhaps even better due to her inexperience. It made it all the more... tender, *wrong.* Like I was defiling something sacred.

But there was nothing wrong with it. I stroked Savannah's beautiful silver hair and ran my fingers down her back, squeezing her ass over that catsuit. She gasped, cried out, and let go.

"I've never been touched there," she said. "It surprised me."

I gripped her cheek tighter. "It's going to be happening a lot now. I'm going to touch you a lot more places tonight."

"Good." She smiled, her cheeks going red. Then she dived on my cock, getting wetter, sloppier. I stretched my legs and fell down on the bed, my body bent slightly to lean against the wall.

"That feels so good." I groaned.

"I'm glad it feels good for you," she said, her lips leaving me with a popping sound, then returned to it, sucking up at my shiny, hard head. While her hands stroked me, she seemed to be reading my sounds, reacting to them. Every time I moaned she went faster in that action, going further with her hand movements.

"What about these?" she said, leaving me again.

"These?"

She stroked my balls. "What do I do with these?"

"Exactly that." I groaned, grabbing a fistful of air and crying out as she stroked my balls, my shaft. It went on for what seemed like hours but was likely a few minutes. The knot in my stomach told me I was getting close.

Too close.

I stopped her and worry drew across her face.

"Did I not do a good job?" She asked.

"No, it was too good. I got close to finishing." I stroked some hair from her face. "And I want to do more things with you."

"More things?" Her eyes lit up with nervous excitement. I had never seen such emotion from her. It was as intimate as the very act of sex itself. She lost every inhibition, every act of caution, and was giving herself to me, more than just her body.

I got up, stepped out of my jeans and tore my shirt off, then climbed on top of her, gently pushing her down on her back and spreading her legs. That line of buttons, going from her neck to between her legs, was mine to undo—one button at a time.

I undid the top one.

And then another. Savannah breathed heavily. Watching me, letting me do what I wanted with her.

We kissed again. She reveled in it, grabbing me and stroking as I towered over her.

Removing button after button, I finally got to just above her navel. Then, I spread her top apart, revealing her breasts. Her nipples were a perfect pink, with lots of little bumps surrounding her hard nub, which I grabbed. She cried out in submission as my fingers pinched at her nipples. I stroked and twisted, not too hard, but enough to give that little bit of pain so she knew I was taking control.

For now, all she had to do was lay there and let me break her in. I thought that she wouldn't need much leading after this. Something told me that it wouldn't be long before she was bouncing up and down on me like it was the only thing she was good for.

But she was good for so much, and I was going to show her. Starting with what lay between my legs.

The scent of her sex had already permeated the air. A passionate, needy smell that had me raging hard, almost painfully swollen with blood. As I continued to undo her bottoms, I kissed her perfect, soft stomach, the faint lines of muscle betrayed its softness.

She moaned in submission.

"Take me," she cooed. "Don't be gentle."

I stroked her hair and then grasped at her neck. She gasped and grinned.

“I will go at the speed I decide is best for you.” My voice was husky with lust.

She nodded, biting her lip.

It was time to finally remove her catsuit. I pulled at her shoulders, then lifted her butt up, and she came free of it, her legs in the air above my shoulders. They rested, fully extended, on my shoulders. Her skin was so soft against my hands, her silky legs spreading apart at my touch.

She was hairless, smooth, and beautifully symmetrical. Glistening wet, ready for my attention.

I fell down into her, kissing her neck, her breasts. Pinching, grabbing, while she groped at me, grasping and stroking before it left her reach.

"What are you doing?" She moaned.

"Tasting you," I said.

"Oh, I didn't know... That was a thing people do to women?"

I looked up at her. "By how good you smell, how could I not?"

I grinned, and she ran her fingers through my hair. "Whatever you think is best."

"Oh, this is the best, believe me."

She smiled.

I kissed her navel, then further down. I was faced with her perfect slit. So symmetrical and untouched. Her bead escaped from the folds as I took in a steep, long breath, shuddering as her scent enveloped me. So sweet and tantalizing. I couldn't stop myself from kissing it first. A soft, gentle kiss against her folds, right on her spot.

Her body trembled beneath me. She was so warm, like a bomb ready to explode at the slightest touch. I darted my tongue out against her, licking, her folds opening for me to give me more space as they pushed apart from my efforts.

She tasted divine.

A gift from Gia.

I devoured her. My tongue lapped at her as she soaked my mouth. My fingers slid between her folds, gently squeezing in her soft entrance. The softness was contrasted by the way she clamped onto my finger. So tight, I closed my eyes and pictured how good it would feel wrapped around my dick.

I pushed in all the same. Slowly in and out, while Savannah's perfectly textured cave squeezed around me. One finger was enough for now. How would I fit? It was going to.

"I'm... What is that? Oh." she writhed in delight at the discovery of her own emerging release. *Was this her first time doing that?*

I increased my rhythm while she soaked my mouth, screaming. She could scream as loud as she wanted but nobody would hear her. In the dead of space, we were the only things that existed.

The universe was ours for the taking. And it all started with her first orgasm.

"That was, that was so good." She grabbed me and pulled me up, devouring her own taste from my lips. I got into position over her, pushing her legs back slightly as I pushed my end against her opening.

"Ready?" I asked.

She nodded. "I hope so."

I pushed in, and her eyes went wide with emotion. It was almost like it was so much she couldn't even scream. She just let out a soft whimper as I pushed her walls apart with my head. She was so tight it felt like she was strangling me.

And then I was inside her.

Savannah panted, breathing in and out, she was covered in a thin shiny layer of sweat, giving her a beautiful hue.

The smell of our efforts filled the shuttle.

While my legs shook, I kept still despite every instinct telling me to submerge into her.

"Is it ok?" she asked.

I nodded. "More than ok." Then I slid inside, and she screamed. Then she wrapped her legs around me, hooking her feet as I fell into her, submerging, filling her, stuffing her, and making her mine.

"Oh my. Oh, oh!" Savannah panted. "It's so much. It's..."

"Good?"

"It's incredible," she gushed, arched her back.

I slid through her. Each time her entrance got further accustomed to me, swelling around me and getting softer—less of a tight grip and more of a loving hug.

I wouldn't last long, and I told her as such.

"I'm close," I said. My vision was blurred with euphoria like that of a release. But I hadn't even had it yet. I looked at Savannah with desperate pleasure.

We were one.

"I don't want to get you pregnant," I managed to get out between slow, steady thrusts.

"You won't." She held her hand over the mound, spread open.

"Are you going to stop it?"

"I'll try," she said.

Good. I wasn't sure if I would have been able to pull either way.

I let go.

Slamming down into Savannah, I pushed the whole weight of my hips into her, gaining speed, turning animalistic, my body drenched with sweat. She wrapped her arms around me and my chest pressed against hers. The pendant rested on her breasts, where it dangled from my neck. It fell down beside her neck as I crashed into her, thrusting with all of my might until finally I went blind.

I throbbed hard, twitching with release after release. It felt like more than I had ever done before, draining me dry as each spasm gave me a more powerful orgasm than I had any right to have.

The twitches wouldn't stop while she cried out in her own orgasm. She writhed beneath me, taking my entire length as my body crushed her hand. I hoped in that last moment of clarity that she could stop it. The last thing we needed was her getting pregnant.

But I would have loved it, and part of me hoped it didn't work. Knowing that I had made her mine in that most primal, final way would be the ultimate bliss.

She was mine all the same, regardless of if my seed took.

Finally, it ended. I fell beside her, slipping out, still twitching as she looked down at her reddened blossom. Pearls dripped out of it.

"Wow," Savannah exclaimed.

Her back arched, her hand pressed her mound, and I watched as all my offering spilled from her, sliding between her ass cheeks and thighs.

"Wow." Savannah repeated, then she started laughing. Incredible laughter as she wrapped herself around me and pressed her mound against my twitching still-hardness. I held her tight.

"That tired me out," she said.

"The sex, or pushing it out?"

"Pushing it out. It's... doing stuff like that is hard. Being that precise and focused. Especially after all that. I didn't think it would be that good."

"It isn't usually that good," I said.

"What do you mean?"

"I mean, it's always good. But that was out of this world."

She stroked my cheek, and we stared into each other's eyes.

"When can we do it again?" she asked.

"Already?"

"Mmm." She stroked herself, then winced a little. "Nope, I'm way too sore."

"Me too. I need a break. I'm completely drained." I stared up at the ceiling briefly, my fingers sliding against her smooth back, and then I said, "You seem like a different person."

"Well, I have changed a lot."

"No, I mean, from like, an hour ago."

"Hmm."

She said nothing, staring out of space, towards the vast murky brown planet of Caria. I wondered if I should have mentioned that. The post-sex daze had ruined my caution, made me feel like I could say anything.

I needed to fix it.

"Whatever happens, I'm here for you."

I wrapped my arms around her tight as she turned to push her butt into me. Her hips gently danced against mine, pressing into my softening dick, which was still twitching.

"It's an interesting planet," she commented.

"It certainly is."

I sat up, eyes wide in alert, suddenly remembering her.

"Daisy."

"Who is Daisy?" she said. But there wasn't any alarm in her voice.

I sighed and sat against the bed. "My horse. I forgot to make plans for her."

She turned her neck to face me. "Violet would remember. I may have only briefly met her, but I know she cared for you deeply. She would remember anything you forgot."

"You're right. But still. I left my gun too."

"We could go and get it. It's only there."

It's only there. It sounded so easy. And it should have been. But we had already gone, mentally I had left. I couldn't go back with my tail between my legs.

I rested my head against the pillow, closing my eyes, tiredness overcoming me like a spell, my whole body drifting off into a restful slumber.

Savannah slipped from my grasp, my hand fell to the bed, and I drifted off.

"Where are we going?" she asked.

I opened my eyes, my vision blurry from my knocking at the gates of sleep.

"Pradorix."

Gentle taps of her finger on the screen, then, my arm was lifted, and her warm naked body pressed against me again. Her curvy, soft butt pressed against my groin, and I wrapped my arm around her mid, pulling her tight against me as she pulled the covers over us. Then I was gone to the world.

15

"Go with the nice lady, don't fuss."

If she was so nice, then why did my mother look like that? It was a strange expression. My mother's mouth smiled, but her eyes were fallen.

"Harlen?" another voice prodded at my consciousness. "Harlen?" Again.

My arm was being shaken. My eyes darted open.

It was still nighttime. *No, I'm on the ship.* Memories came flooding back.

"Huh?" I asked.

"You were yelling." Savana sat beside me, naked, stroking my hair. Warmth instantly flooded me, and I pulled her in to kiss me.

She kissed me again, then her nose crinkled. "Your breath."

"Yours isn't so hot either," I said, grabbing her and pulling her down to the bed. She lay above the covers, I below it. My hand stroked down to her ass and held it. "I don't care."

And then my stomach audibly rumbled.

"You're hungry." She smiled.

"It's been a while since I ate."

Savannah slinked up from the bed, stretching, which lifted those gorgeous round asscheeks of hers. I watched her go to the other end of the small shuttle. Raising her hand to bring forth a machine, she pressed a few buttons of a touchpad. After a gentle hum, the machine brought forth a plate. She put it on the top of the counter and then did it again, bringing both dishes to the bed and handing me one.

I slid my hand over her hip, holding her while resting the plate on my lap, which was no mean feat, considering how hard she made me. Those thoughts quickly left, however, as I devoured the food like an animal. When was the last time I ate? Far too long ago. Our meal was the bland food I had been reared on. Tofu, potatoes, no sauces, no flavoring, and yet, it was a veritable feast to my eyes and mouth.

When I finished, she stroked my arm, laughing at me endearingly. "You needed that."

I nodded. "I need something else now." Taking her plate, which she had been pecking at like a bird, I put it on the ground and pushed her down to the bed.

It was even better than the last time. After stroking Savannah to bring her to wetness, I pushed myself inside her tight walls. She winced at first and then spread her legs wide, wrapping them around me and pulling me in. We rolled around the bed in a fiery passion. Our bodies were connected as one.

When we finished, I was thankful Savannah had a spare toothbrush, as well as an atom cleaner, for showering. This ship had the most updated technology I had ever seen. I was impressed as I was mortified that planets such as Caria lived as they did, all because Earth-2 didn't see fit to colonize them.

And if they did, then everything that made Caria unique would be gone. So what was the correct answer?

"We'll be there soon, I expect." Savannah ran her fingers through my hair, and I did the same to her silver hair. Soon enough, after we cleaned our bodies and lay clothed against the bed, hands held and squeezed tight, the spec became a dot in the viewscreen. It turned to a healthy green orb, and as it began to fill the screen, I gasped at its beautiful fields—impossibly neon.

"I had no idea they were so bright," I said.

The wood of a Pradorix tree had always been a dark black to my eyes. Barely obvious it had even been wood, save for the grain.

The ship flew around the horizon of the planet, searching for the dock as I stood in awe.

"Me neither. I've never been here. It's different from Earth-2. The brightness there is..." she pondered for a word.

"Artificial?" I suggested.

"Yes." She nodded.

At first, there seemed to be a huge chunk missing from the planet. It became apparent what it was as it centered on our view, in the center.

"So that's the pit," I mused.

A vast, colossal circle, surrounded by snaking trees. All snarling around it in chaotic branches, like they were angry at its affront to nature. The great pit was a dark, dirty brown, and when the ship approached its side, I thought it no surprise that the space dock was right beside it. I saw more details of the pit as we got closer, platforms, little spike pits inside it. It was a gladiator's pit, more monstrous in scale than any imaginable colosseum. The stands must have been able to fit the entire planet's population and then some.

We approached a great clearing and the ship slowed. A large metal platform grew to dwarf us as we approached. There was a parking spot free between two freighter ships, and I was amazed to see the ship decide where to park. I asked about it.

Savannah had just finished buttoning up her bodysuit. "It's not an AI. The Head Master considers those sinful—a life not worthy of creation. I think it's just a regular computer."

I hardly thought of AI as a life, more like an intelligent computer you didn't need to press buttons on. I didn't know what Savannah thought of that. Her expression had been blank.

The ship descended, the viewscreen filled with a lively dock, stuffed with ships of varying sizes and quality, workers, tradesmen, and all sorts of people bustling and chatting, silent behind the screen.

The ship landed with a gentle thud. The platform fell, and we stepped out into the world.

Fresh, clean air—almost damp with condensation, I took in a deep breath and was shocked at how easily it went down in lungs, no microparticles of sand to scour then. The grated platform was holed, like a grated gate, so that the condensation would drip back down into the planet with ease.

The planet should have been dark, the way trees surrounded the sky at every turn. I got dizzy looking up at them, gargantuan compared to even the mountains of Caria. And yet, the bright, neon leaves illuminated us in a calming green glow.

I hadn't seen so many ships since I had been on Earth-2.

They came in all shapes and sizes. From great big ones that could hold an army to tiny shuttles barely large enough for their pilot. All of them were metal, some painted and some left clean—none were the strange white pureness of the Gia shuttle. Despite their variety, we still stood out more than a pressure rocket in the desert. Dressed in overalls, the orks and humans that worked on the lot, as well as some pilots, marveled and whistled at our unassuming lightbulb of a ship.

They looked at Savannah too. Her hair and eyes attracted attention almost as much as her ship.

I made a fist at them looking at my woman, but soon realised if it was out of attraction, it was more because of her white hair and eyes.

"What are *they* doing here?" one worker whispered to another.

I slid my hand over Savannah's hip, claiming her, hiding her. If they knew about Gia, then they'd know such an act would be unheard of. And besides, public displays of affection make people uncomfortable. I was counting on it.

"We should get you a hat, and some less conspicuous clothing. I know you've not got the robe anymore, but that bodysuit is hardly subtle."

Her eyes flickered a little wide, but she showed no emotion. Had she defaulted back to her old ways now that we were around people? Would she only show herself to me?

I liked the thought of that for me, but not for her. Even if it was like seeing her emotionally naked, she should still be a regular person for herself.

Her words said she agreed with my thoughts. "Will I be able to choose new clothes?"

Perhaps I read into them how I had felt when I had first

brought clothes. I felt at being able to provide her that opportunity.

"Whatever you like," I assured her.

It would also give us a chance to explore the town, and look for our mark.

We paid our fee with the dock worker at a counter and were ready to head into the city, but a ship landed just before us, stealing my attention. It was beat-up, parts of its holes bent where space asteroids had hit it. It seemed like it shouldn't have been able to fly. When it landed, it trembled as if relieved it had made the journey.

The man who exited it scratched the back of his head in embarrassment.

A dock worker yelled at him, "Where'd you get that pile of junk?"

"The guy I got it from upgraded to a new model. Gave it to me for nothing."

"You gonna fix it?"

"Ha, what's the point? This piece of garbage is gonna get sold for scrap."

The great mechanical ship had so many different sections, each seeming to have been retrofitted. They all threatened to fall apart at the slightest nudge.

Savannah yanked at my shirt. "Harlen, there's a queue behind us."

I came to my senses and took Savannah's hand, leaving the counter.

"Welcome to Pradorix. Have a nice stay," the ticket attendant said as we left.

We walked down the many steps to the town, where the floor turned to a comfortable dirt path, snaking through trees wider than towns. The paths were large enough for cars to pass, which occasionally some did, but the pedestrians stood to the edges of the street. The drivers waved politely as they passed.

If I worried about attracting attention before, now the crowds grew, that worry dampened. All different kinds of people, clearly from other planets, visited the tourist destination of Pradorix. It would have been hard to tell who was from here and who was a visitor had it not been for the garbs of the locals. They wore plain loose fabric in earthy colors, as if they wished to be seen as one with the planet.

"How about here?" I asked as we approached a clothes store situated in a large metal hut. It would have looked like any other generic black metallic building, had it not been for the glowing blue metal sign.

“Looks good," she said simply. I squeezed her hip and kissed her on the forehead, which caused her mouth to flicker.

"Good girl," I told her.

She gasped, putting her hand to her mouth in surprise.

I smirked. "Ha, that did it. C'mon, let's go in."

16

The bell jingled on our entrance.

The store had a plain black decor, almost gothic, from the color of the wood. Calming pastel lights illuminated the room to a kind of relaxed, calm vibe. Racks of clothes stretched in every direction, all in it the fashionable earthy tones of Pradorix.

The shopkeeper, an old woman, bid us good morning.

"Ma'am." I nodded at her.

Savannah quickly left me to excitedly dart towards the underwear section. I grinned at the shopkeeper, but she merely smiled back, letting us know she had seen all kinds of folk here.

"Found something you like?" I asked, standing next to Savannah in the bra and panties aisle.

She picked up a plain white thong with a matching bra and said, "I've never owned anything like this before. Everything I have is so plain and..."

"Boring?"

"I was going to say uninteresting, but yes."

"Try it on."

"Try it on?" She frowned quizzingly at me, then whispered up close like it was a secret, "How will I pay for this?"

I looked at the price tag and tried to hide my surprise at how expensive it was. I hadn't been in a clothing store since I was a teenager. I had no bearing on how much things should cost. Back on Caria, we made everything ourselves.

"I'll buy it," I said.

Her eyes glowed with adoration at my simple solving of the problem. I wanted to grab and kiss her, but a guy walking past caused her to stand up straight and hide the panties as if it was some secret shame. Her face rested back to normalcy.

How would I tell her that emotions weren't a crime? It would likely take a while for her to get used to it.

Savannah walked over to the cashier, and with all the proper decor of a princess, said, "Excuse me, may I use the changing rooms?"

"Of course you can, dear."

Savannah's cheeks went red, then she came back to me, whispering, "Harlen, why don't you pick out some outer clothes for me?"

I frowned. When I had left Earth-2, picking out my own clothes has been a great source of pride. Even though what I could get - and steal - were essentially tatters, it was *my* tatters, not the robes I was forced to wear.

"Are you sure? Wouldn't you rather pick them out yourself?"

"I trust you." She darted her eyes around the store and quickly tiptoed to plant a kiss on my cheek. She then dashed into the changing rooms, closing the curtains behind her. The shopkeeper beamed at me, and it was my turn to go red in the cheeks.

It's funny how you can fuck the life out of someone, but

a little public display of affection can go a long way to making you feel sheepish.

I browsed the store, not particularly caring that I was in the women's section because of my purpose to be there, and found a medium-length skirt, beige-colored, and a tan loose blouse shirt. There was a knitted beanie hat too that I thought would look cute on her, as well as hide her hair.

I knocked on the wall next to the curtain. "Savannah, I have your clothes."

"Come in!"

I frowned, not knowing if that was allowed, but the shopkeeper was busy serving another customer, so I darted inside, quickly closing the curtain behind me.

My jaw dropped.

Her bodysuit lay crumpled on the ground. Savannah stood there in just the white bikini and panties. The mirrors behind her showed every angle of her body. Her gorgeous butt cheeks hugged the thong material to where they rested above her hip bones, and the bra accentuated the curvy thickness of her breasts.

"What do you think?" She was grinning from ear to ear, clearly proud of how she looked.

I slammed into her, our lips crashing as my hand slid over her panties, causing her to shudder.

I whispered into her ear, "I think we're gonna have to buy 'em, seeing as you already tried them on. Maybe a couple of sets."

Her hand went for my bulge, and then there was some chatter outside, bringing me back to reality. I moved back from her, aching for her as she tickled the tip of me.

"I got you these," I said, feeling powerful that I could stand and talk to her while she stroked me. There was no rush now. We had all the time in the world to fool around.

She just beamed, saying nothing as she took the clothes and looked at them like they were made of gold.

When I stepped back out into the store, I was greeted by the chime of an alarm from the speakers above the cashier.

"A new challenger has entered the coliseum—the fierce Lexly of Wraxon. He will be fighting a Skradog! Prepare for battle when the sun goes down. Tickets twenty credits."

"How often does that happen?" I asked the cashier.

"Oh, about every day," she hummed.

"And they volunteer for that?" I found it odd how such barbarism could be normalized.

"Sometimes," she mused while checking something on her till. "Sometimes they're criminals. We have no prisons on this planet. The pit is law, as they say."

I tried to remind myself that things were different everywhere, and what would be normal on Ciara would offend her just the same. Still, the casualness with which she talked of such brutality shocked me. If it happened every day, it would become as normal as anything else on this strange planet. And I was no better anyway. My whole life had been a battle.

The shopkeeper's expression became brighter as she looked past me. "Well, don't you look gorgeous!"

I turned, and my jaw dropped almost as much as it did when she had been wearing just the underwear. Savannah wore the knee-length skirt, loose-fitting blouse, and hat like she was born to wear it. She strolled beside me with her head held high.

"What do you think?" she said, her hand sliding under my arm.

"Wow, just *wow*," I said, proud that such a beautiful woman could be on my arm. I had been with many women before, but just fucking them and having one on my arm like this was different. This felt more... real. She was mine, and I was proud to have her.

When I paid, I noticed her eyes glancing at the dwindling contents of my wallet, but she said nothing out of politeness.

Then we left the store, hand in hand.

I knew we weren't just on this planet for fun—we had a purpose. And yet, I couldn't help but let it fall to the back of my mind as we walked the bustling market stalls. I started to feel that this place's riches rivaled even that of Earth-2. The naturalness of it had fooled me into thinking these were more simple folk. With the many stores selling all kinds of things, the markets flourishing with business, it told me that things were actually fairer here. Everyone seemed equal, be they tourist or local.

We passed a particular stall with giant red fruits hung on display. It seemed appropriate that after our bland dinner on the ship, we got to try something that had actual *flavor*.

"Have you ever seen anything like this before?" I said.

She shook her head as if waiting for permission to speak.

"Savannah." I took her cheek in my hand, making sure she would hear me fully.

"Yes?"

"You're allowed to want things, you know. Just say, and I'll get it."

"It's not that." She pursed her lips. "I saw how much money you have. What are we going to do after? Where are we going to stay? I guess we could head back to the ship. But there's only enough food for another few nights. Then what?"

"We could always fight in the tournaments," I joked.

She hit my arm playfully, then quickly went back to her regular expression. "That isn't funny."

"Listen. I always figure it out. I've made it this far, haven't I?"

But I knew that was a good attitude when I only had myself to worry about. Now I had Savannah in my care.

Then it came to me. The pendant, it still hung under my shirt. "I've got some jewelry I can sell. Don't worry. It will all be fine."

"You do?"

"Yeah. I forgot about it."

I neglected to mention that it was the very pendant around my neck, knowing she would have thoughts about it. I knew I should have told her, but she would only have convinced me not to. It was just a pendant. Just a family heirloom. If we sold it, we'd be fine for a good while. And I didn't need that long to find *more* coins.

"We'll be fine."

She frowned at me. "I may be naive, Harlen, but I am not stupid. I've seen you with all your clothes off. The only bit of jewelry you've got," She poked it through my shirt. "is *that*."

I grabbed her hand and smiled at my being caught like a naughty child, then said, "Well, I meant it."

She scowled at me. "It shouldn't come to that."

Taking our whispered words for romance, the market stall worker shouted, "A Trellon to share for the lovebirds?"

Glad for the excuse to move on, I went into my wallet and dug some coins out. I exchanged them for the big red fruit we'd been admiring. It was bigger than my head. From afar it looked like a tomato, but its skin was more like a peach, soft and begging to be bitten into.

"Besides, this is gonna fuel us for today. What else would we spend money on?"

She eyed the great fruit with wonder. "You're right. Better this than beer."

"We've got enough for a couple of them, too," I said.

Around us, couples were holding the big red fruit in both their hands. It seemed customary to eat it together. So I held it out to Savannah, and she grabbed it with the other hand. Then we took a bite together. Its sweet flavor explosion made my heart race. It had been a long time since I had eaten something so succulent.

Savannah, on the other hand, had already gone for a second bite. "This is incredible," she said after gulping it down. Her voice was contemplative. "Just incredible."

"Yeah, it's pretty great," I agreed.

"No. Like, really incredible."

"I know!"

"Harlen, you don't get it."

Our eyes met—that little flicker of auburn in the plain of her whites caught my eye again as we looked into each other. She knew I got it then. We were perhaps the only two people in the galaxy who did.

We took another bite together. Eating conservatively, but healthily, until the last piece was there. We took a bite together, our lips meeting in the center, and we hugged tight.

"What now?" she asked, swallowing and wiping the fruit from her mouth. She got a little bit on the side of her cheek, which I rubbed off, causing her to scrunch her nose at me.

Sliding my hand into hers, I turned to face the crowd. Every so often, a truck or car would drive past, beeping its horn at tourists that would get in the way.

"I suggest we find a nice bench and watch the world go by. Maybe a van with The Hardest Wood is gonna drive right past us, leading the way to their headquarters."

It was unlikely at best on such a massive planet, but this was its capital, so it was worth a shot.

We found a nice little green patch amongst the dirt path, where a few benches had been propped up. Savannah rested her back on me while I hand my arm across the bench. It was comfortable, and I put my arm around her, stroking my thumb across her stomach.

"They all seem so happy," she remarked.

"Even without being able to move things with their mind," I said, kissing her forehead over her hat.

Like most planets, Pradorix had a healthy mix of ork and human. However, they seemed much more suited to coexisting here, unlike Caria, where the orks tended to keep to themselves and start fights in bars.

I shared this observation with Savannah.

"Well, it is the middle of the day," she remarked.

"Good point. I suppose I am idealizing this place a bit too much. It's all at the cost of that great big pit. What do you think about it?"

I was eager to hear her thoughts. In fact, I wanted to listen to what she thought about most things. It was a darn sight different from my saying whatever I could while barely listening until it was time for them to spread their legs.

Except perhaps with Violet—I cared what she thought, and I pushed that heart prang deep down until I didn't have to think about it.

"Every planet seems to have a prison or a colosseum or something like that. What did your planet have?"

"Me," I said bluntly.

"Well, it's one way to earn a living."

"It *was*. I always told myself that I wasn't the only bounty hunter on the planet, and at least I was one of the good ones, only going after bounties that deserved it. I still think that, I reckon'."

She fell down my chest. I stroked her cheek, looking at her, while she considered my face, then she said, "You did what you had to do. We all do what we have to to survive in this galaxy."

"You know what I need to do now?"

I flexed my kegel muscle, making myself twitch under her head. She giggled and dove her head into my groin, wrapping her arm behind my waist.

Her voice was muffled in my shirt. "Besides, if you weren't there, doing all that, then I wouldn't have been able to save you,"

"Excuse me, darlin'! I think I saved you."

Her face unearthed from my clothes, with the most heartwarming grin I ever saw. "So." She sat up. "Who else are we going to save?"

"The galaxy." I put my arm back around her. "We're gonna save the whole damn galaxy."

I closed my eyes in bliss, but she began tapping at my arm rapidly.

17

Savannah shook my sleeve and yelled, "Look!"

Across the road, a truck drove by as pedestrians moved out of its way. For a moment, we were faced with the logo as the truck passed right by us—The Hardest Wood.

Are you kidding me? That easy?

We jumped up from the bench, running hand in hand. A few people yelled, 'Watch it!' as we interrupted their casual stroll. Thankfully, the road only weaved in one direction, and by the time we got to a crossroad, the van was parked at the lights, waiting for them to change.

Its indicators were flashing left, so we turned that way, running as fast as possible. I was thankful it was another long road, so that we could gain some speed on it when it got caught in traffic. By the time it drove past us, we thought we would lose it. Crowds of people were growing, and it was about to hit a traffic crossing.

But then it turned into a building, and we were able to catch our breath.

"C'mon." I gripped her hand, clammy from our exertion, and took her to the other side of the road, which faced the building. There was a small parking lot, so we were able to hide behind a ledge and watch.

"It's not a very big building. Must be mostly underground," I remarked.

"A bad place to be trapped if we were caught," Savannah said, then frowned at me with a kind of half-embarrassed laugh.

I looked at her with pride. She was leaping head first into this dangerous lifestyle—*my* lifestyle.

"What?" she asked at my look.

"Nothing." I shook my head. "So, I guess we'll have to sneak in. Shame about the men guarding it."

"That's not a man."

I hadn't given them much study, choosing instead to look at the building for point of entries, so they had been blurs to me before. Now that she pointed it out, I could see it wasn't a guy, but an ork.

A female ork, and not like any I had ever seen. She was tall for a female—had to be close to seven feet. And although her hair was tied up in a tight bun, its bright violet-red color still shined under her hat—as did her face. She didn't have the ugly snarl of an ork, or that pig nose they all shared.

For all intents and purposes, she was a beautiful woman, just a green one with tusks. Perhaps that made her even more so.

"What do you think?" Savannah asked, putting her hand on my leg.

"I can take the guy no problem, the ork though? I'm sure with your help we could team her no problem. But-"

"But?" She ran her hand up my thigh.

"The guards are right there, on the street. People are constantly walking past. Someone would see us jump them."

"If only there was a way for you to convince someone to sneak you in." Savannah ran her fingers further up my thigh, stroking between my legs.

"Is it really the time for *that*?" I laughed.

To my surprise, she asked, "Don't you think she's cute?"

I stroked Savannah's cheek. She looked so adorable in that beanie, but those lips constantly needed kissing. "You know, I'm learning more and more about you. You're quite the voyeur, aren't you?"

"It's interesting. I want to see how you do it."

"Do what?" I groaned as she stroked me harder.

"Seduce women. You must be very good at it."

"I'm not bad." I shrug.

"Somehow, I think that is an understatement."

"So the plan is to seduce her and convince her to let us in." I frowned. "Hardly seems feasible."

"Have you ever been with an ork?"

I shook my head. "Orks aren't usually beautiful like that, at least by human standards."

"She must be half."

I nodded, pulling her hand off me.

"What will you say to convince her?" she asked.

"I'll think of something."

"You always do." She rested her head on my shoulder.

We watched the guards, and I studied the ork for longer, noticing more about her. Beneath that plain shirt and pantsuit, there was a tantalizing thickness to her. Her ample breasts could barely be contained by her white shirt. I imagined she had to have it specially made for her, but it still couldn't accommodate those mounds. Her thighs, even standing upright, threatened to break through those pants with their impressive muscles.

"Thoughts?" Savannah asked.

"She could probably squeeze me to death with those."

I thought Savannah would reprimand me for losing focus of the mission, but instead, she said, "I'd like to see her try."

I shook my head at her, smiling. "What else would you like to see?"

"Well. I want to be there when you talk to her, erm, what's it called, flirting? That thing you used to do with me sometimes, back on Earth-2."

"You knew?"

She nodded. "I enjoyed it."

I grew warm. But then we sat in silence against the wall. We occasionally took turns glancing over, but it stayed unchanged for what felt like an hour.

Finally, talk arose across the street. We lifted our heads just over the edge to see the guards' replacements coming to let them off shift.

"About time," the ork grumbled. Her voice was strangely deep. As if she was putting it on, to appear more like 'one of the guys.'

The other guard she had been standing with bid her a good night and asked if she had any plans.

"No," she said bluntly.

When she walked away, in the direction of the street we had come in, the two new guards looked at each other. They snickered, clearly at her expense.

"Must be tough being a half-ork," I said. "Too tall for a woman, too pretty for an ork."

Savannah grabbed my arm. "C'mon. She's getting away."

Thankfully, she walked slowly, taking her time like most orks. Anyone walking towards her was forced to get out of her way.

We only had to trail behind her. When a group of girls

walked past, they waited until they were long past her before turning back to look and snicker.

I sensed the heat radiating from the ork, almost like an aura of shame.

She heard it all, but didn't let it affect her.

And when she turned left into a bar, I knew why. She was going to drown her sorrows.

I could relate.

"Poor thing," Savannah said. "Maybe we should find another way in."

"Are you getting cold feet? We're only sneaking into the building. She shouldn't be working for such an evil corporation anyway. Not on a planet like this, where you can do anything for money." I grabbed her hand and her fingers slotted into mine and squeezed. "Do I gotta remind you that the stuff they make kills people?"

"You're right." She nodded, pursing her lips.

"Besides, I could use a drink. Let's just go and sit in the back."

We entered the bar, and the bell jingled to alert the entire room to our presence. The ork had chosen to sit in one of the corners and was nursing something clear. I imagined it was pure rubbing alcohol or something just as foul. If Klargen was ork beer, then that had to be their vodka.

Jazz music played, which meant we could whisper to each other. We had taken our seats at the other end of the bar, where we could see her, but it wasn't quite so obvious we were watching, due to the tables and other patrons in our way.

Once we were seated, a waitress came over and asked us what we wanted. Savannah immediately turned to me. Her expression was utterly blank, revealing nothing of what I imagined was her anxiety about knowing little about such things.

"Two beers for now," I said.

Once the waitress left, I suggested to Savannah that she look through the menu and pick out something new.

"But I wouldn't know what to pick."

"You can pick anything you want. It doesn't matter. That's the beauty of alcohol. You find the stuff you like over time. Just avoid anything from that section." I pointed to the list of stuff too strong for a human.

She grasped my hand under the table, and the waitress brought over our beers.

I sipped mine, watching the bar. There were two girls, dressed rather ridiculously, I thought, in the way that meant it had to be the height of fashion, but impractical so. Heels far too impractical for a city where every path was grated. So much makeup it was obvious it was to hide their attractive appearance, but it just heightened it, what with how poorly it had been applied.

So they were 'cool girls'.

I sat up at the bar. I judged them to be around eighteen or nineteen, something in their desperation to appear old enough to be here told me they weren't. I found this peculiar, as the sign said no one under the age of twenty-two was allowed admittance. So if they were allowed to be in here, wouldn't it be best not to flaunt themselves at the bar's counter? The barman seemed not to mind, flirting back with them.

Personally, I thought they were kind of ugly. They were both caked in makeup and had this rattyness about them both. It was like their status, and not their looks, had afforded them to be looked at as attractive. Between their flirting with the barman, they made eyes at the ork, whispering and giggling in a way that was apparent to everyone in the bar.

"She's just sitting there, by herself. What a loser," one said.

I gripped Savannah's hand tighter.

"Careful, she might eat you if she hears you," the other replied.

They burst into another fit of cackling. I instinctively grabbed for my pistol, finding the infuriation similar to getting ready for a fight.

But that would have been entirely inappropriate. They were just being mean. That was hardly a crime—and this wasn't my bar to protect.

The ork continued to sip at her drink. I noticed that her shirt was undone now, all the way down to her cleavage. She merely sighed and continued drinking. Perhaps going to her happy place, where people didn't mock her.

A crunched-up beer mat hit her in the face. She winced but didn't react, not looking at the girls as if they would go away if she didn't make eye contact.

Savannah whispered, "How can that girl get away with that? She's just a little blonde thing. That ork could crush her."

"And yet, *that* ork ain't. She's just sitting there, taking it."

I looked at the girls, bubbling hatred rising up through me. It would've been easier if they were guys, I wouldn't have thought twice about getting up there and smashing their heads together. The barman would have probably turned a blind eye too, nobody stands for guys picking on girls. But this was different. Nobody wants to see this kind of thing. It makes people uncomfortable. They'd rather just look away.

"Why aren't we doing anything?" Savannah asked, grabbing my hand under the table.

"Why do you think?" I asked, raising my eyebrows.

"Hmm," she pondered, tapping her chin with her finger. "If she isn't reacting, there must be some kind of reason. Perhaps a social hierarchy."

"Bingo. She could easily crush her, but she doesn't because of the repercussions."

The girls giggled again.

"So she can't do anything." Savannah frowned.

"But *we* can." I squeezed her hand as I got up from the table, sauntered over to the bar, and leaned over to the barman right beside one of the girls, asking him for some napkins. She smiled at me.

"Ma'am," I said in as polite a manner as I could.

When the barman passed me some napkins, my shoulder jerked back and hit the girl's glass, which poured all over her lap. She screamed inappropriately loudly, like something truly awful had happened, which I suppose it had to *her*. I bet she never had to deal with any problems or work for her life. So she just spent it picking on people.

"Beg your pardon, ma'am." I flashed a look at the beautiful ork, who was now eying me with interest, but her eyes were half-narrowed in suspicion.

I bounced my eyebrows at her and smirked at the ork.

"Are you not going to apologize?" The ratty-looking girl demanded.

"Ever so sorry, Ma'am. Here, take this." I handed her the napkins the barman had passed to me.

I headed back to the table and slid my fingers back into Savannah's hands. She took a sip of her beer and glared at me with a half-smirk while I took a victory swing of mine.

"Your turn," I said.

"Me? What am I supposed to do?"

I cocked my head at her, and then she nodded, suddenly understanding.

The girls chatted again. The one whose pride I had wounded was scrunching up the ball of tissue, preparing to throw it at the ork, while the other rested her elbow on the table.

Savannah lifted her hand, and the girl's elbow fell, making her face plant the counter.

The ork smirked, then quickly hid it. When the girl composed herself, cheeks going red from embarrassment, she reached for her drink, but it slipped out of her hand and fell onto her lap.

"What is wrong with your bar!" she cried.

The barman looked panicked, putting on a casual voice in an attempt to placate her. "Nothing. It's fine. The drinks had been sat there this whole time."

"When my father hears about this!" She threatened.

He held his hands up in defense. "Whoa! Whoa, wait, I'm sorry! Drinks for you lovely ladies are on the house. Let me fix you another, anything your pretty little heart desires." He beams a charming, manipulative smile as if trying to placate a child throwing a tantrum.

She stood, crossing her arms at him, her skirt flaring to show a bit of her thighs. I hated her far too much to care about that, not when I had Savannah next to me—and that ork on the other side of the bar.

There was no use denying how I felt about her.

The girl clearly couldn't argue with free drinks, as she said. "Well, fine! But fix the bar, or no amount of free drinks will save you from my father's wrath."

I snorted, and she turned on me.

"And just what is so funny?"

I laughed again. "Oh, it's just, when you said wrath, you sounded like some kind of crazed superbitch. It's just liquid, honey. Your clothes will dry. I'm sure you can afford new ones."

"Clearly, you can't." Her nose wrinkled in disgust.

I looked down at my somewhat-worn shirt. "Hey, I like this shirt."

The girl's eye caught Savannah, however, and she did a double take at her silver hair, strands of it coming out from under her beanie. I put my arm around Savannah instantly, like it would protect her from the girl realizing a Disciple of Gia was on her planet.

The girls strutted out of the bar with their noses in the air.

The ork immediately stood up, strolled over to us and asked, "May I sit?"

I held out my hand to the free chair. "Please."

18

The chair seemed hardly suited for such a tall woman, but it easily took her weight. The ork crossed her legs and leaned back, placing her hand on her knee, studying me.

I was immediately distracted by the way her shirt bunched up around her open cleavage. The faint hint of the curve of a green breast showed. I gave it a controlled glance, for precisely the right amount of time, to let her know I was interested but not lecherous.

"Why did you do that?" she finally asked.

"Do what? We were just enjoying a nice drink. That barman should really get that counter fixed," I said and then sipped my beer.

She smiled.

Like her tusks, her teeth were sparkling white, gleaming from the chandelier above us. She must have spent a great deal of time polishing them.

I offered, "Can I get you a drink? Klargen?"

She snarled. "No way, that stuff's disgusting."

Savannah was back to her lack of emotion. I squeezed

her hand, wishing to tell her that if there was ever a time to not do that, it was now.

"I'm guessing that's no rubbing alcohol you've got there either."

"Vodka soda."

I clicked my fingers at the barman, not caring it was rude because of his apathy to the ork being bullied.

"Another vodka soda for-" I turned back to the ork.

"Maple." She smiled, her cheeks going rosy. She then asked, "So what are you two doing on Pradorix? Honeymoon? Date? You don't seem from here." Her voice was hopeful. I wondered for which part.

"That obvious, huh? We're not on our honeymoon," I took a swig of beer.

"Oh? I see." The ork glanced at my hand around Savannah's hip.

I turned to Savannah. "What do you think? It's been kind of like a date, hasn't it?"

She remarked, "I've never been on a date. If this is one, then it has been interesting."

"Interesting?" Maple asked, taking another sip of her drink.

The waitress put our new ones on the table.

"Savannah finds lots of things interesting, if you catch my meaning." I smiled at Maple and put my arm further around Savannah.

Savannah interjected, "I must ask. Those girls, they're... nothing. You could have killed them with a fist."

The ork sighed. "You don't go pummeling the boss's daughter and expect to keep a job."

Savannah leaned over the table. A flick of her silver hair fell over her face as she asked, "Is your boss the Forest Pit King? We're looking for him."

The ork howled with laughter.

I needed to teach Savannah how to be more subtle in conversation. At least she was good at sneaking around and observing. *Ah well, we all have our skills.*

"Why is that funny?"

"Nobody sees that guy. You really aren't from here, are you?"

"Can you explain?" I asked.

Maple leaned forward, the front of her blouse opening more. My pants twitched, and as if she could read my mind, Savannah stroked her hand on my thigh, the tips of her fingers against it.

"He's the most secretive man in the galaxy. The only time you see him is in the pit."

"In the pit?"

"Well, at the top of it. He never misses a show. Why do you think he's got that name?"

I shrugged. "Thought he just liked digging holes."

Maple smirked and took another long sip of her drink, then she glanced at Savannah and said, "Excuse me, I need to go to the lady's room."

She stood up.

I gave Savannah a little nudge. "Don't you need to go too?"

"No, I went on the ship."

Maple nodded, stood from her chair, then sauntered off towards the bar. Her pants hugged her butt so tight I thought they might rip. It was so big, impossibly so, even proportioned with her great stature.

"What do you think of her shape?" Savannah asked casually, taking another sip of her beer. Then she burped, covering her mouth in shame.

I laughed, kissing her on the forehead. "Do you have any

idea how cute you are?" I ruffled her hair over her hat. "You should open up more. If you're on guard, she'll be on guard."

"You seem to be doing quite well with her. I believe she is attracted to you."

"True. But it's for you I say that. I want you to be more open with people."

"So we should reveal why we were here?"

Why does it seem like every time she takes a step forward, it's two steps back.

"No, I just mean. Smile more, I guess," I said.

"I see."

After a while, the ork returned from the bathroom. My eyes bulged out at her cleavage. Her buttons were now undone to her abdomen.

"Hi!" Savannah said, too many decibels too high. Her grin was ecstatic.

Maple shook her head, laughing as she said, "You are a strange lady."

I said, "She's gorgeous, though, isn't she? How lucky am I? Sharing a table with two beautiful women?"

"You do not think I am beautiful." The ork waved her hand in a way that said, '*Stop. No, continue.*'

Savannah leaned into the table, "I do too. You are absolutely gorgeous. I don't understand how those girls could pick on you. They were clearly jealous."

"Jealous? Ha!" Maple laughed.

"I mean it. They were stick figures, and not attractive ones. You, on the other hand—well, I'm jealous."

The ork gazed at Savannah.

I downed the last of my drink and noticed that we had all finished ours. Were we tipsy? I clicked my finger at the barman, and he brought another round over so fast they were seemingly already made.

"You've got a nice pair yourself," Maple said.

Savannah's cheeks went bright red. I squeezed her thigh under the table.

Maple said, "So you never told me why you were here. I mean, I assume you were joking before when you said you wanted to talk to the King."

Savannah was about to speak, and I quickly grabbed her leg to shut her up. "Why would I? When I've got two queens right here," I interjected.

Maple snorted. "That was very cheesy. Like something my dad would say."

"You liked it, though," I said, downing my beer. How did I finish it so fast? I didn't remember starting it.

"It was funny," she said.

* * *

As the night went on, we drank beer after beer. regaling stories and opinions, finding we shared many.

At the end of the night, I was thankful I had just enough coin to pay for it. I didn't have a piece more. *If this wasn't the right lead, we'd be screwed.*

We stumbled out onto the street.

Maple mumbled quickly, "Where are you two staying tonight?"

"Oh... I guess we will find a hotel or something," I said. I may have been drunk, but I still knew the perfect time to stumble over words, to suggest something unsaid.

"No way!" the ork yelled, startling a couple of guys walking past us. "You'll stay at my place. I have a spare room!"

"We don't want to put you out."

She shook her head. "My momma always told me to

accommodate friends, and you two are the first friends I ever had."

My heart broke at her drunken revelation.

"C'mon, guys." she sang, walking off ahead of us.

Savannah whispered to me, "She's so nice, *and* funny. Who wouldn't want to be friends with her?"

Maple yelled over her shoulder, "You two coming?"

"We're coming!" Savannah sang, then suppressed an adorable belch.

I said, "People are funny. No, I don't mean funny that way —when someone is a little different, they tend to get ostracized instead of included. I guess that's one of the benefits of being a Subject of Gia—everyone's the same."

"And the downside is, I don't understand any social conventions. I just don't get it. Why would anyone exclude *her*? Even sexually? When she is so clearly suited for intercourse?"

I smiled at her bluntness. "Like I said, people are funny. When one powerful person says something, everyone else tends to believe it. We're not from here, so we can see her for what she really is."

"Beautiful," Savannah said.

Perhaps it was an effect of the alcohol, but Pradorix was more beautiful than ever at night. The leaves high in the sky now glowed gently, basking the black streets in a warm hue that seemed the perfect brightness. Lulling us into a warm sense of comfort.

I felt it all around, or perhaps it was merely that the whole city was drunk. There seemed to be no shortage of bars on a planet where recreation was as important as wealth.

We caught up to Maple.

"Do you like living here?" I held out my arm for her to take.

She eyed it at first, and I wondered if she was thinking how it would look for a seven-foot woman to be taking a man smaller than her arm. But I wasn't exactly short, and when her hands slid onto my shoulder, she seemed to grow warmer with confidence.

We strolled down the street, the three of us arm in arm. Others walking towards us had to get out of our way, but we didn't care—I was the king of the street with my two queens.

Maple said, "It could be worse. I could be on Orkulus, not that I've ever been there. But judging from the orks here, I don't think I'd like it."

Savannah replied, "We left our home planet too. We didn't like it there either."

"So, where do you live now?"

Neither of us answered, and Maple didn't ask another question. We made our way away from the busy streets to a row of houses. The road was quiet, the house lights were mostly all off.

She hummed to herself until we stopped at one.

"This one's mine."

The house was two stories high with a well-kept garden where beautiful flowers grew across the walkway.

"You're not like any ork I've ever met," I confessed, alcohol increasing my honesty.

"I'm not an ork. I'm not human either. How many of those have you met? They don't even have a name for me."

I said nothing, electing to pat her back. She squeezed my arm, which made it go dead, and my male mind immediately wondered how my rod would fare in those hands.

"Ok. This way."

The lights were all off, and she didn't need to turn them on because she lived there. Savannah and I, on the other hand, followed her closely, lest we trip over any rogue nightstands.

What we *could* see in the darkness was clean and well kept. In the corner, white eyes flared to brightness, causing me to reach for my gun.

"It's just me, robot. I have guests," Maple said.

"Disarming," the robot said.

After making our way upstairs,she stopped at a door, "This room's yours. I'll see you in the morning. If you need a drink, the kitchen is that way. The bathroom is opposite."

I wished her goodnight.

"Good night," she said back, humming gently to herself as she stepped off down the hall, the Pradorixian wooden floorboards whining under her steps.

"I'm exhausted," I said, taking Savannah's hand and turning the light on, immediately shielding my eyes as the blinding white startled me. Savannah quickly buried her face into my chest. I shut the door behind us, found a bedside table light, turned that on, and then turned the main light off.

"That's better." Her voice was softer, less reserved now that we were alone.

She wrapped her arms around me, looking up at me with her bright white eyes, the brims filling with tears.

"What?" I asked, laughing awkwardly, but she squeezed me tighter.

"That was the best day of my life," she said, matter-of-factly.

We crashed onto the bed. Kissing, I pulled Savannah's top off, and she leaned back against the bed. My drunken stooper took in her new white frilly bra as she spread her legs and revealed her white panties under the shirt.

I stood up, tearing my shirt off, and she bit her lip at the sight of my muscles, making me go hard in anticipation.

However, by the time I got my jeans off and got down to her, we began kissing, and tiredness overcame me. Combined with the alcohol, I simply could not get hard, which made us burst into laughter, for she was trying very hard with her hand to make it happen.

"I'm glad you had a good day today," I said, cupping my hand over her white panties, holding her secure.

"Apart from all the murder," she said.

We looked at each other and then burst into laughter.

"How is that funny!' She slapped my chest and pulled her arm around me. "What have you done to me?"

I shook my head. "I don't know. I shouldn't be laughing either. What a crazy fucking day."

"It's new for me! You do this all the time."

My smile faded a little, but the laughter subsided. "Not with you."

"We better not make a habit of it," she said, stroking my cheek as she looked up at me.

"You're right, let's leave the murdering to once a week,"

She snorted. "I can't believe I'm laughing at that. What would my mother say?"

Our laughter subsided.

I hugged her tighter. "If she possessed any sense, she'd say she was proud of you for all you did today. You stood up for yourself, you had fun, and then you defended someone else who needed help. That's a lot of things to do in one day."

"Shall we try and not top it tomorrow? Can we just relax and figure out what we're going to do?" she asked.

I'd almost forgotten we had a purpose here. I could very well have left it all behind. Caria seemed too far away now. I didn't have to worry about Cane. Or whatever lay in the deep dark pits of that tower.

I shivered.

"Are you cold?" She cuddled closer to me. Her warmth was so comforting as she stroked her hand up my chest and grasped her fist around my necklace. "I always thought this was so pretty."

"Maybe you should have it then."

She shook her head. "I have you. That's enough for me."

"Mmm," I mumbled, staring up at the patterned ceiling. I reached for the light switch and turned it off.

"There is one problem." She yawned.

"What's that?"

"You're too great to keep to myself."

Silence, but I thought I'd let that go unsaid for long enough.

"Savannah."

"Yes?"

"Do you got, like, some kind of fetish for watching people?"

"Hmm." She tapped my chest with her fingers. "I suppose it's something like that. I'm not sure."

Her hand snaked down my abdomen to grab me and stroke me, causing it to twitch hard, but we were on the cusp of sleep, so I grabbed her thonged ass cheek and squeezed, making her eep and jump closer into me.

"We can find out what it is together."

19

A strange voice in a strange dream asked, "Are you coming back?"

Birds chirped, neighbors chatted merrily. Noon had broken, and the world was alive.

The half-orc, half-human, *what was her name?* Maple. Her voice carried up the stairs and through the door.

Another voice like pure Klargen. A woman—her housemate?

"When will they be awake?" she grunted, the aggression evident in her voice.

"I'll go and wake them soon, Mom," Maple replied.

My eyes opened wide. I shook Savannah awake.

"What." She yawned, hugging me tighter and reaching for me. I grabbed her wrist and took it off.

"You must have got in late last night," a man said, his voice clearly human.

I had no idea what sort of man could go toe to toe with a lady ork. If he was powerful enough to be seen by her as a warrior worthy of seeding her, I would have to think twice about what I said around him.

There was a knock at the door.

"Hello?" I answered.

It opened, and Maple poked her head in, and then glanced down at us in the bed.

Savannah's near-naked body was wrapped over mine.

Maple stared, then, realizing she forgot herself, looked away from us.

"Would you two like coffee and breakfast?" she said to the wall.

My stomach grumbled, and the thought of coffee spurred me to forget any possible awkwardness.

"Sure, sounds great."

"Alright, come down when you're ready."

She shut the door, and Savannah giggled into my chest and said, "Oh, I just froze. I didn't know what to do."

I throw my leg over her, taking her body in mine. "I don't think she minded."

I kissed Savannah, then I got up from the bed and put my clothes on while she did the same.

"Good thing we didn't do anything last night," she said.

My head pounded. I shouldn't have stood up so fast.

I rubbed my head and said, "Although we were hardly quiet, so we may as well have, judging from the things we talked about."

"What did we talk about?" She lifted her arms to let her blouse slide over her head, and her expression was very different when it was over her.

I felt I didn't need to answer, as it seemed she had remembered.

Before leaving, I grabbed my gun belt from the floor and then decided that I probably shouldn't bring it to the breakfast table.

When we stepped out into the hallway. A battle-ax was displayed proudly on the wall.

It was reinforced with jewels across a hilt made of an exquisite stained wood I assumed wasn't Pradorix wood, as that would throw off balance from the shined double blade, which *was* made of it.

I pinched Savannah's butt and said, "C'mon trouble, let's see what they made for breakfast."

Walking down the stairs, the smell of fried food permeated my nostrils. It smelt so good I quickly forgot about the ork woman and her certainly frightening husband.

"Hello there." A small man appeared from around the stairway, making me jump at his chipperness and small stature. The man in an ironed striped shirt held out his hand and beamed, saying, "My name's Freddy."

He couldn't have been taller than five feet. I held out my hand to the white-haired balding man with an impossibly infectious grin on his face. Behind him, sat at the table, his ork wife stared venomously at us.

Through my hungover pain, I stepped out of my body and heard myself say, "It's great to meet you! You have a beautiful home. I'm Harlen, and this is Savannah."

Savannah waved awkwardly and flashed a smile that lasted a second. It must have taken a lot for her to do that, and I appreciated the effort.

I walked over to Maple's mother, who was sipping on a bright red liquid. I wondered how I could eat when sitting across from whatever was in that glass. But it would have been insulting to do otherwise.

She grunted, "Glasha." and took my hand, squeezing it, cracking a few muscles.

My eyes widened in pain, and somehow, I thought Glasha must not have been the one to name Maple.

"Mother!" Maple cried.

I tried to ignore that Maple was wearing nothing but a long t-shirt. Her breasts shook with every moment.

Glasha smiled through her tusks and said, "He has a strong handshake. I approve of your friend."

Relief came over me as I shook my hand free of the pain and said, "I was going easy on you. If we had an arm wrestle, I don't think you'd be so lucky."

The whole room went silent.

And then she grinned again and said to her daughter, "Why is this the first time we're meeting your friends?"

"Mom!"

It was strange, watching an ork in her twenties complain like that, but there was something cute about seeing how embarrassed she got.

"Sit," Glasha commanded.

Savannah and I took chairs beside each other while Maple loaded the table with bacon, fried tomatoes, and eggs.

A classic earth-2 breakfast. Nothing could be a better hangover cure.

"Here you go." Maple placed a mug of murky brown liquid next to mine, and my heart jumped before I'd even tasted it.

I felt the soft tickle of Savannah's lips against my ear.

"What is that?" she asked.

"It's coffee. Try some. It will wake you up."

Across the table, Glasha watched us, between taking sips of that red liquid I hoped wasn't Klargen, considering how early in the day it was. I supposed there must have been a morning drink for orks too. It wasn't something I'd ever seen back home in the bar.

Savannah took her mug and brought it to her lips, taking

a sip. Her eyes opened wide in delight, and she took another.

"Good?" I asked.

"Incredible. I feel so awake." Savannah licked her lips, savoring the taste as she closed her eyes and sighed blissfully.

When I took a sip, my reaction was not dissimilar. "We don't have coffee where we're from," I explained to Glasha, whose dark red eyes bore into us.

"Both of you?" She looked between her and me, glancing at Savannah's white hair.

Freddy interjected, flicking at his bowtie, "Now dear, the only grilling that should be happening is for the bacon."

She smiled and leaned back, holding a hand open. "Forgive me. I'm interested in my daughter's friends." It came out more like a grunt than words.

"Mom, you're embarrassing them, and me too," Maple complained again.

I held my hands up and said, "It's fine! We're guests in your home."

Savannah was currently wolfing her food down. But that only caused Glasha and Freddy to smile at the compliment. I rubbed her back while she went bright red with embarrassment and swallowed.

"I apologize. I forgot myself." She sat up straight, wiping her lips on a napkin.

"When the food is this good, it's easy to forget your manners," I said.

"Hear, hear!" Freddy said.

"How did you two meet?" Glasha asked.

I said, "In an old tavern. We got talking and had a great time. At least, I think we did. We drank a lot."

"You're only young once!" Freddy cheered.

"They..." Maple began to say but then cut herself off.

Glasha lasered in on her daughter. "What did they do?"

Maple looked down at her bacon, running her fork around it. "It's embarrassing now."

The mom's demeanor changed so rapidly it was like she wasn't even an ork, even with the grunting voice. "Sweetie—be proud of who you are. These two fine warriors - and it's clear they are warriors, no matter how they try to hide it with their human politeness - saw you fit for friendship. What more proof could you have of your worth?"

But Maple had gone quiet, shutting herself down like I wish I could do to the robot noisily cleaning the pots and pans.

Glasha stroked her daughter's back. I didn't know orks could show worry or sympathy. It was clear she loved her daughter very much.

"There were these two girls. Nasty little things." I explained, taking turns to look at the husband and wife.

The ork wife slammed her fist on the table. "Those bitches. I know who they are."

"Mom, please!"

"Why did you let *them* do something and not *me*!"

The husband spoke up, "Sweetie, we've been over this. They're the daughters of two of the richest CEOs on this planet."

Glasha leaned back on her chair. "I know." Then she smirked at her daughter. "We could tag them. One punch from each would cave their ratty little faces in."

Maple smiled back at her mother and said, "You know we can't."

"Why not?" asked Savannah.

I found myself wondering the same. Surely a few bouts in the pit were right up any ork or half-ork's street.

I asked as much.

Maple said while staring at her bacon, "It's not the pit we would have to deal with. It's crossing the Forest Pit King or any of his right-hand men."

Her mother groaned. "I can crush them all in a fight. As much as it pains me to admit, there is a time and a place for battle."

"The last man that crossed him ended up dead in a ditch," Freddy explained.

"Cowards. Not a fair fight," Glasha spat.

I was starting to like her more and more.

I said directly to her, "I hate that. I need to look a man in the eye when I fight him."

There was a twinkle in her eye. "So you *are* warriors. I can see it as plain as day."

I looked at Freddy, who nodded and smiled, then Glasha, who glared at me approvingly. Finally, Maple, who was still looking down at her plate.

"We haven't been entirely honest with you," I said, letting out a tense breath.

Savannah stared at me. Under the table, she grabbed my hand.

The clock on the wall ticked. The family was all silent, waiting for my following words with bated breath.

I took another sip of coffee and said with complete sincerity, "We came to talk to the Forest Pit King."

Of course, they all laughed. I had wanted them to.

"Nobody talks to him," Glasha grunted.

"This is important. My planet is in danger," I insisted.

I explained how on Caria, a Pradorixian gang, under the guise of a building company, was crafting a dangerous, life-endangering drug, and I came here for answers—and to stop them.

Maple asked what the company was called.

"I think you know," I said solemnly.

"You tricked me?" Maple said, her mouth then moved to form more words, but none came out. Instead, her shoulders drooped.

"We thought if we-" I stopped myself from saying 'seduced,' "*befriended* you. You would help us sneak in. But something happened—we found ourselves befriending you for real. Seeing how great you are. How great your family is," I took in a shaky breath. "I had to come clean."

I stood out from the table. "Savannah and I will be on our way now. We'll find some other way to speak to the king. It's evident to me that there's more to this than just The Hardest Wood. We don't need to involve you at all. We'll just go straight to the king."

"Even attempting to speak to the king is tantamount to volunteering for the pit," Freddy said, in a moment of rare seriousness.

"And besides. Who said you were allowed to leave," Glasha added.

Savannah and I glanced at each other. *Will there be a fight?*

"Not when there's so much more of your story to tell," Maple said, still frowning but focused on us.

Freddy became animated and said, "Oh yes! I agree. For instance, how does a Subject of Gia come to leave the sect and wear the garbs of Pradorix? Might it be a riveting love story?"

"You aren't angry?" I asked the room, but I looked to Maple for the answer.

"My mother taught me I needed to be smart—smarter than any human. For people to take orks seriously, they need to try twice as hard. So. I knew you were watching me in that bar. I knew you were looking for some opportunity to speak to me. And-"

I waited with bated breath.

"I knew that whatever *'mission'* you were on did not succeed when we had that much fun. I knew I could trust you. And I thought if your way to trick people is to stick up for them, then how bad could your mission be?"

She stared deep into my eyes, but traced her finger around her glass, as if to center herself. "You were clearly not from here, and that's why I invited you back home. I-" but she suddenly went red, realizing that all eyes were on her.

"You were right." I turned to the parents. "She may not have been our friend before last night, but I speak for Savannah and me when I say I'm glad to call her one now. You two as well. You did a marvelous job raising her." I took a breath, anticipating the reveal that was new to myself too. "If my parents were half as caring and powerful in both measures as you two, I suppose things would have turned out very differently."

"You wouldn't be instinctively reaching for that absent gun on your hip like we're to do battle, for one thing," Glasha said.

I laughed. "I don't even know I do it."

Savannah rubbed my thigh. "You always do it, I don't mind. It makes me feel safe."

Silence then, as the room soaked in our overly tender moment.

"So!" Freddy rubbed his hands together. "Tell us everything."

"Everything?"

Glasha leaned forward, stabbing her fork into the table, which only resulted in the fork bending against the

Pradorixian wood. "Every. Little. Detail." She grinned, baring her blood-stained teeth at us.

I looked at Savannah. "Well, we both were Subjects of Gia..."

I went through it all. How I had left the sect, why I had done it. How I had stowed away on a rare supply run to Caria, where I had heard people lived like in the cowboy stories I loved to read. How I was taken under the wing of a seasoned bounty hunter, and a kind bar owner - I gulped at the thought of her, pangs of guilt stabbing at me - but Savannah squeezed my hand, until got to the part where I was standing in front of The Hardest Wood's base, escaped from the fight with the Gia Knight, barely with my life intact.

That was when Savannah interjected. "If my mother is secretly buying some kind of drug, I need to find out what it is."

"Why don't you ask her?" Freddy asked.

"It's not that simple," I explained.

"I don't think I would have a warm reception back home, not that it was ever warm before. And well-" Savannah's voice suddenly went louder, she yelled to the ceiling. "The universe doesn't revolve around Gia!" I squeezed her hand under the table. "Sorry." Her cheeks went red.

Freddy said, "That's what we like here. Someone who can think for themselves."

* * *

The day went on, and even though I had tried to make excuses for leaving, the parents insisted we stay.

And how could we resist the comfort of their home? It was clean, tidy, and we partook in many conversations, sharing our individual stories. Glasha told me how she had traveled over from Orkulus and met Freddy in a bar, much like we had met their daughter.

“He was the only man who wasn't scared to talk to me," she said, grinning through her tusks.

Freddy got up from the table and stood beside his seated wife. He was the same height as her sitting down.

"How could I resist such a beautiful little minx?"

They began making out. While it was sweet, it was also kind of gross and earned much-deserved complaints from Maple.

"Some people don't have parents that love each other," Glasha said, her giant hand dwarfing Freddys on her shoulder.

"It's true," I remarked.

"Very true," Savannah added.

* * *

After using their shower, which was incredibly powerful, we had a day of relaxation and then heavy drinking. The family seemed to have a shared love of getting wasted.

I stumbled up from the chair, the room spinning around me.

"M'lady." I held out my hand to Savannah, who giggled, holding her hand in front of her mouth, suppressing a burp. Then I turned to the family. "If you excuse me, I think it's time for my lady to sleep. And then we shall be out of your hair. Thank you for the wonderful hospitality."

Savannah got up, and then I crouched down and threw her over my shoulders. She laughed and hit her fists against my back but soon gave in when she realized resistance was futile.

In our room, I threw her down onto the bed, tearing off my shirt.

"Should we do this with them there?" she asked.

"I'll just have to gag you," I said.

She gasped as I took off my belt and tied it around her mouth, she bit down on it, and we began having our way with each other, silently as we could. Our movements were slow, measured. I pushed in and out of her with great meaning, the slowness of it, our bodies pressed together softly and deeply, made it all the more intense. Finally, as I slid through her dripping wet folds, I went blind with light, releasing inside of her. At the same time, she bit down on the belt I had tied around her, eyes glazed with desperate pleasure.

* * *

Savannah poked me awake.

"What," I grumbled.

"They're talking about you."

"Hmm?" I rubbed my eyes, opening them to the pitch blackness. "What are you talking about?"

"Ssh." She put her fingers to my lips. "Just listen."

I grumbled again and then piqued my ears, hearing nothing at first but whispering.

The words became clearer.

"Honey, you shouldn't do it." Glasha grunted.

"But I want to!" Maple protested.

"I know he's cute, but that does not mean you should risk your life for him."

"Mom, it's not just that."

"So you *do* think he's cute?"

I smirked. Savannah hugged me tighter, kissing my neck and rubbing herself on my thigh.

"Mom! Anyway, he's with Savannah."

"All I'm saying is, I saw the way he was looking at you too. And she didn't seem to mind. These foreigners have weird ways." Glasha said knowingly.

"I can't believe what you're saying." Maple's voice got louder.

"I just want what's best for you."

"Well, maybe finding out what's in that building is what's best for me. I don't even know what I'm guarding."

"You're paid well enough to not know. You don't like it? Find another job."

"But I *like* my job. I just stand there and talk to the other guards. I don't have to deal with any customers."

"But you do have to deal with those guards that are laughing behind your back." Glasha sounded strong, but I could tell there was hurt there, at the affront to her daughter.

"Everyone laughs behind my back! Ork! Humans! Everyone." There was silence then. Had she never spoken that before?

I made a fist while Savannah kissed my neck again.

I whispered, "I'm going out there."

Savannah nodded, and I slid off the bed, grabbing my clothes from the floor.

The dad chimed in, "I'll tell you who won't laugh behind your back. Harlen, now that's a real man. He says what he means, and he does what he says—honorable."

I chuckled and looked at Savannah, who cocked her head and smiled as if to say, *'you, honorable?'*

Opening the door into the hallway, I shielded my eyes

from the bright light and stepped out, then climbed down the stairs.

"I couldn't help overhearing," I said, entering the kitchen.

"Sorry, were you sleeping?" Maple said, smiling at me and then darting her eyes to the table.

The three of them looked at me, sitting in those same spots they had been before. Clearly, they had stayed up drinking, but due to their tolerance, it hardly seemed to affect them at all.

I liked this family.

"We were discussing your proposition," Freddy said matter of factly.

"I don't remember proposing anything."

"And yet here we are discussing it," Freddy said.

"So, what did you decide?"

"I'm gonna help you sneak in!" Maple blurted out, red eyes wide. She grinned, while her parents frowned at her. She continued, "There's an opening when my shift partner goes to the store. You can sneak in and see what they're up to there."

"And what happens to you?"

she slammed her fist down on the table. "A warrior laughs in the face of danger."

Her mother smiled but shook her head and said, "A warrior knows when not to be foolish. Better to live to fight another day."

"That sounds more like a human than an ork," Maple retorted.

"Yes, that's what your father taught me. If he didn't, do you think I would still be standing here? I was foolish then. You would be wise to take heed."

"I think she should do it," the small man said. They gawped at him.

“You're an adult now. You make your own discussions and your own mistakes. They're not going to blame us for it, but you. So, if you want to put yourself in danger, so be it."

Glasha grunted, "You would send your daughter off to death?"

He smiled at her and said, "Do you have so little faith in our little warrior? I've seen her fight. You trained her."

Silence for a bit, I didn't particularly need to be there for this, but I spoke up all the same. "So, what's the plan?"

"Tomorrow, two o’clock, when I'm on shift, my partner always goes to pick up something from the store, leaving me alone. That’s when I'll let you in."

"That simple, huh."

"That simple." She nodded, then stood up, breasts pushed out, nipples showing through her top. "Get some rest. Who knows what will happen tomorrow."

I shook my head, heading back to my room, where the big ax displayed opposite the door. I ran my finger across the hilt, dust collecting on my digit.

They were no warriors, I thought. Ork or no ork. Once Glasha married that small man, nice as he was, they had settled into human ways and passed them on to their daughter. Was it fair of me to lead her down this path? If the Pit King and his right-hand men were as dangerous as they say?

But they said she was an adult, making her own decisions.

Making her own mistakes.

20

"Ready?" I warned Savannah.

We waited on the other side of the long, busy street, across from The Hardest Wood. Cars bustled past and people merrily went about their day. Between their movements, we watched Maple stand guard, talking to her coworker.

Eventually, the other guard walked away from her, just as she predicted.

"Now!" I grabbed Savannah's hand, and we walked briskly across the street, almost getting run over by a car whose owner beeped and yelled out the window for us to '*watch the road!*'

Finally, we got across, and Maple opened the door for us, leading us into the secret building.

There wasn't a soul in sight. It was an unremarkable entrance to an office building with an empty secretary's desk. Black wood, unpainted, like every other building on the planet.

"What now?" Savannah whispered.

"This way, let's look for someone that works here," I said.

We took the stairs down into a dark and empty warehouse. Building materials lined up across great racks. The more we walked, the bigger the room seemed to get. No matter how we tried to quiet our footsteps, they seemed to echo down the hall, alerting anyone who could hear to our presence.

But not before we heard them.

A couple of workers turned the corner ahead of us. I grabbed Savannah and pulled her to the side of a rack, out of their view.

Then, we headed between two of the long racks, walking briskly but quietly, heading for where they had come from.

A corner of the warehouse, with no door— a dead end.

"Look." Savannah pointed to the ground at a trap door— unassuming, but not hidden.

We glanced at each other, and I said, "Only one way to go."

She nodded and lifted the door up with her powers.

"Show off." I smirked.

"I haven't done it in a while." She grinned.

I climbed down the ladder, the pitch-black broken up by eerily familiar, dim orange lights. My heart raced, and I held onto the rungs tight as my hands got clammy.

Could *they* be here too? Those things I kept unsuccessfully pushing to the back of my mind. That haunted me whenever I closed my eyes.

"I don't know what we're gonna find down here," I whispered up to her as she held her hand out to silently shut the trap door, shrouding us in darkness.

"Isn't that the point?"

"I mean, It could be something bad."

"It would be anticlimactic if it wasn't."

"Will you listen to me!" I hissed. "It might be what I saw on Caria."

“I see." She paused as our feet tapped against the ladder, pondering my words, and then finally said, "We face them together."

Had she seen through my false attempts at hiding the true horror of that cave?

"Together," I agreed, feeling better that we would have eachothers backs. I didn't have to do it alone, and neither did she.

The ladder went forever. I didn't need to consider what would happen if another worker climbed up here. How would we explain our presence?

"We might have to fight someone on this ladder," I whispered.

"Have you ever done that before?"

"There's a first time for everything," I said solemnly.

Downward we climbed. it seemed to never end.

The smell of wet metal perforated the air.

Finally, down below, the orange light stopped, illuminating a puddle, which shone back up at us.

I dropped down, and then Savannah joined me, nodding.

We headed into the deep, dark tunnel, having to crouch until we were met with a gated door, which I pulled open. The floor was gated too, that same wood. Thankfully, this one was stable on my feet. I could not see how far the depths below went, but I didn’t want to find out the hard way.

It was a lab, similar to the one I visited before, but without the great drums. Instead, there was a testing kit on the table. vials, beakers, a computer.

I sat down and clicked on the screen, but of course, there was a password.

"What now?" Savannah asked, crossing her arms. "Why would they hide this all the way down here?"

The place was empty, a dead end.

"Because they didn't want anybody to see it or find it." I leaned back on the chair, staring at the illuminated computer screen, and said, "We're going to wait."

"Wait?" she said.

"Wait. These scientists can never fight. They're always so keen to give it up, especially when there's a gun pointed at them."

"You won't kill them, will you?"

I stepped up off the chair, frowning when it wouldn't budge from the push of my knees, and walked over to Savannah. She was sitting against the wall with her arms crossed. Long strands of her silver hair broke from their designated place to rest over her face chaotically. Taking my gun out, I resisted the urge to do a few finger flips as I showed her the side.

"If you ever need to use this, not that I imagine you will with your gift, these notches denote the strength."

She watched my gun with interest.

"This one—stun."

She nodded. "And the next?"

"*Very* stun."

"Really?" She smirked.

"What?" I laughed. "It's like a stun, but more of it."

"And what about the next one?"

"This one, you have to hold your finger down to charge. It's called *'kill, or stun a bigger thing.'*

Savannah slapped my shoulder. "You are so silly."

I scoffed, grabbed her, and crashed my lips into her.

"I'm the *silly billy*," I said in a stupid voice, then started tickling her. She cackled with laughter.

"Stop it! we're supposed to be undercover."

"That ladder goes on forever. Nobody will hear you... fall to my mercy!"

I tickled her some more, and she lifted her knee, trying to get away from me. I stopped, giving her some mercy and our laugh subsided, leaving us staring into each other's eyes.

Our kiss was soft, tender. My hand slid up Savannah's blouse to touch her bare skin, stroking up to her breasts, squeezing over that soft, patterned fabric.

The gate shut with a slam.

"What the hell?" I broke the kiss, grabbing my gun and aiming at the door.

There was nobody there behind the gate. I traced with my eyes to a wire that traveled upstairs. Then, I took in more of my surroundings.

I shouldn't have let my guard down. I should have known better.

I couldn't see anything out of the ordinary, though.

The floor beneath us split.

Because of the weight of everything on it, it was instant. My ass hit the grate before it fell vertically, and then I was floating in the air.

Savannah was too. Her hand shook, she winced with concentration. Around us, the desk, computer, and chair all stuck to the now horizontal floor like they were nailed down.

"You're gonna have to teach me how to do that again."

"Yeah, maybe." She gritted her teeth, arm shaking. "I can't hold it much longer. Not both of us."

I looked down to the deep below. Some of the things on

the desk—testing equipment, samples of the drug, had fallen down the dark slide.

"Savannah, there's no way but down. You'll need to save your strength to stop us from hitting whatever's down there." I reached out for her. "Come here."

She looked down, worry strewn on her face as she floated over to me, both arms shaking, and I held her secure. The horizontal floor was too far for either of us to grab.

"Let's drop." She grabbed onto me, and my stomach entered my chest.

She gripped me so tight I thought I would have bruises from her fingers. We slid on the smooth surface, falling almost vertically down—we could see nothing, and only hold onto ourselves for security.

"You're gonna need to look down," I shouted. The rushing past our ears made my own voice hard to hear.

We slid for ages, yet, it seemed to get more horizontal with time. We slowed. Until finally, once it had turned flat, we slid out into a *thankfully* bare room. The floor became that grated metal wood, and we rolled, my joints hurting against the hard surface.

I rolled off her, and we lay on our backs.

"That was fun," she remarked.

I laughed. "Could have been worse."

A neon flash appeared, blinding me momentarily. I held my hand out from the brightness, squinting at it until the light became an arrow. A red and green arrow pointing away from the direction we had come.

Grumbling, I sat up, checking I still had my gun and it was safe.

“You in one piece?” I asked.

“She rubbed her head. “As Gia made me.”

Pushing myself up from the floor, I got up and helped her up.

“We might as well follow it.”

She smiled. “We have nothing better to do.”

“Having fun?” I said as we walked down the dark hallway.

“I'm not *not* having fun.”

“That's the spirit."

There was a light at the end of the tunnel.

"I've had enough of dark tunnels," I remarked. "It seems like this week all I've been doing is climbing into dark tunnels."

She smirked at me.

"What?" I asked.

The light got closer, as did a tapping around. Intermittent clicking and clacking, the hairs on the back of my neck stood up, and I kept my hand on my pistol to draw if I needed to.

"Nothing," she said.

"Go on," I said, quieting my voice. The clacking grew louder.

"It's just, climbing into dark tunnels."

I stopped, squinting at her. "Savannah Knight, are you being naughty?"

She smirked. "It sounds dirty."

"If this is how you're gonna behave every time we go on an undercover mission, I'm leaving you at the ship.”

She nodded, but her smile grew. "No, of course, you're right, and you weren’t the one tickling me a moment ago."

I stopped, slid my hand down the small of her back to grab her ass. "Good point. It does sound dirty, though. I swear, if we make it out of this, I'm gonna bend you over and..." I stopped my words dead, letting her imagination gill in the gaps.

"*If* we make it out of this." She cooed. "We should take this seriously."

"Girl, I'm as serious as the day I was born."

But heeding her, I took her hand, and we walked down the hallway, flashing arrows guiding our way. The light at the end of the tunnel got bigger. The tapping was less intermittent.

A man coughed.

I pulled my gun out and pressed my face against the glass of the door, looking left and right.

21

I looked through a window pane.

One light bulb hung from the center ceiling, swinging above a tight-suited man standing at a desk, typing away on a computer. He was so slender, he looked like he might fall over if the wind blew too hard.

I opened the door, holding Savannah behind me, and pointed the gun in both directions in case of ambush.

The walls were made of doors. Each was identical to the one we had come out of.

"Hello, sir," the man said politely.

I eyed him. "What is this place?"

"Registration center," he said, clearing his throat and then typing away, peering over his spectacles.

"Registering for what?"

He frowned at me over his spectacles. "The pit."'

My eyes darted to all of the doors, expecting at any moment for someone to burst out and start firing.

"That won't be necessary. Unless you plan to fight the doors, and I warn you, they pack a wallop if swung hard enough."

"Explain," I said, deciding I would be fast enough to draw if he lied. I put my gun in my holster.

"Did I not?" He arched his brow.

We stood there, waiting.

"If I must." He sighed. "When you were trespassing, stealing, fighting, whatever it was that you were doing that led you to walk through that door, you volunteered yourself for the pit."

"We didn't volunteer for nothin'."

"Oh? Then how did you come to walk through that door?"

I said nothing. Savanah just frowned at me, shrugging.

"So what if I shoot yer." I reached for my gun.

"Then my colleague will come to take my place, and your registration will be delayed."

He said this as if it was no more a nuisance than running late.

"What if I shoot *that* guy?"

"It will be further delayed. Meanwhile, your prize money will be growing with each... shooting."

"Why would the prize money grow?" Savannah said.

He peered at her over his spectacles, saying nothing, as if that was answer enough. After an annoyed sigh, he asked, "Shall we begin?" and clicked away on his computer while we stood there, perplexed at the oddness of the situation.

"Name?" he asked.

My eyebrow was in a permanent furrow, Savannah and I looked at each other and said our names simultaneously.

"One at a time, please."

I stepped forward and said, "Harlen Gray."

He clacked on the keyboard, then asked for my age.

"Twenty-seven."

Clack clack clack.

"Sex?"

"Plenty." I winked at Savannah, and she snorted.

"*Sex*?" he repeated, unamused.

"Male."

"Occupation?"

I paused for a second. "Bounty hunter."

"Preferred weapon?"

I pulled my gun out of my holster. "This."

"Hmm, let me see."

I pulled it back. "No way."

"Then it will be taken from you."

I looked around the empty room. "By who? You?"

"No. I am here to take your registration. There are others dedicated to handling you."

I made a fist. "Ain't nobody handling Savannah."

“Then I suggest you let me see your gun. I'm not going to take it from you," he insisted.

Deciding I could sock him in the face long before he pointed the gun at me, I passed it over. He placed it on the desk, took off one set of glasses, put it in a case, and then pulled out an identical set. Wiping them with a cloth, he put them on.

"Hmm. Photon." He ran his finger across the notches, pushing them up and down as he asked, "Barometer working?"

"It works." I grit my teeth.

"These usually come as a pair. Where is the other?"

"At the shop."

He tutted. "If this is the weapon you wish to use, I see no reason to stop you, although we have far better in the store cupboard.”

He handed it back to me, and I twirled it before putting it back in the hoster, explaining, "I’m rather attached."

"I can see that." He then yelled over me as if trying to reach someone at the far end of a hall, "Next applicant, please!'

But Savanah was only right beside me. She stepped forward.

"Hello." she grinned shyly.

"Name?"

Clack clack clack.

"Savannah Knight."

Clack clack. A bead of sweat dripped down his hooked nose.

"Age?"

"Twenty-seven."

Clack. The bead dangled off his nose's tip.

"Sex?"

"It's fun?" She said.

We burst into laughter, but he was entirely unreactive.

"C'mon! That's funny." I said, kneeled over.

"Sex?" he repeated again.

"Female."

"Chosen weapon."

"These." She held up her hands, made a gun with one of them, and then blew off her smoking finger barrel.

I had never been more proud of her. Also, I realized she was a bit of a dork.

"A disciple of Gia, it will be interesting to see what you can do in the pit," he remarked.

The man in the suit walked over to the wall, held his hand up to a slot, and a protruding block machine groaned mechanical noises until a sheet of paper fell out, and then another.

He walked back to the desk, put the paper on it, and

then pulled something out of the drawer. I reached for my gun instinctually.

"Please, stand by the wall."

We walked over to the wall, where he stood before me, took a photo, took another, then pulled the tiny picture from the camera and stuck it to the sheet.

"Now, if you could go through that door." He pointed.

"Is that it?" I demanded.

"Yes, and if you wouldn't mind moving along, I have another appointment due. I don't believe you would wish to be in the same room as my next volunteer."

Somehow, I doubted anyone was too much for Savannah and me to handle, but I said, "C'mon, Darlin', let's get to the bottom of this."

I held my arm out for her to take, and she grinned, slotting her fingers into it. We headed out the door he had pointed to until we were led to an elevator, where we entered, and pressed the only button there.

It shook, taking us lower until finally, it stopped at another room.

We left the elevator and were greeted by another identical-looking man standing at a desk computer.

"Oh c'mon!" I groaned.

He held his hands out. "Sheets, please."

"And then what? More waiting?"

He coughed into a fist, then clacked some more on his keyboard.

I said, "You know, you remind me of a guy I've met before. Do you have a brother?"

He typed some more and then repeated, "Sheets, please."

We handed them to him, and there was more clicking on the mechanical keyboard.

"Please wait in the marked room to be called."

"How long will that take?"

Clicking, clacking. A drip of some water in the corner of the office.

"Approximately an hour."

"I swear to fuck, we better be seeing the Forest Pit King himself after this."

"He will be there, yes."

Savannah and I looked at each other.

"Well, I suppose we had better go to the waiting room." I took her hand and walked through a door-adorned hallway, each with a number outside in black. One of them was turned on, a bright orange 3. Inside, the room was nothing but two Pradroxian wooden benches on either side of the room.

I groaned, and we sat down on one while Savannah leaned her head on me.

"Well. We've got time at least for some peace and quiet."

"It's been a while since we had that."

She hugged me closer, gripping onto my shirt. I stroked her beautiful silver hair and kissed her forehead over her hat. Savannah took it off and fixed her hair.

"Say..."

"Hmm?" Savannah's silver eyes stared up at me, almost shining. *Was that flicker of auburn growing bigger?*

"I never did ask. How exactly does it happen?"

"What happen?"

"Ascension."

"It's forbidden to talk about," she said bluntly.

I cocked my head at her.

Her mouth flickered a smile. "Oh right. Yeah. Well. Remember the platform the masters stood on when we had to display Gia's gift?"

I nodded, stroking her beautiful white-silver hair while

she ran her fingers across my abdomen, twirling a single digit, slightly tickling me.

"They pushed it out of the way, and then there were these staircases going down. We all headed down there together, into this room full of mist. The mist was thick, warm."

I felt my heart speed up. I gripped onto the bench with my free hand. *Was I finally discovering what it all was?*

"And, we all sat in a circle around this... It was like a fountain of water. I think the mist came from there. We sat around it and meditated. My eyes were closed, but this blue light appeared. It was so bright I could see it through my eyelids. Even though we were supposed to keep our eyes closed, I darted one open for a second. Everyone else's were closed. The light seemed to come from everywhere. I couldn't figure out its direction at all. It started to dim, and everyone's hair had gone white! I quickly shut my eyes, and then we were told to open them again.

"Is that why..."

I wanted to say the auburn mark in her eye, but she caught my meaning, as she nodded. "Mother was displeased. She said I disobeyed Gia, and that I was lucky that Gia had only left me with this mark in my eye to remind me every day. But, I think it *did* please her, in a way, because ever since then, I was the perfect little Subject of Gia."

"So... Do you think she is real?"

"How could she not be? It all happened."

I tightened my lips and said, "I can't argue with that."

"Do you ever wish things went differently? That you stayed and took the gift?"

I pondered a second to honestly think if I did or not.

"Not in the slightest." I pulled my gun out and twirled it. "Besides, I got this."

"You're so good with it," she said, stroking my abdomen, getting a little lower.

"And you're great at moving stuff around with your hands, Darlin'."

"We make a good team."

"What else could we need? They're crazy if they think whatever's in that pit is gonna be a match for us. We're gonna get that prize money no problem, then we'll be set."

"And do what next?"

I tapped my chin. "I'll figure it out."

"You always do." she beamed at me, then pressed her lips into me, stroking her hand down.

"Nope." I grabbed her wrist.

She gasped. "Are you denying me?"

"Not before a fight. I need all my *chi* or whatever it's called. And also, think how good it's gonna be after."

She sighed, resting her head on my chest, stroking down her back, and squeezed her juicy ass. "It's gonna be so good."

I closed my eyes, keeping my hand on her butt as we waited.

22

A ding rang out around us, like an alarm clock's hammer hitting its bell once.

Neon words appeared on both sides of the ceiling, *'Get ready.'*

The platform shook and vibrated. I clambered off the bench, shaking out my stiff joints. Savannah stood up too, stretching and yawning, and then there was another noise.

"What is that?" Savannah asked, eyes darting with panic.

Her question was answered as we got closer to the surface, the sounds of a crowd loudly cheering for us broke through the ceiling.

"That's a lot of people," I remarked.

Finally, a light appeared from the window of the door. Blinding at first, then my eyes adjusted to see the ground. The door clicked—a lock unlocking. I opened it, and we stepped out to the thundering applause, but we were still in a tunnel, so it couldn't have been for us.

"How many tunnels are on this goddamn planet?" I said.

But Savannah said nothing. We stepped out into the

light, and if the applause was thundering before, then it was deafening now.

The colossal pit engulfed us. High in the sky, cloud wisps surrounded the seats, where whistles, trumpets, and screaming cheers attacked us. My head spun looking up at it all, unable to take it all in with one gaze. I had to keep looking around to get it all in my vision, so I focused down at the vast empty space before us. The traps and platforms we had seen on our arrival to the planet were gone. It was just a gargantuan bowel of dirt, in which we were but two tiny ants.

A voice boomed through unseen speakers, "Ladies and gentlemen."

Both Savannah and I darted our eyes up, where lights shone on a section of the circle.

The man, from this distance, would have seemed an average size if there weren't people next to him. He was a giant and barely human in appearance. His skin had black metal plates on it. I couldn't tell if it was armor or a natural part of himself. It was like he was one of the very trees that grew on this planet, uprooted and given sentience.

The Forest Pit King stared at us, observing with a blank expression of disgust. His blinks were slow and measured, or was it that time seemed to slow in his presence?

A man beside him, if I squinted, looked vaguely similar to those underground, although this one seemed to have more of a *flair* about him, sounding less stuck up as he spoke.

He yelled into the microphone, "Never has it been said that The Forest Pit King is unfair. These two broke into private property, a heinous crime. Perhaps you think, well, it's only somebody's business. But when they entered a simple building company warehouse and found nothing but planks of wood, where would they break into next? Your homes?"

The crowd booed at us. I gripped Savannah's hand and said, "Well, he knows how to stir up a crowd. Wish he'd get on with it."

"For the first time in history, falling from the grace of Gia. Led astray by a rogue cowboy. It's a story for the ages, and tonight, we get to see it play out."

I closed my eyes and took a deep breath. "We got this," I said to Savannah.

"I never had a doubt," she responded.

The announcer's voice turned to a venomous snarl. "Send out the Gratars."

The crowd roared a cheer. It would have been an improvement on the boo's, except they were cheering for not us.

Miles away, so far that it was a spec, the door opened, and something slivered out, tiny in the distance. Two lizards zooming with great speed, each carrying something on their back. They stopped and stood up on their hind legs, tongues darting out, tasting the air.

"They're smart," I warned her.

"How can you tell?"

The lizards reached behind their backs and pulled out two swords.

"Oh."

"Yeah."

They darted towards us. Which would have taken a while if they weren't so damn quick, galloping across the dirt like pressure rockets. And then, like boulders from a catapult, they leaped in the air with impossible height and momentum.

To land on us, swords at the ready.

I set the gun to kill, aimed, then squinted one eye to get a shot. I knew I wouldn't need to charge up the shot. It was dead in the crosshair before I even fired, and when I did, the crowd gasped at the purple light that hit the lizard in the heart, causing its body to spin in the air as it fell towards me, landing at my feet.

It was no bigger than a small dog.

Meanwhile, Savannah had stopped hers in the air. The lizard flailed, trying to grab onto something nonexistent. She thrust her hand down, slamming it down into the ground with such velocity that it landed with a bloody splat.

More cheers arose from the crowd.

"They're cheering for us this time," I said. "See how that works?"

"Yeah." She grimaced at what she had done, then looked at me for approval.

"The Gratars were trying to kill us," I reassured her.

She nodded. "Us or them."

"Good girl."

In the speakers, the announcer yelled, "Let's have a round of applause for our convicts!"

He paused for the cheers, then interjected, and they hushed at his words. "But—you didn't really think a simple *Gratar* could take them down, not when they came all this way from Earth-2."

Boos.

"These Earth-2 rogues think they can disturb our peaceful way of life. Little do they know, all roads lead to the pit. Shall we send in the next beast?"

"How are you holding up?" I asked Savannah, who shook out her hands and stretched her neck.

"Bring it," she said with stern-faced determination.

"You're beautiful." I grabbed her and kissed her.

The crowd cheered, which caused a grunt into the microphone.

“Like I said, a *few* Gratar couldn’t take them down, so how about *many*?"

Lizards sprang from the door, pulling out their swords and spreading across the pit in an attempt to pincer us.

Savannah and I ran to meet them. I aimed my gun at the first one but missed it because it was so far. When he got closer, I shot again, but it dodged, then flung itself at me, its sword gleaming. My purple blast made short work of the airbound lizard. He fell to the ground with a thud, replaced by his identical friend, who snarled and threw his sword at me—the tip pressed against my chest, stopping dead, floating in the air.

Savannah had her hand out and focused on that, not the lizard behind her, whom I shot. She was panting. Beads of sweat began to drip down the side of her face.

I shot another lizard that was trying to sneak up on us.

Savannah raised her hand for one, snarling and running at me, but it only stumbled to rush back up and chase at me again. My gun was getting hot in my hands. I shot the lizard and then managed to get the last one.

"Are you ok?"

"Yeah. I need-" Savannah panted. "I just need a breather."

The cheers were almost like mocking. Couldn't they see how she was hurting, didn't they care? Or did the rabid crowd thirst for blood because of our supposed guilt?

The voice boomed from the speakers. “Now his Gia pet is out of action. How about a real fight, without her silly powers to protect him."

I stood ahead of Savannah, who tried to stand up, but I held my hand back. "Sit this one out. Rest up, I'm sure I'm gonna need you even more for the next one."

The voice cried out over the roar of the crow, "So, you might be thinking these two were alone in their crime, but in fact, they had a collaborator. The very employee paid to guard that building. Can you imagine such betrayal?"

The boo's were grating on my patience.

"Now fight to the death, but let it not be said he is an unfair king. The winner will receive their freedom. And of course, if that wasn't enough, the reward of ten thousand coins!" Cheers again, louder this time.

I groaned. "Will they hurry up?"

But Savannah was still resting on one knee, catching her breath.

The ahead door opened, and a silhouette appeared.

Maple stepped out into the light wearing her tight work attire, which wildly contrasted the ax on her back. She walked towards me, so I headed forward to meet her.

"Stay there, rest," I called back to Savannah, who grimaced but nodded.

While Maple and I trekked towards each other, it took several minutes until we stood a few yards apart.

I had fought ork's before, but never one with the smarts of a human. I couldn't read her expression, except that of determination. Just like those I had seen on an ork trying to kill me. Would she be mommy's little warrior and prove herself? I gripped my gun tight, not knowing when she would launch her attack.

She dropped her ax at her feet. It landed with a hard thud.

"Did you really think I would fight you?" she said.

"I had an inkling you wouldn't," I lied.

Boos were all around us, the crowd having seen our dropping of weapons for what it was.

I dropped my gun, flared my arms out, and shouted, "We

will not fight each other." more boos. I called again, "You'll have to find some other way." But there was no way for them to hear me.

"It appears the accused has something he wishes to tell the crowd. What do you think, should we hear him out?"

They all booed.

“Now, if he were an unjust king, he wouldn't let the guilty plead their case. Bring the cowboy a microphone."

I turned to Maple. "Do you trust me?"

She squinted. "About as far as I can throw you.”

"That's pretty far," I remarked. "But I'll be the one throwing you around."

She grunted, biting her lip as she made a fist, and nodded.

A man walked out at a brisk pace, identical to the many guys we had seen in the halls prior. He pushed his spectacles up his nose as he hurried towards us, a long cable trailing behind him.

I crossed my arms, tapping my foot as I said to Maple, "Quirky guy, your king."

"It's annoying," she said.

Finally, the man got to us, turned a switch on the microphone, and held it out but didn't give it to me. I snatched it from him, which caused a tut, and spoke.

"Hel- " It fed back a piercing whine in the speakers, so I pulled it back from my mouth. "Hello."

"Hello, Harlen Gray, of Earth-2," the man up top responded.

Beside him, the Forest Pit King watched with grimaced interest. Was he in pain? Or did he despise us that much?

"Yeah, nice trick,” I said sarcastically. “But I represent the planet of Caria. Ring any bells?"

"I believe I've heard of it. Yes," the king's man said, nonplussed.

I looked up at the crowd in that giant coliseum and all those people staring down at us. I wasn't dizzy anymore, but more determined than I had ever been.

This isn't just for me, I had others to fight for.

"We won't fight each other," I spat.

"Then you'll fight and likely die together."

"Yeah, about that—see, we don't actually want the prize money."

Gasps erupted from the seats.

"Pray do tell, what is it you want?"

"An audience with The Forest Pit King."

That got laughs.

The Forest Pit King raised his finger, and the crowd went silent. He leaned forward, and it seemed like it took an eternity to get his mammoth head next to the much smaller man. He whispered something into his ear.

Then the speaker said, "The king... accepts." More gasps burst from the crowds. "But, you will fight the most fearsome beast we possess. No one has fought it and lived to tell the tale. Armies have trembled before it. If you can beat it, you may have an audience with the king."

I passed the mic to the man beside me, who *'ahhem'ed'* and trotted off, wrapping up the wire around his hand as he briskly returned.

"You're gonna need this." I bent down to pick up Maple's ax and threw it to her. She caught it in one hand.

I picked up my gun, and we walked back to Savannah, who seemed to be having a brisk word with herself. We grabbed her arms and helped her up.

"Rested enough?" I asked.

She stretched her hands out, then her neck. "Just about."

"After this, we're gonna go to the bar and get drunk. Deal?"

"Deal," they both said.

"Ladies and gentlemen, for the first time in eons, woken from her eternal slumber. Taken from the great planet of Orkulus. I present to you—the Klargite Queen."

I gulped. My heart fell into my gut. *Queen? How big would it be?* The pit was big enough for an impossible creature, but I had learned by now that no creature was impossible. It would need to at least be able to fit through that door. That was still very big.

I gripped my gun but the sweat on my hand made it slip.

"How'd that end up here?" I spoke rapidly. My hand went clammy.

Maple explained, "She cannot be *the* Klargite Queen, but simply a queen."

"Oh," I said, a little more positively.

"She will still be very big."

"Oh." I deflated.

"Have you battled one before?"

"Kind of," I said, gripping my pistol tighter.

"How can you *kind of* battle a Klargite?"

I tried to make my voice deeper. "Well, it was a nightmare. I'm not the biggest fan of spiders."

I stretched my neck back and forth in preparation for the upcoming fight. I closed my eyes, took a deep breath, and brought myself to calm. When I opened them, a sea of tiny little spiders were surging out of the doorway. They ran up the walls, escaping where they could. They were followed by bigger ones. Regular sized Klargites. Maple grunted, stepped forward, spinning her ax a few times, and brought it crashing down on one, splattering blood everywhere.

Savannah and I looked at each other, eyebrows raised, while Maple held her ax up high and roared fury.

"She's meant for this," I said.

Savannah nodded. "We're lucky to have her."

My turn next, I ran forward, closed one eye, and shot the leathery spider beast in the face, causing it to splatter.

"Your turn, make it flashy," I said to Savannah.

She nodded, her lips went tight, eyes glaring. She ran forward, hands raised to lift a spider high in the air, and slammed her hands together. It went out in a firework of blood.

"Fuck me," I exclaimed with genuine surprise. "I didn't expect that!" I looked at my girl with pride, then when I turned back, my jaw swiftly dropped.

The crowd hushed to a quiet fright.

Two black hairy legs as thick as my body thrust out from either side of the doors.

More came out, and then they pulled the body out with it.

Of the beast's dozen eyes, the outer ones' eyelids flared back, due to its leathery skin getting stuck as it struggled to pull its body through the tight enclosure. It hissed in anger, causing a great green mist to surround us, but Savannah caught it, whipped it up into a tight, compact ball, and fired it back at it.

It landed on one of the creature's eyes, but it merely blinked it off.

"Are you not tired?" I asked her.

"I'm getting better at it," she said, grinning. "It must be like a muscle."

"Now is a good time to flex it," Maple said, flipping her ax as she ran forward with a battlecry.

I joined her. Savannah followed behind as we ran towards our inevitable death.

The beast slammed a razor-sharp pointed leg down on Maple. She dodged out of the way and swung her great ax, chopping an insignificant portion of it off, causing the beast to hiss and roar, releasing more spit from its venom sacks.

Again, Savannah caught it all, whipping it up like a spell and firing it back at the beast. But sadly, its venom had no effect on it. It shrugged it off as nothing more than an annoying fly.

It reared its body up high.

"It's going to charge at us." Maple yelled, running back beside us.

I aimed my pistol at its belly, "I've got a charge of my own." I held the trigger, and the gun shook. My hand trembled as the light grew so bright, the sights of my weapon became overcome with it. It was all I could see.

I fired, and the beast flung backward into the wall. My vision quickly turned to light as the aftershocks of the blast seared into my sights.

I blinked it off, and in those blinks, the Klargite Queen recovered, stamping on the ground and flashing it's great pincer teeth at us.

It charged. A stampede of rumbling drums drowned out the cheers of the blood thirsty crowd.

I would have been forgiven for my legs freezing. I would not have been blamed for cowering. Of all the things I had seen in my life, a whale sized spider with the fury of a raging bear, spit dribbled from its pincer teeth was high on the list of terrors.

It wasn't the highest.

"Well, no use standing like sitting ducks," I remarked as I began running forward.

The girls joined me, running in my wake.

"Savannah, can you lift it up?" I yelled.

"Got it."

The Klargite lifted into the air, but she couldn't stop it dead due to its incredible speed and strength. It flew towards us as if it had jumped, its legs spindled everywhere.

"Maple, act after me."

I ran ahead and dived underneath it, skidding on the dirt as I held down my trigger. My gun grew hot, shaking as the blast charged up. I doubted it would work much after this one, so I had to make it count.

If only I had my second gun.

I went directly underneath it, seemingly in slow motion. Its belly was faintly striped, its leather skin covered in tiny hairs. I blasted the photon up into her belly, exactly where it had hit before. The leather carapace split some more, burning where the wound should have been. I prayed it was now fragile.

My skid led me outside of the Klarkgite's orbit.

“Maple, you know what to do," I called.

"Right." She ran underneath the beast, aiming her ax and throwing. It swung with terrifying velocity, the waves of air morphing around it and making a zooming sound. It perforated the wounded skin with ease. The ax tore through the flesh and embedded in it, the handle sticking out below.

"Drop it!" I yelled to Savannah.

She didn't need to be told twice. The Klargite came crashing down, the handle pressing directly down on the ground and piercing the creature.

I ran around it to grab Savannah and pull her away from its trajectory.

The beast's arms flailed around, it lifted itself up, remaining legs shaking. Only we could only see the ax had embedded entirely inside it as blood dripped out below. The crowd gasped in their wonder of what would happen next. They didn't know what we did.

We had won.

The spider crashed, covering us in dust, letting out a whimpering screech, before whimpering out to a void.

The crowd cheered, and I knew *this* was more important than even killing the beast, so I grabbed both the girl's hands. "Cmon, let's get on top of it."

I climbed, and Maple helped Savannah get up as she was weak from her exertion.

We stood atop the beast, in the center of the ring, soaking in our thunderous applause, our arms raised. Goosebumps peppered up my arms, a shivering excitement.

The dust began to settle.

"Is that all ya got?" I yelled. They couldn't hear me, but I didn't care. It was for me, not them.

"Ahem," the man spoke into the speaker, but the crowd cheered louder. "Ahem!" It seemed to make them yell louder.

Maple's eyes were bright, astonishment written across her face. Savannah just looked shocked. She was panting and catching her breath.

I was somewhere in the middle.

Finally, the voice said, "The Forest Pit King wishes to speak."

In an instant, the cheering ceased.

23

Way above us, the announcer held the mic out for the king. It looked like a toothpick for him to snap.

His voice rumbled a deep, groaning sound, "Good."

Savannah held her hands out in exasperation, still panting. "Good? Is that all?"

"Good? What does that mean?" Maple asked.

"It means we won. C'mon, help her get off this." I climbed off the Klargite Queen and then held my arms out for Savannah to climb down onto, as Maple helped her get down.

"Shall we go then?" I asked.

"I'm gonna need that ax back," Maple complained.

"We'll get it back later.” I stretched, realizing how sore my muscles were going to be. “Now I don't know about you guys, but I could use a beer."

"Fuck, yes," Savannah said, laughing as she blinked rapidly. "A beer and a shower."

A trumpet fanfare blared through the speakers.

"Ladies and gentlemen, you saw them fight for your amusement. You saw them win in the most spectacular fashion this planet has seen since the Beast of Beatrix! Please, put your hands together for Maple, Savannah, and Harlen!"

The cheers meant nothing to me compared to stage left. A great door opened up. It had been invisible against the stone wall. It groaned as it shook up, revealing a dark entrance for us to enter. Silently, we made our way towards it. Tired, dirty, but alive—and victorious.

"You guys do this sort of thing a lot?" Maple asked.

"Only on weekends," I quipped.

"We also have a lot of sex," Savannah said.

I glanced at her, eyes wide. But her stare was blank.

"I see." Maple's cheeks went cherry.

I *still* needed to teach Savannah good social skills—or perhaps, I didn't. That might've opened a door that was only ajar before.

Through the doors, attendants with towels and cups of water handed them to us. I gulped down the precious fluid.

"So, what's next?" I asked the guy. "By the way, we're gonna need that ax back."

"Yes, The ax will be returned to you, but first, a shower. Then, the king wishes to speak with you."

Maple interjected, "Got any beer?"

He eyed her terrific height with alarm at first. Then he nodded. "Some will be brought to you. Now, if you will, please follow me."

We followed the man out of the tunnel to a private-looking car park, where an unassuming black car waited for us.

Once inside, we said nothing. all of us closed our eyes. I contemplated the last few hours, and I could only assume the girls were doing the same.

The car drove out onto the main highway towards the palace.

The highways widened, buildings thinned out around us until we were on a dirt road, ducking and weaving between the trees because of their great thickness and height.

The car finally drove through an enclave of large trees.

Space opened up to a great metal castle. Covered by the neon tree leaves above, it seemed like it had grown just as naturally as the trees had, and had not been built by hand—and yet, it was definitely like a castle, just like those I had seen in books.

From the outside, the castle seemed to have many points and rooms. It was perfectly symmetrical in shape, and while castles were usually big, this was even more so, I assumed to accommodate the Forest Pit King's large size.

"Finally, a house where I don't have to kneel down to get through the doorway." Maple said, clearly thinking similar.

"I wouldn't get too comfortable. You're crazy if you think I'm gonna leave you here."

She said nothing, so I leaned back, my arms around the chairs backs where the girls sat. Savannah leaned her head on my shoulder, sighing, while Maple got a little closer but was still unsure.

We were gonna have to spell it out for her.

The castle door fell down around a beautiful mote, and the car drove inside, parking just outside the main gates. Before we could react, two footmen approached either side of the car and opened the doors. We got out.

"So what happens now?" I asked the footman.

"The king will see you tomorrow. Until then, he invites you to enjoy the finer aspects of his castle—the baths, the foods. The exquisite beds."

"Sounds like my kinda guy," I whispered to the girls as

the footman led us up the carpeted runway. "Why do we hate him again?"

"Maybe it was something to do with making us fight for our lives, for the amusement of others?" Savannah remarked.

"Good point. It was fun, though."

She shook her head at me. While Maple said, “It was fun. Savannah is right though, what if this is a mistake?"

"Listen, girls." I turned around and put both my hands on their arms, looking up at the tall ork, then across to Savannah. "You really think he would invite us all the way into his private palace, and wine and dine us, just to kill us? Seems like a whole lot of effort."

"No," Maple said.

"Trust me," I implored them. "This is all part of my plan."

"I trust you," Savannah said quickly.

"I do too," Maple said more slowly.

We took measures of each other then, reading it on our faces as if the words had not been enough, and we all had to make sure we meant them.

"C'mon.” I turned around and put my arms out for them to take. "That bath has our names on it."

The footman had been waiting patiently. He made no comment as he turned back around to lead us into the great castle.

Inside the foyer, it made us look like ants. Everything was bigger. Giant mirrors adorning the walls, and chandeliers on the ceiling held up by rigid thick metal chains.

"This way to the guest's chamber, please," the attendant said.

Inside, there was a veritable feast. Across tables were plates of meat, breads. And of course a variety of colorful fruits that I thought must have grown on Pradorix. There seemed to be a section for foreign foods, the likes of which I wondered if were even edible, as well as, of course, *Klargon.*

"See what I mean?" I grabbed a chicken drumstick and took a bite—chicken had never tasted so good, at least, I hoped it was chicken. I gulped it down and neglected to question it.

"What do you think this all means?" I said through a bite of delicious meat.

"What?" Savannah inched towards the beers and grabbed a bottle, twisting off the cap. She handed one to me, then Maple.

"You'll see." I grabbed another handful of beers and said to the attendant, "Good sir, might you tell us where the baths are?"

“This way, please."

The girls grabbed a few more beers and vodka and followed as we headed into a giant steam bath, where two attendants stood. This looked like the main room, where it split off into men's and women's sections.

"If you'll excuse us, I think we could use some privacy."

"Very good, sir. We will be outside in the foyer if you need us."

They bowed, and I nodded my head, grinning.

"Oh, if it pleases you, we will collect your clothing if you leave it outside here. It will be returned to you tomorrow morning, cleaned and dried."

"Sounds good to me." I nodded at him, and he left.

"See," I said.

"I'm not getting it. Why would he do all this?" the ork asked.

"It's because," Savannah hesitated to choose her words, "he wants to be on our good side."

"And why would he want that?"

Savannah's lips moved to the right of her face. "Well, it seemed we needed something from him. But really, he must need something from us."

I put the beers down on the ground, pointed my finger at her. "Exactly." Then I tore my shirt off.

"What could it be?" Maple asked.

"Something that he needs to butter us up for first."

"Or something we would want to refuse," Savannah said.

"What could be worse than a klargite queen?"

"*Two*?" Maple suggested.

Savannah pulled her top off, revealing the plain white bra underneath, which cupped her breasts perfectly. Yet, their shape remained precisely as they were if she wasn't wearing it. I assume from never wearing a bra in her life, her perfect breasts never had any support, so they retained their innocent buoyancy. This bra was more about showing them off than supporting them. She slipped off her skirt next, standing in her white thong that rode high on her hips.

I watched, taking another swig of beer, throbbing as I pulled my pants off.

"What is that?" Maple asked as she slowly unbuttoned her shirt.

I was about to say it was my hard-on, but then I looked down and saw the pendant.

"Oh, it's just a pendant. Family heirloom."

"It's beautiful. Can I see it?"

I walked over to her, and she took it in her hands. At the same time, I was continuously distracted by Savannah's body, as she took swigs of the beer, condensation dripping down her fingers from the bottle. She tipped her head back and closed her eyes when she drank it. Hypnosting me as I imagined I was the beer.

"Savannah?"

"Yes?" she asked hopefully. Hopping over to me, her bare feet made soft patter sounds against the floor, her breasts jiggling as she went.

While Maple observed my pendant, I leaned in close to Savannah's ear, whispering, although I'm sure Maple could hear us. "Darlin', why don't you have your bath in the women's section?"

"But I would like to watch," Savannah whispered back hastily.

I raised my eyebrows at her. "Did you just disobey me?"

Savannah smirked, and I grabbed her and kissed her while her finger tickled up against the underside of me.

"Next time?" she said, louder than before. I nodded, and she kissed me again, giving me a final stroke while I slapped her butt.

Then she hopped off.

I admired the way that white thong rode up her cheeks. But I would wait to peel it off and taste what it covered.

Savannah was already tamed, and right then, I had to wrangle a more fearsome, yet just as beautiful, beast.

24

I turned to the ork, taking her hand. Maple towered over me. If I wanted to, I could kiss her breasts without having to bend over.

When we looked at each other, her bright red eyes immediately darted down.

"You seem much more nervous than the beautiful woman I met in that bar," I remarked.

She shrugged and said, “Just ‘cause I’m nervous doesn’t mean I don’t want it. “ Her cheeks went rosy through the green.

I began undoing the buttons of her shirt and said, "I’m amazed this didn't get ripped up in the fight." I kept my hands steady to appear calm. *Was I nervous too?* I was glad that Savannah wasn't there. This was far too intimate of a moment between the Ork and I.

"They're made to be stretchy, so you can move in them—not that we ever saw much action on guard duty."

I undid another button, her cleavage appearing underneath the fabric. She closed her eyes, gasping in the relief of my taking control.

"I should warn you," she said. "I am part ork."

"I know what that means. I met an ork in a bar once. He told me that ork and human DNA rarely mix. You have to time it just right, and even *then*, it's difficult."

"That's not what I wanted to warn you about."

Her shirt was close to coming undone. I gave up and pulled it up her shoulders. She had to help me because she was so much taller, and I gasped at her bra. A bright red, exactly the same color as her hair. I dove my face into her cleavage, kissing her flesh while I held the small of her back. I didn't care that she was sweaty—I reveled in it.

She grabbed my head and pressed it down further into her pillow-like bosom.

Then, I got down on my knees in front of the powerful half-ork, undoing her pants and yanking them down. Her thick green thighs greeted me. I stroked up them, spread her legs slightly, kissed the inside of her thigh, and then the front of her blood-red panties—just teasing her, kissing at the material.

Maple stepped out of her pants, and I stood up.

She sighed. Her lips between those tusks were drawn in a blissful half-smile.

"C'mon." I took her hand and led her into the men's baths.

The bathroom was decorated in calming dim hues of orange and blue by lights and candles placed in aesthetic places all over the steps and shelves. Hand in hand, we stepped into the bath and sat down on the edge, so only our legs soaked in the warm water.

I crawled between her legs and said casually, "I like the coordination of your lingerie and hair. Almost like you thought this was gonna happen."

"A girl can dream."

I got down in the water and yanked her panties down, gasping at the sight of her hairless folds, I stroked around them. Inside her lips was a magnificent red color—the same as her hair and panties. She leaned back in the bath as my tongue slid against her folds, tasting her juices. She was so sweet, like nectar. I couldn't stop as she groaned and moaned.

But I did stop to say, "You're my girl now, aren't you?" Then I returned to licking.

"If you want me to be. Oh, mmm. That's nice, like that."

My tongue darted back and forth against her gem. So much sweat built up, I tasted through the salty sweat to her new release of wetness. My fingers slid through those bright red inner swollen caves.

Then she cried, "Oh god. No way, I can't believe it."

She lifted her legs high, and I pushed back on her thighs and devoured her, lapping rapidly. She screeched and roared until finally, wetness sprung forth like a fountain all over my face. Excitement and endorphins flooded me at the thrill of it. I sat up, wiping my mouth.

Still on her back, she started joyously laughing and said, "I can't believe you did that so quickly."

"I can't believe you've still got that bra on."

Maple grinned at me and sat up, undoing her bra and letting her breasts come free. As she sat up, her nipples were a perfect red color, her breasts so big, swinging hypnotically with each of her movements. I devoured her nipple, sucking on its softness that quickly became hard. At the same time, she pulled my wet boxers down. Her hand grasped me, and she began stroking.

I groaned at the pleasure she pulled from me.

Is she going to make me come just from her hand?

I bit her nipple. She roared and stroked me faster,

squeezing me just enough, then I fell forward. I pushed her down, or rather, she let me.

In a brief moment, I pushed deep inside her, sliding through her soaked folds as we became rabid beasts on the edge of the pool. I couldn't contain myself. I kept thrusting and thrusting. All composure was gone. Reaching up to kiss her, her tusks pressed against the edge of my mouth like we kissed between two prison bars. Then I kissed down her body and bit hard on her nipple.

She growled and roared, "Yes, bite it, harder," she moaned.

I bit as hard as I could while ramming her so fast I thought I was about to release, and then she pushed me off her, I fell on my back, and she climbed over me—reverse cowgirl. Her giant, thick cheeks thrust down on me as she slammed onto it, ramming herself up and down with such force they bounced.

"You feel so good," she cried.

My legs rested in the pool while I lay backward, seeing stars. Looking down, all I could see was Maple's thick ork ass slamming on my hips. Each bounce hurt but gave so much pleasure to me I could do nothing but accept it.

But, I was *not* going to be dominated. There was only one woman who I'd let do that to me, and she wasn't on this planet.

So I got up, and with all my strength, I pushed her into the pool. We splashed into the water, falling under the water's surface as she turned around and wrapped her legs around me. I sunk into her as she stroked my hips and began ramming into each other under the water. With no edge to support us, we had to float in the water with our heads above it, kissing and our tongues slapping all over each other.

"C'mon," I gasped, trying to hold my own against the powerful ork. "Let's get to the edge."

"Ok," she said, panting. It was like she couldn't even help it. It was in her nature.

Was this her going easy on me?

Her back slammed against the edge, she cried out and arched her neck back, and now I had her pinned. I slammed into her again and again, the water splashing everywhere while she screamed and roared with pleasure.

Was she *coming*? I was about to.

"Turn around," I told her, slipping out of her.

Maple obeyed. Did that mean I had won? She leaned over the edge of the pool so her butt was outward to me.

I paused upon seeing that fat green ass outside the pool. Maple's bright red slit begged to be entered. I squeezed her cheeks, spread her ass, and saw her other hole. My thumbs rested on it, my hands pulling her apart a little to see that gorgeous red color inside her slit.

"You're mine, aren't you?" I demanded.

"I'm yours," she panted in defeat.

Is this how all ork's made love? It was like a battle, and somebody had to come up the victor.

There she was, baring her ass to me in her defeat.

I gripped myself, rock hard and ready to release. I slid inside her.

"Now I'm gonna show you what making love is."

"I know what making love is. I mean, I haven't done it in so long."

She pushed her ass out further, begging me with her body.

"Not the way you deserve," I said.

This would take all my restraint, but I slid my head inside her and then slowly entered. *Slowly.* Her walls strangled me, she squeezed her muscle around me, but I slid through her, in and out. She gasped and shook, drool spilling from her lip.

"What are you doing?" she asked.

I gently caressed her cheeks, grabbed her hips, and stuffed her, getting all the way to the tip, giving one push, and then pulling back out until only the tip was inside. Each movement was deliberate.

"Giving you the slow fuck you deserve." I said. "So I can admire your beautiful body, bent over for me."

"It's yours," she cried. I pumped a bit faster. With every thrust, she clenched around me.

I needed more of her. I sucked on my thumb for a moment, getting it wet with spit, and pressed it against her asshole. She gasped, her whole body froze, and she started trembling.

"Oh, you like that, do you?"

"I don't know." She shook. I pushed further into her, making it twitch inside her. "I don't know, but I want to try."

"You'll try anything for me, won't you."

"Anything."

Maple shook, and I pressed my thumb against her asshole. She was completely submissive to me now. She was mine in every which way, and it was time to push further boundaries.

"Even share *me*?"

"How could I not? Someone as amazing as you can't have just one woman, can he?" She arched her neck to look at me. Those red pupils went wide as she gasped.

I pushed my thumb into her ass,and she screamed while I began ramming into her with my hips.

I grit my teeth. "Playtime's over."

I lifted one leg over the pool, thrusting down into her.

With each thrust my hips pushed my hand down, making my thumb go into her ass, where I wiggled it around, hooking her.

Gripping Maple's fat cheeks with the rest of my hand, I slammed in and out of her. She screamed and moaned in her pleasure, clearly coming again, *for the third time?*

It was time for me too. I pulled my thumb out, grabbed Maple's forearms, and with all my strength, pulled her back, so she was standing against the edge of the pool. I wrapped my arms around her mid, reaching up for her neck and grabbing it, then began rapidly ramming her whimpering body. The seven-foot woman stood there powerless to my member, taking it all with all the pleasure I could give her.

I went at that rapid pace that could only mean there would be no turning back. My vision swelled with a haze of euphoria. I gripped Maple's breast, digging my fingers into her flesh, and then I went blind.

I twitched inside her, filling her with everything I could give. As my balls tightened, I yelled out involuntarily, falling as she slammed into the ground. I laid on top of her back, the incredible muscular ork like a mountain I was claiming. I twitched as I released inside her.

And then we were done.

I pulled out of her and saw myself twitching.

"Stay there." I told her as she lay whimpering, her hips trembling.

"Fuck." She groaned. "It feels so good. I can still feel it. What have you done to me?"

I ignored her whimpering words as I stretched her cheeks apart and saw the perfect white pearl in her redness.

"How was that?" I asked her, slapping her ass and then sitting beside her.

She crawled to lay her head onto my lap, her tusk

stroking against me as she nuzzled into my lap. I stroked her hair.

"Well, it's a good thing I had to quit my job," she finally said.

"I think you got fired, Darlin'."

She looked up at me, her eyes glassy with that pet name that I had only ever called Savannah. I stroked her hair, looking down at my seven-foot ork goddess proudly.

"Next time," she said, kissing me. "Don't go so easy on me."

I wanted to laugh. Instead, I said, "Shall we go and get Savannah now?"

I went to get up, but she opened the door instantly.

"You were listening?" I raised my eyebrows at her.

She looked down a little shyly. I realized now she was completely naked.

"I'm sorry, I couldn't resist."

I shook my head at her, tutting. "We'll have to find a suitable punishment for you, Darlin."

She smiled as she hopped over, barefeet patting against the wet floor, and climbed into the pool on the other side of me, resting her head on my legs.

"My girls," I said, stroking their heads. Making sure to give each of them equal strokes, they both had broad smiles on their faces, but while Maple lay spent, Savannah kept rubbing her legs together, trying to generate heat or something.

"So you didn't touch yourself?" I asked.

Maple lay silently during our conversation, content in her comfort.

"I..." Savannah said with hushed breath.

"Go on. We're listening."

"You didn't give me permission, so I didn't think it was right."

"Good girl," I said, stroking her hair, causing her to beam warmth.

"So I can now?"

I sat up, causing the girls to raise their heads in alarm, as they were both on my lap. "Nope, I think we should go to bed, don't you, Darlin'?"

She nodded, disappointed but obedient.

"Good girl."

Maple stood up, stretching, then realizing she was completely naked, went to cover herself up.

"We're not strangers now," I said.

She smiled. "Oh, yeah."

Some bathrobes were hanging on the wall. I noticed a larger one for Maple, a regular one for me, and a smaller one for Savannah.

I went over to the wash basket and held it out. "Ladies, dirty washing in here."

When Savannah grabbed her dirty washing and put it in the basket, I noticed her nipples were pebble hard. She saw my turned on expression and reached down to stroke herself, pouting at me, as if the physical act of it would convince me to let her.

I grabbed her wrist. "Did I say you could do that?"

"Please," she moaned. "I need it."

"I told you, you would need a punishment."

She pouted but nodded. "Fine." Then she slipped on the bathrobe while Maple did the same.

We stepped out into the outer hall in our luxurious robes. I left the washing basket there. Then we grabbed some plates of food and beers and met the attendants outside. I asked them if they could get our washing, and they nodded, immediately jumping to attend to us.

The remaining man said, "If you'd like to follow me to the guest bedrooms."

"I think one bedroom will suffice," I said, smiling at my girls.

They followed dutifully behind me. Maple carried a few plates of food. Savannah had as many beers as she could while I gnawed on a drumstick in one hand and drank beer in the other.

* * *

There was A four-poster bed just big enough to fit all of us, draped red velvet curtains and soft velvet pillowcases. A beautiful patterned rug on the floor felt springy against my feet.

After brushing my hands off and washing them in the sink in the room, we sat on the edge of the bed in our robes, drinking and laughing and recalling how we had defeated the great beast. We marveled at our unique abilities and how well we used them together.

I grinned with pride and said, "I gotta say, girls. I couldn't have done it without you. I'm a lucky guy."

Savannah looked at Maple like an understanding came upon them, then she gulped and said, "We're lucky to have you."

"She's right," Maple admitted. Before you, my life was... not great." She looked down at her lap but glanced at me repeatedly. "I mean, my parents were great, just the other stuff."

I wanted to tell her that it was ok. Just because one part

of her life wasn't bad, didn't mean it the rest of it couldn't be. Mine hadn't lacked in the places hers had.

But before I could say that, Savannah said. "Mine neither." Savannah said. "I feel like I'm finally a person now —like I have my own thoughts and feelings and... desires. I was just a shell before."

I leaned back on my elbows, admiring my girls.

Maple sat tall and proud as she said, "And I don't have to be ashamed of who I am when I'm around you. I feel like what I am is good."

They looked at each other again, smiling. I got up from the bed, smiling at them, and said, "Up."

They stood. I took off my robe, pulled the bedsheets back, and climbed in.

Their robes fell to the floor, revealing their beauty.

They climbed into the bed on either side of me, hugging me, their thighs raised on my body. They both kissed either side of my neck. Savannah kissed with her soft, pouty lips, while Maple's tusks were hard-pressed on either side of her wet kisses.

Dainty hands stroked over my member, bringing me hard, and giant ones squeezed at my balls. Their licks and kisses on my ears tickled the microscopic nerve endings, making me shudder in delight.

Then, Savannah's head went below the covers, and her lips wrapped around me. I was sore at first, too sensitive, but the pleasure overrode it, and I was brought to completion, releasing in her mouth.

She came back with her mouth firmly shut and an adorable grin on her face.

"You didn't swallow, did you?" I asked.

She shook her head, grinning naughtily, her silver hair messy all over.

I raised my eyebrows at Maple. "I think you know what to do."

She leaned over, and their lips met, giggling as they kissed. Then when Savannah's tongue came out and met hers, swapping the come she had taken in her mouth, they moaned in delight as it dribbled over their chins. I took Maple's hand and placed it on Savannah's breast.

Maple caressed and pinched it. It twitched in its defeat, but I was just content to watch as Savannah grew hotter as my release dripped down their chins.

I stroked both of their heads. "Good girls."

They giggled and kissed more intensely. Savannah reached for Maple's breast, but I slapped it away.

"I didn't say you could do that, did I?"

She moaned in submission, placing her hand on Maple's cheek instead as their kiss grew more passionate. Savannah was writhing all over, doing anything she could to generate friction between her legs.

"I think that's enough for now." I pulled them apart and laid them back down. Savannah pouted and laid on my arm, hitting a fist against my chest in frustration, but she knew she would do nothing but obey me.

"Oh, and don't even think about using your power, or there'll be even more significant repercussions."

Meanwhile, Maple rested comfortably on me. Even for her size, she still fit nicely under my arm when she laid down, and I was soon greeted by the gentle snoozing sounds of two beautiful women.

It didn't take me long to join them in slumber.

25

Dawn broke.

Warm green light filled the room. I sat up and yawned, admiring the two girls in my bed.

I kissed both of them on the forehead. Savannah smiled, keeping her eyes closed. At the same time, Maple opened them, visibly confused for a moment. Then she saw the mess she had lain in, and a massive smile across her face grew.

"Come back to bed," she moaned.

"Cuddle each other," I said as I got out.

I needed a shower, and thankfully, there was one in the next room.

"Ok, but just cuddling," Maple said as Savannah crawled into her arms, resting her head on her breasts. "I'm not really into girls."

I yawned, picking up a bread roll from yesterday and gnawing at it. "You seemed into them last night," I said.

"It's different if you're there—I mean, Savannah, you're so beautiful and sexy, don't get me wrong."

Savannah opened her eyes and looked up at the pretty

ork, then kissed her on the cheek. "It's ok, I get it. I'm kind of like that too."

"Savannah is a bit of a pervert," I explained. "She wants to share me with other women."

"Oh." Maple grinned. "That works for me. I like being with another woman, for you, Harlen. I don't know why. It seems wrong, so it's hot. I wouldn't want to do it when you're not there to see it, or you haven't allowed it. I like doing it because you tell me too." Then she opened her eyes and looked up at me, resting her hand on Savannah's silver hair, stroking it. "I'd do anything you tell me to."

I walked back over to the bed, kissing her forehead and then doing the same to Savannah, whose nose scrunched up.

Then I said, "Good—because you're my girl. I'll look after you forever."

I grabbed Maple's hand and placed it on Savannah's breast, she pinched it, and Savannah cooed, trembling. I could tell how badly she wanted it.

"Not until I say it's allowed, Darlin'."

I said to Maple, "Don't let her touch herself until I say so."

"Yes, sir." She grinned.

Then I left her there. I left them hugging each other tightly while I went to the shower and got myself clean. I hadn't brushed my teeth in a while, so the new toothbrushes there were a welcome sight.

Returning clean from the bathroom, I saw the two girls were sitting up in bed, helping themselves to some food. Three neat piles of clothing were on the table.

"They knocked, but we told them to leave it outside," Savannah explained. "We didn't think you'd want them seeing us naked."

I smiled. "You thought right. you two are mine." I strolled over to the clothes and began getting dressed while Maple slinked off the bed rather seductively and said, "My turn."

I sat down beside my beautiful, naked Savannah, who fell beside me, rubbing her body against mine. She was boiling hot, warmth emanating from between her legs like a blazing fire. She hugged me tight. I stroked her back, grabbing her ass, which caused her to tremble.

"I know it's hard, just a little longer," I said.

She groaned but nodded at my domination of her.

"What do you think he'll say to us today?" I asked to distract her from her neediness.

"Hmm," She tapped her chin in thought but didn't respond.

So I said, "Maybe he's going to murder us brutally for making a fool of him in the arena."

She gasped, but I grinned at her, causing her to scrunch her nose up at me. "That isn't funny."

I shrugged. "It's like I said, why would he do all this for us if he didn't want to get on our good side?"

She stroked her finger around my thigh. "And if he didn't want to get on our good side—well, we've dealt with worse."

"You think the three of us could take down The Forest Pit King inside his own castle?"

She grinned at me. "Easily."

We fell back against the bed. "I think so too."

After a while, Maple strolled naked from the bathroom, going to her pile of work clothes, frowning at them. "I never got to pick out new clothing," she complained.

"We'll get you something nice at the store," I remarked, tapping Savannah. "Cmon lazy butt, it's your turn."

She sighed. "But I was *so* relaxed." Then a mischievous smirk broke on her face.

I wagged my finger at her. "Don't even think about it. I'll know if you did."

She pouted, huffed, and said, "Fine." Then she hopped off to the bathroom, leaving Maple and me alone.

Maple slipped into her tight work attire, then her boots. She glanced at me before looking down, smiling.

"It's your turn. Come here."

"Oh, ok." She came over and laid beside me on the bed and put her head on my lap.

It was strange seeing the giant women so small and timid against my body, but I had tamed her. She was mine. I stroked her hair and back, reaching down to that gorgeous round ass and squeezing. I said, "I don't know what's going to happen next, but wherever we go, violence and battles seem to follow us."

She made a fist. "I'll murder anyone that tries to hurt you. My ax is yours."

"And what else of yours is mine?"

She hesitated a second. "My body, and..." She went bright red.

"Go on."

"I'm embarrassed to say, but my heart is too. It's all yours."

I squeezed her ass. "Good girl."

Once we were all ready, we followed the attendants to the main foyer, climbing the grand staircase.

"The King has just finished his morning appointments and is ready to see you," one informed us.

I said nothing as the girls walked on either side of me.

Up the staircase, we entered another big booming hallway adorned with carpets of intricate patterns. I assumed they were from languages I wasn't familiar with.

Finally, we reached a grand doorway with two guards on either side. The doors were three times the size of Maple in height, the wood looked aged like it had been built millennia ago, and yet, I was sure only a battering ram could break through it.

"The King will address you now," one guard said, and the two of them pulled open the door. They did not look weak, but it still took them a lot of effort to get the doors open.

Through the doorway, I could see him, all the way at the end of a long church-like hallway, atop a throne befitting for only someone as tall as him. We stepped inside and found our footsteps echoing down the chamber. The walls had strange writing, similar to what I had seen on the carpets.

He watched us, tiny ants to his colossal size, and I thought I would perhaps have preferred to face another Klargite Queen than get into a fight with him.

His great body was covered with planks of Pradarix wood, twisted and formed around his body like armor, except it seemed a natural part of his skin, acting as clothes as well. It adorned everywhere except the areas of joints that needed to move.

The King leaned over to a table on his side and drank from a cup, water dripping down his metal chin. His arm movements were rigid, robot-like, due to the lack of movement afforded to him by his armor-flesh.

"So you're gonna do the talking, right?" Savannah whispered.

"It hasn't steered us wrong so far," I said back. "*Mostly.*"

I grinned at her, and she smiled, diffusing some of the

tension, but Maple's shaking while holding my arm remained.

When we finally stood before him, I wondered if he expected us to bow, but I neglected to. Regardless of his great structure, I was his equal, and he needed to see me as such.

"Howdy," I said.

A great rumbling groan that shook the floor formed the words, "you fought, impressively."

His voice seemed to come from everywhere at once due to the tremendous booming timbre of it.

"We did ok. So what did you want to see us for?"

I knew I had some balls on me to ask that, when we were the ones who had demanded to see him.

And yet he grumbled painfully, "to ask for help."

Savannah grabbed my arm.

I said, "Now, I wonder what three simple criminals like us could do to help the king of a planet."

He groaned again, breathing deep, slow crackling sounds, savoring the moment before each word because it clearly hurt him to talk.

"On this planet, you are not criminals."

I said nothing.

"We are powerful," he said, getting to the point, "but our power, means nothing, next to Earth-2."

His words were jumbled, painful, so he says only that which is necessary.

Savannah crossed her arms. "What makes you think we can do anything? We're just three people, and that's a whole planet. Look what we had to do to get your attention."

He paused, breathing in that gargled, crackling breath, and said, "We cannot, enter the temple. We do not, have the power, to do it." Then he leaned over to take another slow drink of water.

"It's me," Savannah said.

He groaned in agreement, taking great pains to nod. He said, "Never, has a Subject, of Gia left. You are no longer, a disciple, and yet, you still, wield their power. And *you*." He looked at me, and I saw the way his eyelids drooped, *just how old was he?* "A man who, can convince, a Subject, of Gia to leave. This is something, my power, as king, could never achieve."

I wanted to shrug and make a joke about how I fucked it out of her, but it didn't seem the appropriate time.

"Don't forget Maple."

He groaned again. The bags under his eyes, deep pockets of tiredness, seeming to have grown over centuries. "The three warriors, that beat our, most fearsome, beast. You will help us."

"But why?"

He leaned over to the table again, picked up something I couldn't see, and shakily threw it towards us. It landed at the edge of the platform.

Kane. A small baggie, but I'd recognize the stuff anywhere.

"Oh," was all I managed to say. "I should have probably seen that coming. It was them all along."

"What do the Gia disciples have to do with this?" Maple said.

"They were buying some when I got to the hideout," I explained. "The hideout that had The Hardest Wood on the name, by the way. A company formed and based here." I turned to the king. "Why should I not believe that you're behind it all and are leading us astray?"

He sighed again. "What did you find, in the base, on Pradorix?"

"Well... nothing."

"Nothing, a test site. Ordered the company's creation, seemed nothing out of the ordinary, ordered scientists—why? We cannot, find out. They are, too powerful. We do not, have the, gift your, woman possesses."

Savannah began to say, "But I'm just-" I held my hand up to her. Now wasn't the time for her modesty.

I stood taller and said, "We need gold if we're gonna do this, as much gold as you can give us."

"Gold is nothing, to what will happen, if the Gia, gains more power. They are, already beyond our power. But if they, can grow, then they will, be too much, for the combined might of the, galaxy."

He breathed in a long, deep breath. The cracks were louder than ever before. It sounded like something inside him snapped off.

"If they succeed, then, balance will be lost. All planets, will belong, to them, all planets forced to, follow the doctrine of Gia, whether they, have the gift or not."

Savannah's head was shaking back and forth in a visible panic. "But what can we do against my mom?" She crossed her arms and rubbed them for self-comfort.

I turned to face her and took both of her arms in my hands. "Listen. It all leads back there—the hideout, the drug, the knights, what else could it be leading to? We need to find out, not for *him*." I nodded at the king. "For us, for Caria, for Earth-2. For all the people on all the planets that deserve to live freely. We need to find out why they're using that drug and stop them. It might be hard. I don't know how we'll do it, but-" I let go of one of Savannah's arms and took

Maple's, so I was touching them both. "We'll do it together. I told you, remember? We're gonna save the galaxy."

Savannah choked. "I thought you were joking."

"Maybe I was, but I never thought I'd be here, with you two, in this place, having done all we have. What's a little more?"

Leaving the girls, I turned back around to the king, stepping up to his great platform. His eyes went wide, mouth opened with fright, but I merely held my hand out for him to shake as I said, "We accept."

He brought his around to grip mine with great effort, and I felt that for as great as his height was, he had no strength at all. That which he had done to himself, or had been done to him, whether biologically or augmentation, was his downfall.

And I realized he was not an arrogant king, dismissing his subjects, but a recluse for fear of what would happen if they touched him. He only allowed himself the simple pleasure of seeing burglars getting mauled by giant spiders.

Well, everyone needs a hobby.

"Thank, you," he said. "I do not, have long left. I cannot die, knowing the harmony will be disturbed. Please, my assistants will give you, all the gold you need. It is the one thing, I am not suffering for."

* * *

We left the palace.

Maple had been reunited with her ax.

In the limo, we sat silently, contemplative. Then, Savannah sat forward and announced, "What is the plan?"

Her skin was pale. She seemed over-animated, like she was overcompensating for her nervousness.

I grabbed her hand and said, "When I left, your mother told me that she would share with you all the knowledge that was kept from her as Deputy Master, all the ancient lore kept secret by the then Head Master."

"She did not," she said softly.

"That's what I thought. Well, it's there, so I guess that would be a start."

"In my mother's room," she said.

"And is there not one particular time when she is promised to not be in there?"

She nodded. "Ascension."

"So, we wait for ascension, sneak into her room, find out the biz, and then take it from there."

“Do they have a gladiator pit on Earth-2?" Maple asked. By her tone, I couldn't tell if she was hopeful, curious, or both.

"Nope, just a good old-fashioned prison to rot and die in."

"That's a disappointment." She frowned.

"I wouldn't worry too much. By the way our lucks gone, you'll have more than a few folk's heads to split open with that ax."

"If your good luck persists."

"Ha, yeah, *good* luck."

Savannah gripped my arm tighter, and I knew the error of my words. Those *folks* I mentioned were Gia's disciples. The closest thing she had to friends and family until she found us.

And then, of course, there was her mother.

26

We were back in Maple's family kitchen, standing with Glasha and Freddy. Maple was in her room getting changed.

"Of course!" Freddy, clapped his hands together. "I'm so proud of you—what you did in that arena, it was incredible!"

Glasha walked forward, put her gigantic hand on my shoulder, and squeezed it. "She could not have done it without her clan—her warrior friends. You are worthy of standing by my daughter's side."

"Hear, Hear!" Freddy cheered.

I looked at them both and said, "I'll make sure she's well looked after. You have my word."

Maples's voice rang from the hallway. "Ready to go?"

She appeared in the doorframe, wearing brown leather hotpants with draped leather tassels between her legs. She had on a bra of similar leather material that pushed her breasts together. And, of course, she held the ax on her shoulder.

I had never heard an ork squeal before, but her mother managed it, positively bouncing with glee. "Look at my warrior!"

Maple instantly went red. "Mom! Don't embarrass me!"

There was a warmth in me. Savannah and I smiled at each other, and I knew she was thinking the same thing I was. Maple shouldn't have been as embarrassed as she was to have parents that cared about her. But it was her *right* to be embarrassed. She was fortunate for it.

A hand on my shoulder, I looked down and saw Fraddy struggling to reach up to it on his tiptoes as he said with a contrasting authority, "You know, ork women are a handful. You sure you're up to having one in your team?"

I nodded at him. He didn't quite know how true his words were. Or maybe he did, and he was giving Maple away to me?

"I can handle it," I said.

He smiled, tears brimming in his eyes. "I know you can. I didn't need to ask." Then he held his hand out for me, and I shook it. "You're a good man, Harlen. She's lucky to have a friend like you—both of you."

I nodded, holding from saying thanks, as I felt myself getting choked up.

"Now." Freddy dusted his hands together. "How about one last drink before you hit the road. What are you all off to do again?"

Savannah slapped her hands together. "Beer!"

But Maple responded to his question, "Dad, I'm not sure you want to know."

He nodded. "No, I don't suppose I don't—alas, we will cheer for it all the same."

Glasha went to the fridge to pull out two beer bottles for us and two red, corked glass bottles.

"Mom, I am *not* drinking that."

"It's customary to have a drink of klargon with your

mother when leaving the nest. Besides, this isn't just any klargon. It's special."

"You don't mean-" Maple's jaw dropped.

"This is from the queen you killed. The King sent it over specially, as an apology for putting my daughter in danger." She stood up proudly. "Not that you were in any danger. You handled yourself marvelously, like the warrior I raised."

Maple looked visibly touched. "Well, ok then, just this once."

"Actually, can I get one of those too?" I asked.

Everyone looked at me with surprise.

"What, it's real klargon, right? That means humans can drink it."

"This isn't just real klargon. This is the special stuff. From a queen." Her mother gave me this look. It was like she was proud of me, like I was her own son.

"Me too," Savannah said. "I would also like to try some."

"Freddy?" Glasha asked.

"Why not!"

Glasha went back to the fridge and handed out the two bottles to us, I popped the cork, and my eyes rolled with the repugnant aroma. Something was swimming inside the viscous red liquid. I hoped, at worst, it was just a chunk of meat.

"To Harlen—on three, two, one."

Everyone said '*to Harlen*,' and how could I not take a big gulp of the stuff then?

It poured down my throat like vicious scraping cuts. The chunks went down with it, and I swallowed, my head went dizzy, and it came back up, but I grimaced and swallowed again.

I looked around.

Freddy looked exactly as I expected, as I assumed I did.

While Savannah, Glasha, and Maple were downing their bottles. It glugged down Savannah's throat, the red liquid dripping down her cheek until she finished it all and gave off an unladylike belch.

"What." She looked at me, blinking rapidly.

I didn't know whether to be turned on or disgusted.

"How was it?" I asked, astonished.

She whispered to me. "I've got the Gia power stopping it from hitting my tastebuds. I didn't want to be rude."

Glasha stood with her hands on her hips, staring at Savannah, visibly impressed.

The streets of Pradorix were bustling with tourists and locals. Life had gone on after our pit battle, and yet, I didn't feel an ounce of enviousness for their simpler, easier lives. That isn't to say I wouldn't have enjoyed being able to lavishly shop and drink and rest in a comfortable bed. I'd had my share of that in my travels alone, but I had something else—a calling, a purpose, and two contrasting yet gorgeous girls by my side to see it through with me. The unknown of it all was a scary thought, but it was my own thought, not given to me, but shot by my gun and carved by Maple's ax, and the debris pushed clear by Savannah's powers. Nothing could stop us.

We strolled down the pathways of Pradorix without a care in the world, even though we were attracting attention. I wasn't surprised. A guy walking with a seven-foot ork and a Gia subject dressed in regular clothes was bound to turn heads.

"It's gonna be a tight squeeze on that ship. We should probably get another bed," I mused.

"Are we not... sleeping together?" It was strange to get

such a timid question from a scantily clad seven-foot half ork twirling a battle-ax on her shoulder.

"Oh, we are, Darlin'. We just wouldn't fit on that bed."

We climbed the stairs to the dock, and then as soon as my head poked over the threshold of the platform, I ducked it down.

"Shit." I looked at my girls with warning drawn across my face.

"What is it?" Savannah frowned at me,

Maple already reached for her ax, but I held my hand to stop her, and said, "Take a look."

Together, we gingerly inched our heads over the threshold.

There were Gia Knights everywhere, with metal plating across all their shoulders I bet was made of nothing stronger than tin.

They were holding guard, primarily at our shuttle.

"Friends of yours?" I joked at Savannah.

“What are we going to do?" she replied worryingly.

I glanced at the hulking ship on the end of the dock. It was the one I had seen when we arrived, the one that looked pieced together haphazardly.

"Well, we *did* need a bigger ship."

"That thing? It's a hunk of junk!"

"It's home." I felt a faraway glint in my eye as I stared upon the thing with pride before I had even bought it.

In my periphery, Savannah and Maple looked at each other dubiously.

"Girls, trust me on this. Wait here."

Darting behind ship after ship, avoiding the gaze of the Gia Knights, I made my way to the dock assistant. He sat on a stool leaning on his elbow, looking more bored than I had ever seen a person.

"Howdy, I wanna buy that ship." I pointed.

He laughed.

I held my hands up to *ssh* him, not wanting to say exactly why we had to be quiet.

"That big unwieldy thing?" he yammered. "It doesn't even have an AI. Are you sure you want to buy it?"

"Did you have other plans for it?"

"Yeah, scrap."

"Alright, fair enough." I made a show of walking away.

"Wait!"

I inched behind the rotor of a ship as some Gia Knights looked over.

"Four hundred," he said.

I laughed. "That ain't worth three hundred."

"Three-seventy."

"Are you pulling my leg? You were gonna scrap it. I'm doing the favor of collecting it for you. Two-eighty."

"Two eighty? You said three hundred before!"

"I said it ain't *worth* three hundred." I leaned over the counter. "So, two eighty, final offer."

He paused for a moment.

Deciding I wasn't worth the trouble, he waved his hand. "Fine, whatever. You know you ain't even gonna be able to fly off anyway. Damn Gia guys got the place down on lock."

I handed him three platinum bars, he gave me twenty in coins, which jingled noisily as I strapped it to my belt. Then he chucked me the keys, and I caught it in one hand.

"Thanks for taking it to the scrap yard for me."

"Yeah, we'll see."

I snuck back over to the stairs of the platform, and said, "Ladies, your carriage awaits."

Under the ship, I pressed the keys button. The walkway

dislodged with a clink, dust coming out of the edges, but it wouldn't pull down.

"Savannah, might ye do the honors?"

She pulled at it with her mind, it crashed down, and we jumped behind the ramp.

"Get on, get on." I hurried my girls onto it.

We climbed inside the ship, then I found the controls, pressing the button to bring up the walkway while finding the light switch. The ship glowed in a golden hue, and we saw every inch of its walkways—grated metal. This was nothing more than a transporting ship. It wouldn't do in a fight.

Yet.

Attachments could be brought, as was obvious already by looking at it from the outside.

"It's ain't much," I said.

"It's not much," Savannah agreed.

"But it will be." I stroked the handrail in the deck hallway, then wiped the dust off my hand. "Cmon, let's get to the cockpit."

Our feet noisily crashed against the rusted brown walkways.

Finally, at the starboard, I sat down at the controls.

"I'm guessing none of you know how to fly?" I asked.

"I always used the AI?'" Savannah said.

Maple shook her head.

I pulled out the wheel, which came out with a satisfactory *clunk*, then found the rotors and buttons. They were handily named, white labels over the top of the buttons and switches, hastily marked *after* being installed.

I turned the engine on, the ship roared into life, lights glowed in a multitude of colors, and the ship's screen turned on. The radar was an archaic thing, glowing lights across the screen, indicating the vessel and people in our presence. At the same time, the radar parameters were sketched on in with what looked like a marker pen.

"Well, I guess take off is *'take off.'*" I mused.

I pushed the button, and the ship shook, lifting us.

"It's just like a horse. You gotta tease and coax it into going."

"What?" Savannah looked at me perplexed.

"Nothing. Everyone strapped in?"

I pulled the ship up, and we all flung backward, so the ship was facing the sky. The klargon in my stomach sloshed around, turning it and making my eyes water.

"All ok, ladies?"

They nodded, clearly feeling similar to me.

I put my foot on the gas, and we took off.

Until we didn't.

"Savannah, you're gonna need to do your thing."

I looked out the edge of the rearview mirror. I could see the Gia Knights, all of them holding their hands up, pulling us down.

"Right!" She held her hand down, struggling. "There's too many of them," she said through gritted teeth.

But her efforts were working. Slowly the ship peeled away like their grasps had turned slippery.

But they still had a grasp.

"C'mon girl, you do that, and you'll get a nice reward."

She gasped, the ship fell back down, she controlled herself again.

"I can't do it. They are too strong. I'm barely holding them."

I looked desperately around the control panel for something. Any button that could help. And then I saw *it*. Hastily written in pen, more of a scratch than ink. I pressed it, and nothing happened, but then, a door on the console flung open. There was a box for me to stick my hand into, which made me feel like I would get my fingers bitten off if I did so.

Not having time for such thoughts, I reached my hand in and found a headset.

And then I remembered, the picture on the button was a gun.

I put the headset on and said *'hello'*, of course to nobody.

"Maple." I turned to see her, behind me, lying in the horizontal chair, gripping the handguards. "I think there's gonna be another one of these, next to a gun. Be a dear and find it, won't you?"

She grit her teeth, nodded, and threw the seatbelt off, then climbed off down the hallway, holding onto the handrails. If she fell, I worried she would break a leg.

I heard her yell something in the distance, but then her voice grunted into my headset, repeating, "Found it."

"And?"

"Big gun," she said bluntly.

I heard through the headset, the seat in the gunners room shifted with a crashing clunk, and then she said. "Facing the dock now." There was a slight gag, and I assumed she was being held in by seatbelt alone, and it was currently strangling her neck.

I turned to Savannah, whose hand was hanging off her chair, rigid as she held it down. I didn't ask how she was doing. I could see for myself she wouldn't have long.

"Shoot the Gia Ship." I commanded.

I watched in the rearview mirror as a flash of purple light bellowed from the ship, and the white shuttle blew up in the fireworks, taking a couple of them with it.

Civilians, who had been watching a ship being held in mid-air by the Gia Knights, ran off the dock in a panic.

The Gia Knights did the only thing they could do and continued to hold the ship in place. They were peppered around the dock.

"Maple, show these fools what happens when they cross us."

"Right!"

One by one, a blast replaced a knight. There weren't any bones or robes to show for their sorry existence, just piles of black dirt, their remains charred to a sorry state of nothingness.

Savannah gasped, gaining some of her momentum back, and the ship began to drift off. I put the brakes on, so the power of the remaining Knights kept us floating.

"All of them," I spat into the mic.

After a moment Maple said, "I think that's all of them."

I slammed my foot onto the pedal, and we jerked off, the ship shaking as the sky became black.

And we were away from the planet's atmosphere, heading towards the stars.

Gravity readjusted itself, and I held in my nausea as my equilibrium struggled with it.

27

"We did it!'

Through the speaker an unlocking sound as Maple took off her seatbelt and made her way down a ladder, I could hear her footsteps knocking against the rungs.

Savannah was panting. I reached over to grab her hand, but she was smiling despite the sweat dripping down her temple.

Now that the ship's gravity was stabilized, we could take off our seatbelts and walk around.

"Alright," I said to the girls. "Setting coordinates for Earth-2."

An arrow, clicking every time it flashed in and out, told me to go left, so I turned the ship slightly, and it centered inside the circle.

I stood up from the chair, stretched my neck, and then walked over to Savannah, who still had on her seatbelt. I took it off and stroked her hips, my thumbs resting over her mound. She smiled, then I violently grabbed her and lifted her over my shoulder.

"You're coming too," I said to Maple, who leaned on the

doorway with her arms crossed, grinning tusk to tusk. “Nice shooting, by the way.”

Savannah was laughing and hitting my back playfully with the side of her fist. "What are you doing with me?"

"I told you that you were getting a reward."

I found the master bedroom. It had a huge but uncomfortable-looking bed, as well as a chair and desk in the far corner. The decor was the same brown metal grated wood.

As soon as we got to Earth-2, I was gonna hire a cleaner.

The bed at least looked clean.

"Perfect, “ I said.

I sat her down on the chair and stroked the cheek of the beautiful woman looking up adoringly at me. I went behind her, tore off my belt so hard my gun holster fell on the ground, and pulled her hands behind the chair.

"What are you doing? I thought I was getting a reward." Savannah pouted.

I tightly bound her hands with my belt and then tied that to the back of the chair.

"You are—after you get punished. Did you think I forgot about your punishment for what you did in that castle?"

She whined, writhing around the chair. "Haven't I been punished enough?"

I grinned, grasping onto her skirt and panties and tearing it off in one motion, leaving her only wearing her top. Her bareness glistened. I stroked it and felt it was already wet for me.

"Is that for you to decide? Be quiet now, or I’ll punish you further."

I walked over to Maple, who was standing there watching. "Now that the naughty girl is tied up, what am I gonna do with you?"

We kissed, and Savannah gasped, struggling playfully

against her restraints. I knew she could escape with her powers, but she *wanted* to be tied up. She *wanted* to watch. This was no punishment for her. This was a reward.

Maple and I crashed into the bed. I tore off her bra and bit down on her dark red nipples. She cried out and slammed me down onto the bed, tearing off my pants and devouring me in her mouth. I cried out as she devoured me like it was the first meal she had had in weeks.

Savannah pushed her legs together, trying to create some kind of friction, thrusting herself against the chair.

"Did I say you could do that? Spread those legs for me," I commanded.

Savannah cried out, spreading her legs apart. She positively blossomed, ready to be eaten. If the ork currently devouring me hadn't been there, sending sparks of pleasure through me, I wouldn't have been able to resist.

But she needed to be punished—or rewarded, whichever it was, I forgot. So intense was the feeling of Maple's mouth around me.

I pulled the ork off me and tore her hot pants off, tasting her swollen bead, her folds opening to her bright red insides, a beautiful color. I devoured her.

“I bet you wish I was doing this to you?' I said to Savannah, grinning and then diving my mouth back into the ork, tongue sliding through her folds to slap against her gem.

Now Maple couldn't handle it. She yanked me up by grabbing both my forearms, then wrapped her legs around me, crushing me—not before I got inside her. I bent my legs for purchase and began ramming into the giant woman. We rolled around. She pushed me down into the bed and began slamming herself down onto me, bruising my hips.

Savannah was being treated to a full view of her ass bouncing up and down.

Maybe it was the added naughtiness of it all, knowing she was tied up there watching, but I couldn't hold it in any longer.

I decided I didn't have to. I was captain of the ship, and I was gonna come when I wanted, where I wanted. If I finished now, they were just going to have to wait for me to be ready again. I cried out, seeing lights as I released into the ork. She slammed down into me and took it. I twitched inside her.

"Wow." She gasped, breathing heavily on top of me as she ground herself against my spent member.

"That's how good you felt." I panted. "I couldn't hold it in any longer."

She slid off me and kept her leg raised so I could see the bead of white there.

"We're not done," I said, sighing and pushing myself up on my elbows.

"We're not?" she said, her lips licking between those tusks.

I raised my eyebrows and indicated to Savannah. "Somebody still needs attention. I think you know what I want you to do."

"Tell me." Maple stroked her finger across my chest, kissing me.

"Get off the bed, get on your knees so I can see that nice ass while you do it, and make her come-" I grabbed her neck, not hard, but gently. "With your mouth. And then when she's finally satiated, carry her over here and sit on her face. She needs to return the favor, don't you think?"

Maple didn't have to be told twice. She slinked off the bed, getting down on her knees. Her cheeks spread, and my come dripped out of her as she crawled slowly towards the tied-up woman on the chair.

Savannah gasped, struggling playfully against the restraints. At the same time, Maple got close, pulled the chair towards her, and spread Savannah's legs forcefully.

Maple licked her.

"Fuck!" she cried out at her taste. "I've never... I didn't think it would taste so good."

"She is an exquisite flower, isn't she?" I relaxed against the bed, watching my girl go down on my other. Maple lapped and licked, her tusks pressed against Savannah's thighs as she devoured her. Swirling over it. Savannah screamed. It was the most beautiful sight I had ever seen, and I twitched back to life. I had no doubt I was ready to go again, but I was content to watch for now.

As she lapped and licked, I saw it grow in the Savannah like a jug filling with water. She *ooh'd*. Maple grabbed her thighs in one full grip each, fingers digging into them as she lapped faster and faster.

"She's getting close, isn't she?" I said.

Savannah nodded, crying out.

And then she squirted all over her face while Maple kept licking and licking. If she weren't tied down, Savannah looked like she would have been writhing all over the floor. Her body went in all directions, trying to escape and yet not wanting to go anywhere, while Maple kept lapping.

And then she was done.

"Bring her over here," I said.

Maple untied her, lifted the woman in her arms with ease, then gently placed her down on the bed.

I got up on my knees, throbbing to hardness as I stroked Savannah's hair. "Ready to eat?"

She nodded. "I'll do anything you want." Kissing *me*, her tongue slid over my member.

But I held her back. "I didn't mean me. Did I, Darlin'?"

Maple climbed over Savannah's head, whoser her arms were still tied behind her back.

Maple then put her body upright, looking like a queen, riding her subjects face.

I knelt beside Savannah's head and said, "I'm going to use you now. My cock is already dripping from last time, but it doesn't matter because you're not going to stop whatever might happen. Understand?"

Maple lifted her thighs, and Savannah gasped for breath. "I understand."

I made my way over to her outstretched legs and spread them. Stroking at her with my thumb, I split her apart to see the glistening, sticky wetness.

I pushed inside and gasped.

While Maple sat upright like a queen, it was beautiful seeing Savannah's tongue lap against her. I sucked on Maple's breasts, biting hard on her nipple while trusting inside Savannah. She clenched around me, her swollen walls like the warmest, wettest hug I ever felt. I kept thrusting, groaning as we all brought ourselves to our individual completion.

"I'm close!" Maple cried out.

I began thrusting rapidly, beads of sweat dripping down my forehead, and I grit my teeth, my sole focus to get there first before Maple did.

"Don't you dare," I told her, grabbing her arms as she towered over me.Submissive pleasure drew across her face.

"I can't hold it anymore."

I slammed into Savannah, her inner thighs going pink from the repeated battering.

Even though I was so spent, my eyes crossed, rolling behind my eyelids, and I finished inside her. This time, the throbbing was painful, a desperate release of everything that was inside of me to fill her up.

I collapsed on the bed, panting. Maple and Savannah fell beside me.. Savannah's mouth glistened wet, I kissed them both, and we fell asleep in our mess.

* * *

The journey to Earth-2 was *pleasurable*. We delighted in discovering the communal showers together, a hallway of water where we could pull the curtains back and clean together, but also have privacy if we wished. Not that we often wished it. The three of us were inseparable.

After a quick pitstop, in which we filled up the freezer with vegetables and meat, we hardly had much else to do but cook, stargaze, or regale stories of our youth.

When we passed Caria, a twang pulled at my heart, like the string of a guitar yanked too hard.

"Shall we go back?" Savannah said. Her eyebrows furrowed in concern.

"That's where you're from, Harlen? and your friend. What was her name?" Maple was only being curious, but I still wished I didn't have to talk about it.

"Violet," I said, swallowing.

"We've got room for her now," Savannah said.

"And my gun."

I had missed it dearly, the empty holster on my left hip had almost begged to be filled with a weapon, but I had left it empty, through some odd sense of loyalty.

I shook my head as the brown planet went by. I tried to see if I could see the bar, but of course, it would have been a tiny little spec from this distance. There was no way.

"We might not be coming back from where we're going.

She's no fighter. I can't put her in danger," I said with finality. Savannah stroked my back, and Maple kissed my cheek.

"Hey," Maple said. "It's us. What can't we do?"

I smiled. "We'll come back for Violet. After our mission."

"After the mission." Savannah agreed, nodding.

I watched the planet go by and noted that one of the mountains had a particularly damaging black ring around it. It must have been the place where I had left Percival the Gia Knight.

Before, the ring of clouds was just a white ring with a broken section where the smoke drifted through it. But now it was black, where the toxin had poisoned the whole thing.

"So, by my calculations," I tapped the machinery on the desk, the dusty screen blinking. "we should be at Earth-2 in a week."

"What will we do until then?" Maple smirked.

I stood up, putting my naked body proudly on display. "Ship meeting everyone. My bedroom, stat. It's time for inspection. I want you all in my bed and bent over. I'll be in there soon to see you're kept yourselves nice and tidy."

* * *

And so the days rolled by. With each one, growing anxiety nagged at me at the task that lay ahead.

How would we beat *her* and her army of Subjects?

28

Earth-2 was a ball of technology.

Blocks grew from the orb like metal tumors. Bright lights illuminated them all, their colors converging into a terrible white. I didn't know what to say, so I looked to my girls to see their reactions, having always found it easier to comment on theirs.

Maple's eyes were glassy and full of wonder. "I can't believe it. I've never seen anything like it."

"That's how I felt when I saw your planet," I said. "It's amazing how different they can be." I took my place at the controls and said, "I hope I can figure out how to park this thing, or it will have been a very long trip for nothing." I grinned at the girls.

Savannah slapped my arm. "Not funny!"

I shook my head, dismissing it as a jest, but she was right.

Perhaps the time for jokes was over.

The Tower of Gia started as a point, as we directly faced it, like a finger accusing us. Then when the ship flew to the side, the tower began to loom over us, watching us with its blank stare. Plain white walls, without so much as a window. Unassuming, and yet, saying more than I could have put into words.

Savannah said nothing, holding in a breath. I wanted to comfort her, but I had to focus on flying and not crashing into any other ships aiming for the dock.

"Maple," I said, then nodded towards Savannah. Maple got my meaning and held Savannah's hand, squeezing it in her much larger one.

"Remember, girls. If we're together, there's nothing we can't do."

They nodded. But I knew it wasn't much comfort, not when that tower bore over us.

Pulling into the spaceport was daunting. I kept it slow as the jerky movements brought us closer. It didn't help that the ship's gravity changed to accommodate the planets, and my body fell backward against the chair.

It was a damn sight more preferable than slamming into the view screen, and at least I had the rearview mirrors to guide me. It reminded me of what it must be like to reverse a huge, wide truck.

Finally, though, I righted the ship, and we landed on the platform with a thud that bounced us slightly into the air from our seats.

I tapped the mechanical clock on the counter. "By these calculations, we've got a couple of days left until the initiation starts."

"What are we gonna do until then?"

"What do you think?" I smiled.

* * *

My hangover boomed in my head like a drum, pounding lights in my eyes.

The blinds created a stripped silhouette over us, as the many lamps and neon signs outside never seemed to turn off. If this was the planet that never slept, I was jealous that the girls had rebelled against that idea.

I sat up in the motel in the loneliness of being awake, my girls lying naked beside me, their sweat-covered bodies clinging to the sheets. The small of Savannah's back was a hypnotizing line, traveling down to just where the sheet covered her behind. While Maple's muscular physique flexed and unflexed in her light sleeping. I loved them both deeply, and thought I'd tell them at the first opportunity, I might not have another.

Climbing from the bed, I threw some briefs on, and stepped out onto the balcony, staring at the tower.

Up in the sky, rising far beyond the clouds, the tower loomed. I wondered where my room had been, guessing about near the middle but having no real way of knowing. I peered at a spot on the blank white tower. I imagined and imagined myself in that room, sitting in those uncomfortable beds, devouring book after book.

The cool air made goose pimples appear on my arms, while down below in the distance, a car beeped at a pedestrian. Grime and pollution paved the streets. The city was alive with people.

But they *were* alive. That was the point. *They might soon become Ruby's mindless drones.*

The balcony door was pulled back, and Savannah stepped out, draped in my shirt and nothing else. She came and put her head on my shoulder, I gripped her butt, and she hugged me tightly.

"It's been interesting, hasn't it?" I asked.

"Very," she said softly, then hugged me tighter.

"What if I'm not strong enough?" she asked, looking up at me.

One of her eyes had almost turned a full auburn now. I mentioned it to her.

She nodded, lips closed tight, then said, "perhaps her love is leaving me because of everything I've done."

"Perhaps."

She gasped.

"But so what?" I said. "It'll be cool to see what you look like with dirty blonde hair again. You're your own person now, not Gia's little pet."

She shook her head. "I guess so." But then she scrunched her nose up.

"That's not true. You're my little pet, aren't you?"

She smiled. "Let's get back to bed."

* * *

The week was oddly fun.

Although we had the looming tower over us, we still managed to find things to do, like try exotic foods. Earth-2 seemed to be a hub for all the races, and I even saw a few I hadn't known of since leaving.

We sat on a bench, eating what we had been told was called a *'kebab.'* It was an ancient, delicious, and yet greasy offering from the original Earth.

Maple got distracted by somebody sitting on another bench across from the park.

"What kind of girl is that?" she asked.

The girl minded her own business, licking an ice cream cone. Her fluffy tail bounced back and forth in joy as she tasted the treat, as did her fluffy ears twitching above her head.

"I believe they call her a *kitsune.* They come from a planet very far from here and tend not to travel much from it. I read about them once." I said, then, "It's rude to stare."

We sat back around our table, enjoying our own ice cream.

Then, we took Maple to the local movie theatre after she had exclaimed that she had never seen one. I wondered why they didn't have TVs on her planet, and she shrugged. "Probably too much condensation, or too much interference from the metal of the trees. I don't know."

The theatre was adorned by wooden knobbled hardware, polished to an inch of its life. Still, under the folds of carved wood, grime remained where the cleaner decided they only had to shine that which they thought the customer would notice.

"Savannah and I used to sneak out to come here," I said. "They only showed classic movies, so it was really cheap. We'd scrape up whatever money we could."

"You never did tell me how you got money," Savannah said.

"Ssh, the movie's starting." I grinned, dodging her question.

All throughout the movie, the visuals flared across the screen, but it was like a dream. I didn't see it all. All I could think was, *tomorrow's the day. The day it all ends.*

One way or another, likely with us kneeling before all the Gia Knights, our brains crushed to smithereens.

* * *

Back in the hotel, the priestly robes lay on our bed.

"How did you get these again?" Savannah crossed her arms at me.

"It's Earth-2. You can get anything if you know the right guy," I said proudly.

She scowled, "How do you know the right guy? We just got here."

I grinned, hand on my hips. "They were in the same dive bar they always hang out in. You can get anywhere here if you flash a bit of cash."

Savannah tutted, shaking her head at me but smiling like I had been caught in a naughty act. "You were a rogue before you even left the tower."

We draped the robes over ourselves. Maple's was *just* big enough, she had to wear a large, and her tusks escaped from her hood. But if she tied her hair back tight, you couldn't see the red. She held her ax inside her rope. It was hardly subtle, but nothing about her was, so I hoped her height was overwhelming enough that people didn't study the details of her ax's silhouette.

I, of course, had no such problems, and Savannah looked like any other disciple.

But together, we looked very odd, walking towards the tower through the dirty streets. It was almost comical, and Savannah had to go to great efforts to shield all three of us from the dirt and grime. Usually, it would be no effort for a single person to do it to themselves.

The doors opened for us. The long white hallways lay ahead. Daunting fright filled me, which I pushed deep down and led my women inside.

Initiates of all ages glared at us as we walked. It felt like we may as well be stark naked, all the good the disguise did.

"Just keep walking. Act like there's nothing out of the ordinary."

It was a terrible plan. Word would be abuzz of the strange trio. But, if we had timed it right, every master would be downstairs, unable to receive the news until it was too late. That gave us ample time to get to Ruby's room, find out what we could—and then what? Escape with the knowledge? We could go back to the Forest Pit King. Perhaps with some helpful knowledge to arm ourselves with, we could use his many resources to aid us. Or possibly Earth-2's government would be interested in what we'd discover. It was a flimsy plan, but it was the only one we had.

The elevator hummed gently.

"This is a very strange place," Maple remarked.

The elevator finally made it to the top of the tower, where it opened and showed us the hallway. It was plain and straightforward, with nothing but the blue light in the lower middle to brighten the path.

"This way," Savannah said.

We made our way down the hall. The only thing breaking up the vicious thumping of my heart was our noisy footsteps. We were not a group made for stealth. Hopefully, the floor was completely empty, with no attendees in the rooms, whose doors we could not see in the smooth white walls.

Finally, we made it to where Savannah stopped us. She held out her hand, and the cracks of the door appeared, exactly as my heart started racing a mile a minute.

"Ready?" I asked them.

The door was just ajar, ready for us to push.

We went inside.

The room was plain, a simple rug in the middle, before a white desk. On it lay a bowl filled with golden spheres, the kind we used to practice levitation. I walked over and picked one up, placing it on the desk.

The girls disappeared from my mind. It was only me and the ball.

I raised my hand, focused, but it merely rolled off and landed on the rug.

I shrugged. "Worth a shot."

Savannah walked over to the computer and sat down, clicking on the terminal and letting off a cute little grunt. "There's a password."

"Don't you know it?"

She shook her head.

"Try your birthday," I suggested.

Savannah scoffed. "Surely, mother's would be the one."

"Go on, try yours."

She shook her head as she typed, then gasped.

I walked over to the desk and leaned over the chair.

Meanwhile, Maple was musing over the plain white room. "This place is strange."

After much clicking around, looking at folders within folders that went nowhere, we managed to find one buried under legions of them, called *'research list.'* There was a file in there, we clicked it, and a cold shudder came over me.

"Why is she tracking the deceased relatives of initiates?" Savannah asked.

It was a simple spreadsheet with names running down it. Mother and father sat on the left, with 'deceased' or 'alive' marked next to them. It seemed like most of them had died of natural causes. It was no secret that many orphans had come to study at the tower of Gia, hoping they possessed the gift. Some said trauma unlocked the latent ability.

"She isn't tracking..." I said, then my words trailed off, unsure of how to word it to Savannah. How to spell it out to her.

"What?" Savannah flipped her chair to stare at me.

"Think about it," I said. The answer seemed evident to me.

Savannah shook her head. "No, it's not like that. It can't be."

"Can't it? Then why would she hide the file deep down in all those folders if it was something she didn't want us to see?"

"*Then why* would she use me as her password?"

"Perhaps it was a guilt thing. Ruby wanted to confess to you what she had done, eventually."

Savannah shook her head, then kept clicking around the folders, trying to find something.

"Hey, what's this one?" She clicked on it and found a picture of a pendant in the shape of a thick, gold ring. I gripped the space where mine should have been.

The picture was of a complete ring—no quarter circle.

"What is that?" I managed to get out. Savannah turned to me. Concern drew across her face as she saw my fist, what I was gripping.

"Scroll down," I said.

STOP THEM the voice came from all around.

The walls fell down around us, all but one. Each one pulled down by tired-looking Gia Knights. And at the front of them all, *Ruby Knight*.

Her eyes bulged out of their sockets, thick vascular veins pulsing in the white.

I reached for my gun, but my arms wouldn't move. I watched in horror as the weapon was floated from its holster and tossed aside. There were multiple men holding Maple in place. They struggled but managed to keep her from moving while another floated her ax away.

And I was powerless to do anything. I couldn't protect them. I had failed them. It all happened in slow motion, as if to prolong the torture. I was brought out of it by Savannah's voice.

"Mom? What is all this?" Savannah asked, struggling to move.

"Thank you, daughter, for bringing it back to me."

Ruby moved her hand around the air, frowning. "Where is it?"

"Where's what?" I asked, putting on my best act.

"Where is the pendant?"

"No idea what you're talking about."

"Separate prison cells—all of them."

"What about The Deputy Head?" one particularly tired-looking Gia Knight asked. His eye bags were impossibly heavy. The Knights must have been forced to stay up with her. If she didn't need sleep, why did they?

"All of them!" Ruby walked up to me, and I saw the sweat seeping from her pores. A speck of blood dripped out from one of the particular large veins in the whites of her eyes.

It was like she saw every little part of me, down to my very core.

"We will find it," she spat.

29

I didn't go into the cell without a fight.

And it turns out, Gia Knights now knew how to throw a punch. It was a complete sucker one, considering I was being held frozen, struggling through the sheer force of my will, but it certainly worked to get me in my cell.

My dark *empty* cell. At least it wasn't wet. Hell, it wasn't that different from my old bedroom.

So there I was, laying on my back, staring at the walls. Tapping on my chest, I lamented my bad fortune.

At least I didn't have to wear the stupid robe anymore.

Across from me, there was another cell where somebody slept under a blanket. She snoozed gently, the thin blanket raising and falling in an almost cute way. The pile looked vulnerable like that. I thought they must've been exhausted to sleep in a place like this. I leaned against the wall on my cot and closed my eyes, resting them. I would at least remain in an alert position, so if anything happened, I could jump out of bed.

I wondered how my girls were faring. I had no doubt of Maple. They'd have a tough job cracking her. Which, of course, meant she was in extreme physical danger. But

Savannah—who knew what Ruby was prepared to do to her.

I had to save them.

I closed my eyes and tried to form a plan.

* * *

"*Pst.*"

My ear twitched, I frowned.

"*Psst.*"

I grumbled, "What?" Then I opened my eyes and realized where I was. I had been having the most beautiful dream about a buxom ginger barmaid giving me a bath.

Standing in the other cell was a very petite woman. She had bright blonde hair and a pointed nose and stunning features. It suited her regal-like appearance.

"What are you here for?" she asked, her eyebrows raised high in curiosity.

"I tried to break into the tower of Gia and read some secret files on the Head Master's computer," I said bluntly. "This was after a race across three different planets to get to the bottom of some grand conspiracy, I'm still not entirely privy to. I think it has something to do with Gia, who is a god I just decided actually *does* exist."

She paused for a moment, taken aback, and then snorted. "Yeah, right."

I shrugged. "Don't believe me then." I closed my eyes, crossing my arms to get back to sleep.

"Nah, don't sleep. You're far too pretty to let rot in that cell."

I frowned and opened my eyes. "Do you really think flirting with me from across the bars of a cell is appropriate right now?"

The petite blonde thing grinned at me. "Could be a worse place to do it."

She had a point. I swung my legs over the bed and strutted over to the bars.

She scanned her eyes up and down me from her cell and said, "Hmm. You're not from here. You've lived a life on a harsh, simple, yet hard planet."

"You're observant," I said.

"You learn to be when you're from where I am."

The petite lady walked away from her bars.

I glanced down at the tightness of her t-shirt and leggings that stopped at her thighs. My eyes traveled up to her bubble butt. I wasn't expecting her to be packing something like that when I saw her from the front. It was the kind of butt one got from being highly athletic. It gave me pause to wonder, was there more to her than meets the eyes? I shook my head at myself, just being hopeful. Plenty of girls were born with a nice butt.

She stretched, then came back to the bars. Was that one of her flirting techniques? Let me have a look to weaken me? Or was she a secret agent of Gia?

I mustered a casual voice and asked, "And where are you from?"

She wagged her finger at me. "That's more of a first date question."

"I don't recall asking you on a date," I said.

"What if I get you out of this prison cell?" she asked, eyebrows raised.

I scoffed. "Lady, if you get me out of this cell, I'll take you home right now and bend you over until you're red and sore."

She smirked at me. "It's funny, the things you think you can say when they have no repercussions."

"And what repercussions would that have had?" I crossed my arms, having truly lost any care in the matter.

"I'll hold you to it."

I shook my head. "Unfortunately, I have far too much to deal with right now."

"That's a shame, big strong guy like you. I bet you're just the sort of guy that would teach me *how* to be bent over."

Footsteps echoed down the hall.

"Teach you how?"

She smiled at me. "I've never even kissed a boy."

"Yeah, right, look at you," I said, shaking my head. "This is definitely a trick. They sent you down here to flirt with me and try to get information from me."

"And who are *they*?"

"Someone who clearly knows I couldn't resist a sexy little thing like you that I could throw around. If it's your first time, there's no way you could handle that."

She sat down on the edge of the bed, stretching, her shirt pulled up to reveal her toned stomach—another clearly intentional move.

But it proved how athletic she was. Her petite height might have hidden it from one less concerting, but not from me.

"I'm just messing with you," she said. "I'm not a complete virgin, I've done stuff with myself, so I'd be ready for the main event."

I shook my head. "I can't believe we're having this conversation across the bars of a jail."

"Maybe you can ask for me as your last meal." She licked her lips, wiping her long blonde hair out of her face.

"Maybe you two can refrain from your sinful behavior!" the guard yelled as he walked down the hall.

The mystery woman bounced her eyebrows at me. "They

hate that."

"Not as much as you will hate my shutting you up," the guard said, standing before her.

His thick muscular back showed even through his ridiculous long robes.

"What are you gonna do, make me?"

The girl was clearly insane and not worth the trouble.

The guard put his hand out, and the girl held her throat, her eyes popping wide.

"Hey!" I yelled. "You can't do that."

But the girl grinned. "Just kidding."

The guard looked at his hand. Horror drew on his face. "You did this. Your sinful behavior has corrupted me."

"Maybe go meditate it off." She stuck her tongue out.

The guard stormed away.

The girl dug inside the hem of her leggings, pulling out a sewing needle.

She bit her lip in concentration as she fiddled with the lock.

Meanwhile, I was speechless.

Perhaps if I hadn't witnessed the miraculous act of her stopping Gia's powers, I would have wondered how she'd break open a strong jail lock with a thin sewing needle.

The lock opened.

"How did you do that?"

"I've been picking locks since I was a kid."

"No, not that! The thing with the guard?"

"One out of five men get performance anxiety," she remarked as she looked left and right up the hall and began working on my lock.

I gripped the bars, staring down at her.

"Seriously, how?" I pressed.

She bounced her eyebrows at me. "After."

"After what?" I frowned at her.

"After your side of the bargain. See.” She put her hands on her hips and grinned up at me. “You gave me some long-winded speech about how you got here. Let’s see if you think mine is any more believable.”

She strolled back and forth across the still locked entrance to my cell, tapping her chin as I supposed she was wondering where to start. Then she leaped into it. “My parents agreed to betrothe me to this guy I hate, so the idea of some street ruffian like you taking *it* from me?” She laughed. “It would send them wild! Seeing as you already agreed, it's time to go."

The door opened, and she walked off, but I grabbed her wrist. Her arm was tiny, and my hand circled around it with ease. It made me realize how Maple must feel every day.

She flipped over my back and wrapped her legs around me, squeezing my waist with strength I hadn't suspected she had.

The needle pointed right in my neck, it’s prick against my skin felt cold.

"One wrong word, and I'll stick this in your throat," she warned.

"I have friends on another ward," I said, gritting my teeth.

"Then you better hurry up. C'mon, my place isn't far from here."

She flipped off me and strolled away.

"This ain't how I like to do things," I said, catching up for her.

"Then you better show me how you like to do things."

At this point, I was going to be forced to. She may talk a big game, but she'd never *had* anyone before. I don't care what size toys she's stuck up there. She ain't ever been rammed by someone holding her down like she was nothing but a piece of meat.

And I wasn't small.

A guard turned the hall, but she held her hand up, and while he tried to do the thing, she stopped him. That didn't leave him defenseless, though. He grabbed her and pushed her against the wall, so I ran and slammed my fist into his face.

"Hey, we make a good team." She grinned. "I had trouble with them before."

"Thought you could stop their powers—which you still haven't explained, by the way."

"I can, but not a whole group of them. I guess that's where you come in—my muscle."

"Seemed like you had the upper hand on me a moment ago."

We got to the counter of the jail, where we made short work of the desk clerk and retrieved my pistol and Maple's ax. Then we headed into the dirty, bustling streets.

After convincing her to take a detour to the bar where I had left the pendant, we were on our way.

She put her hands in her pockets and walked beside me.

"That only seemed to work once on people. I'm fast, but I'm not strong. These Gia assholes, they learn fast," she said.

"So you've fought them before," I said, adjusting the heavy ax on my shoulder.

She raised her finger at me. "Ah, you learn too." She shook her head. "You're a smart guy, aren't you?"

"And you're a pain in my ass."

"And yet here you are, still following me."

I dropped the ax, which fell with a violent crash, and grabbed her arm. I then quickly grabbed the other before she could flip. She put one foot to my thigh to climb up me like I was a ladder, but I let go of her arm and grabbed her other leg to throw her down, pouncing over her and putting my knee right between her breasts.

In the middle of the street, a few people gasped. Luckily, the roads of Earth-2 were so scummy people weren't likely to get involved unless it got *really* bad.

I snarled at her, "Listen, you little bitch. I'm not messing around. I've got friends trapped in those cells back there, and you've got the power to help me help them escape, so just tell me what bargain you want to strike with me. Do you want gold? I can pay you all the gold you want."

She gasped, her mouth forming a perfect little 'o'.

I got up and held my hand up to help her up.

"I don't need gold. I have all the gold you could dream of back home." She looked over her shoulder and saw all the dirt I had gotten on her. "Well, now I've got to go back to my apartment and change into clean clothes."

"And then?"

"We'll discuss our plan."

"I'm warning you." I raised my finger. "I have no tolerance for funny business, not after everything I've been through."

She smiled. "I'm counting on it. C'mon, my place isn't far from here."

I begrudgingly agreed to follow her, Hoping that my girls could hold out a little bit longer.

She led me to a tower block, which felt odd to call it, compared to the tower of Gia looming over it. Although it must have been about thirteen stories high.

She entered, and I followed behind her.

I'd reached the end of my rope, and it would only take one last insolent word from her for me to lose it.

30

The hallway was caked in dirt, having not been cleaned for such a long time.

The elevator shook and groaned, and I wouldn't have been surprised if that was the moment it decided to fall and send us plummeting to our deaths.

I crossed my arms while the petite blonde woman looked delighted with herself.

"This is serious." I grit my teeth.

She walked towards me, pointing her finger at my chest. "Oh, Mr. Serious. So serious all the time."

I scoffed. "Hardly."

She winked at me. "C'mon, Mr. Serious. Let's see if we can get some of that serious out of you."

The elevator dinged, and I followed her down the hallway. A luminescent bulb flickered, and then just before I thought it would burn out forever, it blinked again.

We got to her door, where she crouched down before the mat, purposefully giving me a full view of her luxurious, toned behind.

"I swear to god. You're gonna regret all this teasing me.

I've got three girlfriends, you know—two of which I should be rescuing right now."

She gasped. "Oh, Mr. Serious has three girlfriends. How ever will he make time for me?"

I pushed her front against the wall, sliding my hand between her cheeks, lifting her as I grabbed right on *her*. She moaned in submission.

"With a couple of thrusts," I said in answer to her question. "Something tells me a little princess like you is *extra* fertile. I don't think your folks would much like you getting knocked up by a rough felon like me."

"No." She trembled. "They wouldn't like it at all."

I put her down, and she hastily led me into her apartment.

It was a mess—trash everywhere, overfilled bins, and an odd smell in the air wafting from the kitchen. Suddenly I felt rather unattracted to her.

She led me to her bedroom, where at least the smell wasn't as bad. Clothes were thrown all across the floor, though. I had to tiptoe to not step on them with my shoes.

I didn't feel like taking my shoes off, though.

"They're mostly clean," she said. "Don't worry. I don't keep any trash in here. Well, not until today." She winked at me.

But I shook my head. "How can you live like this?"

She stretched on the bed, pulling off her shirt and revealing her petite, perfectly hand-sized breasts in a small see-through bra.

"It's not my fault," she moaned, falling back against the bed. "The servants usually cleaned up."

"The servants? How does someone with servants live in a place like this?"

She sat up. "I told you I ran away. They wanted me to marry some jerk!"

"I thought that was a lie you made up." I walked over to her desk, pushed off her clothes from the chair, and sat down. Putting my elbows on the desk, I rubbed my eyes and asked, "So how did you end up in jail?"

"I stole," she said softly, devoid of emotion.

"Why? You've got enough clothes here."

"Well, I ran out of money, spent it on all these clothes."

"You left home with just enough gold to survive on, and you spent it on clothes?"

"You don't understand!" she protested. I was still rubbing my eyes. "All my life, I've been put in these tight dresses. So many dresses. Do you know how hard it is to fight in a dress?"

"You'd look cute in a dress," I smirked, hoping the comment would annoy her.

"Damn right! But that's beside the point."

I moved my elbow against something hard on the table. it screeched on the wood from its weight. I ignored it and kept rubbing my eyes. I was so tired of it all. *Ruby is making slaves of the world right now and this chick is wasting my damn time?*

"So, how do you pay rent?"

"I've got enough for rent, and I can steal food without getting caught. But I wanted a bedroom to sleep in, one that isn't filled with all this mess. I don't know why I can't seem to keep my room clean."

"If you lived on my ship, I wouldn't allow you to have a messy room like this. I'd make you tidy it."

"Oh, you'd *make me*, would you? And how would you do that?"

I turned to face her and noted that she was only wearing

a bra and panties now, having taken everything else off when my eyes were closed.

I got up to go to her, but something fell off the desk with a thud.

I bent down to pick it up from under the chair.

"Don't worry about that," she said.

But my hand clasped around my pendant.

I picked it up and looked at it, realizing that the guy I left it with had removed the cheaply soldered wire that connected the string to it. Why the hell would he do that? *And* he had changed the color of the engravings. This one was red.

I blinked. "Where did you get this?"

She was on her back, foot pointing in the air like a ballerina. "What? That's just an old family heirloom. Are you coming to bed or what?"

I yanked mine off my neck and threw it at her.

"What did you do to it?" she said, picking it up. What's this string... wait." She looked at it, and then me.

We held each other's pendants on either side of the room.

I got up and walked over to her and said through a calm breath, "This morning I saw a picture of the full one. Today I met you, and you have a quarter." I held mine out in my hand, and she placed hers there, next to it.

They didn't stick together or form into one piece or anything like that. The two pendants just rested on my shaking hand. It was obvious that they were two pieces of the same whole, and that we were still missing two more of them.

We looked at each other.

"Who are you?" she asked. Her pretty mouth opened in wonder.

"Who are *you*?" I said, clapping my hand around the two pendants tight in my hand.

"Seeing as you're a prince, I could probably trust you."

"What?" I scowled at her.

She put her hand in her hair. Wincing, she pulled out a sticky line of tape that stuck to her hair. Strands stuck to the tape as she flicked it off her hand.

Then her pointed ear stuck out.

She did the other ear, and I stood there, mouth agape.

"This is who I am. You jokingly called me a princess before, well I am one—a princess of Elfa."

"What the hell are you doing here? Nobody ever goes in or out of your planet."

She smiled at me. "I escape from jail every week, and you think I couldn't escape from a planet? It was just a bigger prison, with bigger cracks to sneak through."

I opened my hand on the pendants again. They seemed so unassuming.

What purpose did they have?

"What do you know about these?"

"Nothing. Ours was kept secret, handed down from generation to generation until it became nothing more than a fancy heirloom. I didn't even think that it could be one part of a whole, kept by the other royal families."

"Darlin, do I look royal to you?"

"Did I, in that prison cell? Appearances can be deceiving."

Her hand closed around my fist. I dropped the amulet and pulled her in. My heart raced.

I may not have liked her personally, but there was some strange connection between us. Like we had known each other for millennia.

She wrapped her arms around me, and I lifted her up, my groin rubbing against her panties.

"There was a picture of the amulet on the Head Master's computer." I groaned as we fell to the bed, and all the mess in the room floated away. It was just her and me alone in the universe. "They know something about it."

"Well, then I guess we better get back to the tower then."

"After we save my girlfriends. We need them," I said, holding her cheek.

She nodded at me, looking up at me with adoring eyes. We kissed again, our tongues dancing as we rolled around the bed, and she grabbed at my belt.

"After," she said, which I took to mean after we did what we were going to do.

"After." I agreed and sunk my hand into her panties, finding her shaved smooth and wet for me.

She dug her hand into my pants and grabbed me, then gasped, as her fingertips could barely meet around me.

"Bigger than you thought?" I said through a hushed breath.

"Just a bit." She kissed me again, our tongues lapping at each other like a dance.

I climbed over her and pulled my shirt off. She ran her fingers across my many scars and battle wounds.

"You're quite the bad boy, aren't you."

"You've got no idea," I said, pulling her bra off and biting down on her pink nipple. While thrusting my fingers inside her, her smooth wet walls gripped me so tight I thought they would strangle my finger. My thumb rubbed against her gem, and she cried out, writhing on the bed in wild ecstasy. Clearly, she had not been touched like this before.

I licked at the small woman's ears,my tongue darting over their points. She gasped and cried out while I continued with my hand until finally, I brought her to a quick, wet release.

"My turn," I said.

She nodded. "Your turn. Do whatever you want with me. I'm ready."

I looked down at my glistening wet hand, soaked with her juices. "I can see that."

I climbed onto her, towering over the small woman as my *head* pushed against her opening. It was like trying to split two glued tight walls. She gasped and panted.

"I can take it." She closed her eyes, and I pushed inside her.

They split apart, and she grasped the bed.

"Oh, god. I can take it. Don't stop."

I leaned down and licked her ear, whispering. "The safe word is *pendant*."

"Then you better hold your hand over my mouth, so I don't say it." She panted.

I thought that was an excellent idea. So I put my hand over her mouth and pushed deep inside her, filling her so deeply I thought I must have been painfully poking at her cervix. But she didn't let up. She just looked at me with those eyes of desperate, forlorn pleasure, and I began using her body, which clenched around me with all its tightness.

Then I grabbed her and threw her on top of me, pushing her up and down on me like she was my personal little toy. She collapsed on me, spasming as I used her, milking me harder still.

"It's so big." She winced. "But it feels so good, don't stop."

I didn't intend to. Not until I was finished.

"What happens if a human comes inside an elf?" I asked her, grasping her neck and thrusting deep up into her while grabbing at the thick flesh of her bubble butt.

"Why don't we find out," she said and began bouncing on me, imitating the way I had been using her body before.

She was inexperienced, chaotic, but it made it all the better as I relaxed and watched the petite women ride me. She was giving it her best effort.

And she wasn't bad at all.

I was getting close.

"Not yet," I said, climbing up and throwing her off me.

"I'm a princess. Do you have any idea what the punishment is for manhandling me?"

I said nothing, just pulled her legs down so she was prone on her stomach. I pushed my viciously throbbing member into her cheeks, finding her opening and ramming inside, gripping her hip, pulling her up into me.

I went wild while she screamed in ecstasy.

And then I did, too, giving her everything I could.

31

We were done. My senses returned. I climbed off the bed to walk towards my shirt.

"What's the rush?" The tiny elf stretched, then cupped her hand over herself, massaging while I had pounded. Her hand got sticky with my release, and she looked at it with a kind of strange interest.

"Did you not hear all that stuff before? About my friends?"

Her eyes went wide. "Wow, you were so good I forgot. I'm sorry–hey, what's your name?" She bounced from the bed, walked over to me, and stared up at me with bright, adoring eyes.

"Harlen," I said.

"I'll help you." She smiled in a way that made me feel she had mischievous thoughts.

I grabbed her arms. "Ok, but listen, I'm in charge of this mission."

She nodded. "You're in charge."

I walked away from her to grab my shirt and put it on, then tied my belt while she got dressed.

"My name's Selphie, by the way."

We stood outside the jail, conveniently a street away from the tower. It was almost like they *wanted* it separated but couldn't remove all association with it.

"So, what's the plan, Harlen?"

"Oh, it's very complicated, darlin'."

She raised her eyebrows at me.

"We go in and break them out." I grabbed my gun and twirled it, then grinned at her. "You block em, I'll tag em."

Inside, a bored desk clerk was sitting at his post. His robe's sleeves fell down to his elbow as he spun a pen in his finger, dropping it multiple times.

I shoved the gun in his face. "Hello! We're here to visit a few inmates!" I grinned at him.

He raised his hand, but Selphie blocked him. "Nuh-uh!" She grinned.

Weighing his options, the desk clerk immediately started clacking away on his keyboard. "What are their names?" His voice shook.

"Savannah and Maple."

Patiently, he typed with remarkable accuracy for someone who had a gun pointed in his face.

"T-they're..." his voice faltered in his fright.

"Tell me!"

"Floor 2 and floor 4."

I fired the gun, and his head slumped against his keyboard, not dead but stunned.

"Thank you for your cooperation."

And then, for the benefit of Selphie, I spun my gun before putting it in my holster.

"Fancy man with fancy tricks."

Selphie seductively sat on the desk, moving the guard's head out the way until he slumped onto the ground. When the petite elf spread her legs, I walked between them. I grabbed the back of her neck, and she said, "but we both know you've got more tricks with your other pistol."

“You don’t know the half of it.”I grinned, then grabbed her wrist. "But I’ll show you later."

"Oh, you bet."

We made our way down the rows of empty cells.

"But what about your other girls?" she asked as I shot a Gia disciple who was inspecting his nails while leaning against a cell. He slumped against the bars.

"What about them?"

"Won't they get jealous?"

"I have a peculiar arrangement," I said.

"How peculiar?"

"Let's just say you'll fit right in, darlin'."

"With a promise like that, how could I not be curious?"

"I'm warning you, though." I pointed my gun at her. "The rest of the girls know their place."

"And where is their place?" She grabbed me and pulled herself against the wall. I towered over her, cupping her breast.

"Beneath me," I said.

"Even if they're a princess?"

I cupped between her legs. "*Especially* if she’s a princess."

A guy yelled, and without looking, I aimed my pistol down the hall and shot him. "C'mon, let's go find them."

* * *

Savannah was the first we found. She sat on her bed, hugging her knees. Confusion furrowed across her face.

"What? Did you think I would just leave you here?" I grinned at her, she grabbed onto the bars, and we kissed, but we were distracted by the clicking of the lock as Selphie bit her lip and messed with it.

"This is Selphie. She's a runaway princess from Elfa."

Savannah blinked, then smiled, shrugging. "Fair enough. I'm Savannah—runaway Gia disciple."

The door opened, and they shook hands.

Heading down the hall, Savannah used her powers to slam a guy against the wall, then I shot him.

On the next floor we met Maple, who was pacing up and down her cell.

"Maple, Sephie, runaway princess from Elfa, half-ork from Pradorix."

"Charmed," Selphie said, doing a mock curtsy.

The towering half-ork clambered over to the tiny woman and crouched down, leaning on the ax I had just handed her.

"You are an elf," Maple observed.

Selphie flicked her pointy ear. "Ears and all."

Maple smiled, and then with one arm, bound her into a suffocating hug. "I look forward to getting acquainted with you."

* * *

Now outside the prison, we stood on the side of the street opposite the tower. It was much like Savannah and I had done on Pradorix.

"So, here's the plan." The girls all watched me. "We're

gonna go downstairs and meet with Gia. We'll get to the bottom of this once and for all."

"Meet with *Gia*?" Savannah frowned in confusion.

Time for explanations. "There's something I haven't told you." I pause, taking in a breath to even myself. "I've been hearing this voice every time I wake up. I thought it was just a dream at first, but every morning, someone called me, wanting me to come back." *I can't believe I'm saying this after denying her existence for so long, but I don't see who else it could be.* "It's gotta be her. It's got to be the reason I could do Gia stuff that nobody else could. If I can get down there and speak to her, maybe we can work together. Because I don't believe Gia is evil."

"My mom." Savannah made a fist so tight her knuckles turned a milky white. "She can't be allowed to continue this. We need to stop her."

I nodded, both of us knowing what that meant but neither wanting to say it.

"I'll do it for you," I said.

"You might have to."

We headed into the temple, no longer caring about stealth. The disciples walking around doing their daily tasks were stunned to see such an odd group of people in regular clothing. We hurried towards the elevator so fast they did not seem to have time to react.

"Well, the shock factor is one way," Maple observed.

I grinned as we stepped into the elevator. "Wait, let me try." I raised my hand, closed my eyes as it shook and dramatic music played in my head. I grit my teeth, focusing just as I used to.

But nothing happened.

Did that mean nothing would happen downstairs, was my plan really that stupid? It's not like we had another.

But the ork walked over to me like she could read my mind after having spent so much time with me.

"We don't need answers," she said. "All we need to do is stop them."

I nodded. "Let's stop them."

The elevator carried us down to the temple rather unceremoniously. The doorway to the temple was like a little portal.

"Selphie, keep a forcefield around me. I'm gonna step out first. You stay behind in the elevator."

I took a deep breath, cocked my gun, and stepped out into the temple.

The Knights all stood there, in a military position, hands raised like they were guns.

"it doesn't have to be like this," I said.

In the middle of them all, Ruby Knight stood, with this terrifying dark aura around her. "Did you bring it this time?" she smiled, her eyes bulged out of their sockets. Even from here, I could see the red-veined lines.

"So, how's Cane treating you?" I taunted.

She snarled. "You always did mess things up." Her eyes moved as erratically as her head, like she was a puppet being jerked around on strings. She twitched like a snapping insect towards her disciples, but seemed to regard them as inconsequential as she said, "You destroyed our means of obtaining the final medicine before I could grasp it."

"What even was that all for anyway?" I kept my gun aimed at her.

"This." She raised her hand and the tower seemed to dim.

"All that focus, to bring me closer to Gia."

Lighting shot out her hand and struck me square in the

chest. I fell to my knee, my skin radiating with a buzzing electricity.

It *hurt*. Like, really hurt.

I heard Maple grunt behind me. "That's our cue."

My women poured out from the tiny doorway. Savannah brought her hand out and flung her mother so far away from the wall that she slammed against it and crumpled to the floor. I thought I saw the shock on Ruby's face when it happened, but her eyes were already so bulging it was hard to tell.

A Gia Knight trembled as Maple staggered towards her, raising him ax high, ready to slam it through his skull. He just stood there shaking like an idiot.

"Stop!" I yelled. We'd have no more *needless* bloodshed, not when Gia was so close. These knights were just following doctrine.

Maple turned to me. "Aw." She then dropped her ax, grinning maliciously at the knight.

All the knights were shaking, hands raised but trembling, looking to each other for clues of what to do.

I glanced at Selphie, who was shaking like a leaf in a hurricane. It must have been extremely exhausting to keep me protected against all this power. Savannah was helping with her own, but the princess probably wasn't used to this.

"Listen, knights. Do you really want to do this? You've seen Ruby. Is that what Gia wants?" I asked the room.

The knights exchanged glances. Seeming to say to each other precisely what they had all been thinking and too afraid to speak aloud.

"Harlen." A girl stood up, sweat clinging her white hair to her head. "You were always the one to point out stuff nobody wanted to in class."

One gasped, but then another stood up. “He’s right. What she's done, it's not ok."

Another knight gasped. "Did you just speak against the Head Master?"

"Actually, *she's* the Head Master now,” I nodded at Savannah, “the previous one will be retiring.”

The clump of robes against the wall pushed herself up and then flew high up in the sky, lightning flaring all around her. "I don't think so." lightning flashed around her.

"Knights, is this really what you want to fight for? Does *that* look like the word of Gia? Turn away from this abomination and leave us with her."

They got up, and one by one, began to funnel out of the hall, walking past us like we weren't even there.

"Where are you going? How dare you!" Ruby spat.

“You know, I think Ruby's feeling talkative, something to do with the drug.” I whispered, then shouted, "Hey, *Ruubs*. What happened to everyone's parents?"

She grit her teeth, her eyes bulging so wide I honestly thought they would pop out of their sockets.

Lighting crashed down from the ceiling, adding to the sparks flying off her.

"I killed them all, searching for it. What did it matter? They all left you. Do you know how easy it is to convince parents that their child is gifted, special? None of you had it. I gave it to you. It flowed through me like it does now. I am Gia!"

I fell at the news that my parents never left me. I was taken from them.

"What about dad?" Savannah pleaded.

"That weakling? Dead too." Ruby scoffed.

I shot her. It landed right in her chest, exposing her midriff, but she ignored it.

I shot her again. This time her flesh seared, but she continued to ignore it. The more I shot her, her bones exposed, her organs, she just laughed maniacally and then flung lighting at us.

Savannah stopped it, holding the lighting.

I slammed my notch to the very last dial, way past kill, the dials that shouldn't have even been on the gun.

I squeezed, the whole room went white with light. My hand seared, burning as an explosion fired from my gun, making me drop it and crouch as I held my hand in exacerbation of pain.

When my vision returned, there was but a crumpled pile of nothing on the ground.

"Is everyone ok?" I asked.

Grabbing my good hand, they helped me up.

"We're ok. Are you?" I looked up at the three of them.

There was Savannah, with her kindness.

Maple, with her fierceness.

And Selphie, who spat in the face of an impossible adversary, a fierce spirit who I wanted by my side, both to tame and be my ally.

"I am now," I said. "I've got you girls."

They helped me up, and we looked to the stairs in the middle of the temple.

"But." I turned to them, trying to hide the proud tears brimming in my eyes. "I've got to do this alone. She's been calling me, I didn't know what it was, but I do now. I need to see her."

They nodded. Savanna, holding herself together. "I need to tend to my mother. She may have been evil, but she still deserves a proper burial."

I was about to tell Maple to help her, but Maple put her hand on her shoulders and said. "Let me assist you."

Selphie jumped up. "I'll help too! In whatever way, I can."

I left them while I turned back to the stairs and stepped down those carved steps, down into the room, with the warm blue light coming from nowhere, amongst the white steam. I couldn't see anything.

I groaned as I sat down to cross my leg and my knees clicked. I placed my hands on my lap, and closed my eyes to meditate.

Seemingly instantly, a hand delicately touched my shoulder.

When I opened them, the mist was gone. The room seemed entirely unremarkable now except for the white woman before me. Everything about her was pale. Milky skin, eyes, hair, lips. Her nipples were a slightly darker shade of gray.

She smiled and hugged me.

I didn't know how to feel, except comfort. But I knew there should've been more.

"You came. I've been waiting for so long," her feminine voice whispered against my ear.

"Gia?" I dared ask, my voice cracking.

She nodded. Smiling as tears brimmed her eyes.

"I guess I've got some explaining to do," she said bashfully, not anything like how I'd expect a god to act. "You must have so many questions."

I touched her cheek and glanced at her immaculate body.

"Time has stopped here," she said. "We have all of it in the world. I scarcely know where to start."

"What's this pendant?"

"It's a piece of a portal." She smiled, stroking her fingers along it before resting against mine. "All four pieces connect. We built it as a door and gave it to the chosen calamity of each world."

"Calamity?"

"Our word for royalty—one who owned the power to end life on a catastrophic scale."

"But how could I end life on Earth-2? I'm just a guy."

"It was not on this planet."

The implication became clear. The nuclear war that had destroyed the planet of the original earth, caused by the power of the royal family—my ancestors.

I took it oddly in my stride, as I asked, "So why is this tower *here* and not there?"

"When my people die, our ethereal spirit transfers through the planes to settle where we deem appropriate. I came to you, hoping you would find me. But the knowledge had been lost. Instead, this tower was built around me." The white woman snarled with distaste. "I tried to mark all those that had stolen my *love* as they call it. I removed all the colors from them as a warning to others. It was all I could do. It seems that the warning wasn't heeded. They kept coming. So, with all my strength, I called to you. It's not something that is known to happen."

"And Savannah's eye?"

She smiled. "Another cry for help, designed to reach you."

"Well, I'm here. So now what?"

"You must fulfill your end of the prophecy."

I sighed for a moment, looking out into the blank walls. "Time has stopped here?"

She nodded. "We may talk as long as you wish."

My other hand slid onto her hip, and I pulled her close. "After the month I've had, I don't give a crap about any questions or prophecies. I'm gonna fuck *god*. And then you can tell me after."

She stroked my cheek and stared into my eyes. "Technically, I'm not *god*. I'm *a* god."

"Close enough." I pulled her naked body onto me as I fell back onto the stone floor. Her kiss enveloped joy in me, and my hardness rubbed against her as she stroked down on it.

The End.

Harlen and his girls will return!

In the meantime, enjoy this free preview of my current work-in-progress, a cosy fantasy isekai story:

PROLOGUE

Sweat beaded down my forehead and spine. It clung my clothes to my body like a salty glue.

The discomfort from perspiration was secondary to my knee pressing against the hard, dry tree trunk. I leaned into it to steady myself, sinking the rough bark further into my skin. I was a sturdy tripod for the camera in my hands.

Looking down several feet below, I reminded myself it was not heights I feared, but that which falling would bring attention to.

I wiped my hand on my shorts and returned to looking through the viewfinder while my assistant Cassie passed me a towel, having sensed my discomfort. I didn't say 'thank you,' because every word had to be conserved, lest it alerted the tigers.

Wiping the sweat from my brow, I passed it back to the pretty young brunette. She smiled at me as she put the towel back in her carry bag. If she minded that it was wet with my sweat, she did not show it. Instead, she nodded and watched me intently, eager to assist me in whatever way she could.

Cassie herself also glistened from the heat. It made her a

shining beauty. If there was ever a woman that looked like she belonged in the rainforest on an expedition, it was her. My eyes darted to the way her tight cargo shorts hugged the underside of her thigh, revealing that smooth flawlessness broken up by a few beauty spots that were appropriately named.

I averted my gaze from her delicious thigh before I got any more distracted, and she gently smiled at me. I noticed an extra button of her tan shirt was undone, revealing more of herself. Were that many buttons open before? Had she done it when my back was turned, to cool down? Or was it to attract more attention from me?

My break was over.

If I had spent it lusting over my assistant and not resting, then so be it. The new development of our relationship was welcome all the same. I would see how far it would go when we returned to base camp. Work ethics be damned—she was attracted to me, so I would act on it.

On a tree a few yards away, I made out a vague shape hidden inside the branches. Raising my hand, I gave the thumbs up to let my other assistant know I had finished my short break and would return to taking pictures. Now was his turn to rest.

Then, I peered through the viewfinder of my film camera, holding onto the telescopic lens to steady it. I held in a breath of pleasant surprise.

Wading through the river, leaving a wave of water like an elegant cape, the Bengal tiger swam like it was a water-born species. Only the deer carcass gripped in its teeth betrayed its violent nature. Occasionally when its, *her*, head darted up over the water, her furry muzzle gently snarled to show teeth that could bite clean through if it wanted to. They could easily tear through flesh like a hot knife to butter.

Her head emerged from the river first. When the rest came free from the surface, water dripped readily over its body to collect underneath its neck in a flat wave of fur. Its orange, black, and white coat shined more brightly from being waterlogged.

Ordinarily, I would have had enough shots already. Those few alone I would be proud to show the magazine, but I wanted the front cover.

Cassie *very* quietly gasped. I looked at her for a moment, as a warning, to remind her that even the slightest noise would be the end of us. Her cheeks went a little red as she nodded at me, and I smiled at her, knowing the warning wasn't needed. She was a professional, and I had done right to have her on my team, attracted to her or not.

I then heard the high-pitched snarls of a cub, testing its new roar, and I looked back through the viewfinder to see what she had gasped at.

The tiger mother dropped the carcass to the forest floor, watching as her two cubs ran and pounced on it like it was going to run away. Their high-pitched mini-roars echoed through the rainforest as they ran around to leap on it again, fighting playfully for dominance.

Meanwhile, blood showed across the mother's mouth, visible because of the deer's absence—evidence of the violence she committed. She yawned, and then sat down, resting his head on her giant paws.

The cubs gnawed at their prize, pretending they had caught it themselves.

Sunlight beamed through the leaves to reflect off something that hit my eye, causing my eyelid to flicker. I ignored it, being too focused on my work. The tigers did not notice it, so there was no reason for me to either.

The shots I was getting were cover-worthy, each one

froze in my mind as the shutter clicked, until, without checking the number on the camera, I swapped it with Cassie for a fresh towel.

After handing me the cloth, she began quietly rolling up the film inside the camera, ejecting it for another while I wiped my brow. It was almost like surgery. Much like a doctor couldn't afford to drip sweat into the operation, my camera needed to remain dry to function.

We had come too far, and I did not trust the photos Danial would be taking in the other tree. He was not a poor photographer, but he wasn't a good one either.

I could've managed this without him, but he used a digital camera, just in case my film camera failed. I would never need his pictures, but it was good to have them just in case—although if I had to return to the magazine with only his, I would rather get the plane back to the rainforest to take them again.

It was worthwhile to get it on film. They garnered so much more money, and frankly, they looked better. You can't beat that 35mm authenticity.

My eye twitched again. This time having no distraction from the camera in my hand, I darted my eyes to the tree across the fray, where I saw the source of a flash.

It had been a joke.

A few days ago, I had joked to myself that Danial seemed the kind of person to use the flash when shooting a predator. What cruel fate had turned that to reality?

Fury snarled through me, more towards the man's father than at him. It's not Danial's fault he's an imbecile, but his CEO dad for not teaching him otherwise. Damn silver-spooned asshole that he was. The CEO of the magazine I worked for probably thought he could send his son into danger to toughen him up. I supposed I was to be some sort of drill sergeant for him. A lot of good that did, when he was thrust upon me *days* before our flight.

"Cassie," I whispered, "take over."

Her eyes went wide at the opportunity. She looked at the camera like it was made of gold, and then quickly came to her senses as she leaned forward and aimed the lens at the tigers.

Meanwhile, I slowly reached for the walkie-talkie on my hip, careful not to shake the branches as I pressed the long red button on the side.

"Danial," I whispered in the quietest voice I could.

"Yes, boss?" he yelled excitedly. I heard it all the way from his tree, and through the speaker.

"Be silent," I spat into the thing quietly as I could.

A growl erupted. I darted my vision towards the tigers, but only the cubs remained, still gnawing on the carcass, oblivious to any threat. Where was the mother?

I spotted her.

With an impossible quietness, she was wading through the leaves much like she had swum through the lake. Sniffing at the air, she looked for the source of the noise. Sensing that my group of trees bore more of the scent, she sauntered towards us, her claws flaring out from their unassuming furry sheathes.

If she realized the exact tree we were in, she could climb it with ease.

I snapped off a branch and threw it away from us, back away from the cubs. It had been instinct.

Her head darted to where the branch landed, sniffing at the air as she crouched, ready to pounce.

I did it again to drive the point home.

In a flash of speed, she launched at the branches. Her

growl sent a wild gush of adrenaline through me. My vision became a tunnel, the edges like a border of migraine.

Grabbing my walkie-talkie, I whispered, "Don't speak. Don't utter a word. Don't take another picture. Stay silent and don't move until I give a signal."

You fucking imbecile, I added mentally. I would tell him that later when the danger was over. I would also have to hold myself from punching him in the face—not that he wouldn't deserve it. Better *that* than being torn to shreds by the tiger.

Cassie put her hand on my thigh, and the adrenaline surging through me focused right down on it. In a moment of clarity, I thought it peculiar how, in the face of near-death, I could *still* feel that urge.

The clarity left, replaced by throbbing urgency, and our eyes met. She nodded at me, reading it all in my mind—my frustration with Danial, my want of her. She shared them both. Cassie's full lips opened slightly, ready to launch at me, but she restrained herself.

Later, we would not have restraint. Later, we would be like tigers to each other.

I would not be gentle with her—I'd take her like a beast.

In her enjoyment of it, she would be loud—like a feral bitch.

All of this was said in our gaze.

Then, there was some light shuffling of branches, and I returned my gaze to the tigers, having been taken out of my shared trance with Cassie.

They were leaving, mother at the front of the line, carrying the dripping carcass. The cubs followed dutifully, trying to get at the carcass like the mother was holding it for their play.

Danial whispered into the walkie-talkie, quiet, like a fly buzzing in the distance, "Harry."

"What?" I responded without anger or malice.

"They're leaving."

I closed my eyes briefly, calming myself. How could somebody be so keen on their immediate death?

It was time.

I had saved enough money and gained enough contacts. I was going to start a new magazine. *My* magazine. I wouldn't have to deal with any CEOs, any red tape, any silver-spooned little shits. I'd choose my *entire* team, not just some of them.

I'd been planning it for as long as I could remember. It was almost unheard of, a photographer starting his own magazine. Most were content to just take pictures and leave the bureaucracy and the writing and all the business stuff to others while they jacked off in the darkroom.

Not me. I didn't want just a piece of the pie, I wanted the whole damn factory.

I sighed, and spoke into the mic, realizing Cassie's hand was still on my thigh. It felt so natural I hadn't even questioned it.

"That should be enough time," I said into the walkie-talkie. "*Quietly* make your way down the tree and back to the car—and I swear to god, if you make one bit of noise it won't be that tiger you'll be worried about."

With my cameras and equipment securely in our bags, Cassie and I climbed down from our perch. Across the field, Danial jumped down from his.

We converged on our way back to the path we had cut.

"That was wild," he said, loudly and excitedly, despite standing right beside us.

At that, my heart fell to my gut.

Was there something wrong with him? Did he have some kind of mental deficiency?

"Run," I said gravely, with all the severity I could muster. I grabbed Cassie's arm as she leaped into her jolt beside me.

Danial followed.

He was gonna get me fired. If word got out that one of my assistants, and the CEO's son at that, died on my watch, I'd never work again. I'd get blacklisted. All hopes of starting my magazine dashed before my eyes, laid on his chewed-up remains.

I knew, without an inch of guilt, which part of that bothered me more.

But the green Range Rover was several yards away. Jack and Steve leaned on the door, half dozing off. On seeing our urgency, they quickly got inside.

Behind us was a violent roar, seeming louder than thunder. I felt it in my body like a jolt of lighting.

"Get in." I spat, oddly calm as I swung the door open and pushed Cassie in first. Danial got into the middle seat, and I turned to get into the doorway, but the door slammed shut from the force of the beast ramming into me, trapping my hand in the door—a dull pain, mattering nothing compared to the jaws around my neck.

CHAPTER 1

"Are you ok?" It was a woman's voice. Sweet-sounding, full of concern. In my dazed awakeness, I had first mistaken her for Cassie, but *this* girl had a strange old-country accent.

I groaned.

The ground was soft but I still ached. I felt like I had been dropped on my back, but I bore no memory of it. Trying to sit up, a migraine seared across my closed eyes like lightning. I gave up to rest my head against the dirt.

The girl gasped at my movements, and my ears perked at her running away from me. But, she *was* still in my presence.

I frowned at her whimpering.

"I'm ok," I said softly, to not alarm her.

"Good!" she squeaked. "I'm so glad."

I thought at first she was a young girl, judging from her frantic fright, but I had mistaken alarm for youth. *This* voice belonged to a woman.

I don't know what prevented me from opening my eyes. Perhaps it was just a migraine, or perhaps, it was due to the horrific dream I had.

If it was a dream, that meant the decision I made, of finally starting my own company, was untrue. *Well*, that didn't matter. Just because I dreamed I had the balls didn't mean I did not. *Sometimes dreams tell you things, like, if you don't start a company, your head will be torn off by a tiger.*

That old saying.

I was probably off to film the tigers today. I should cancel it, tell that CEO where to stuff it.

I took a deep inhale and breathed out quickly.

The air was clean, fresh, and at the perfect temperature. And yet, due to the heat I had been breathing in the past few days, that was unexpected. I had responded as if it was a toxin, expelling it as fast as I could.

The woman yelped again like a frightened puppy.

My next breath was deep. I took it all in and finally opened my eyes.

The trees flickered sunlight through the leaves. I squinted against the light, struggling to grasp my bearings.

My memories of India weren't false. They couldn't be.

The blistering sweat. The feel of a beautiful young assistant's hand on my thigh. The anger towards the other assistant.

I reached for my neck, and my eyes went wide in alarm. All my hand brushed against was a bristled five o'clock shadow. No bandages, not even teeth marks.

Shaking my head as I sat up, my heavy camera fell from my chest and hung just above my crotch. I laughed at the strap being just short enough not to crush me painfully—having your camera strap be too long was a rookie mistake, one I learned long ago.

Just ahead of me, on the beaten path I had *so wisely* chosen to rest on, was a cart. I couldn't see its contents.

Behind the cart, a pair of trembling knees were being hugged by their owner. Below them were her sensible yet archaic-looking walking shoes. They seemed to be sewn with a thick piece of leather thread, connecting the sole to the rest.

"I won't hurt you," I said to the girl, and my mouth spoke the next words before I had even thought of them, "I appear to have lost my memory. Could you help me?"

I always had a knack for bullshitting my way out of a situation, and what's more, it was not technically a lie.

Her knees in that long skirt stopped shaking slightly, but not entirely, betraying her still rattled nerves. "You need my help," she decided. It wasn't a question.

"Yes. I thought I might ask you a few questions? I seem to be of perfect sense, and yet I can't quite recall where I am."

I was making sure to speak in the most polite and eloquent tone I could muster, to give myself an air of noble birth. If this was a poor part of *wherever I was*, it would suit me to speak above my station. I would get more help if they thought I had money. That had happened to me before, in Sudan on an expedition.

I sat up and crossed my legs. If she thought I would pounce to attack her, she would at least see it would be difficult from my position—sitting as one friend would with another.

"I suppose I can help with that," she said. The knees behind the cart disappeared, and sunny blonde hair bobbed up from the top of the cart. Below her fringe were the brightest blue eyes I had ever seen.

My brow raised in surprise.

I appeared to be in a simple country, where technology was scarce. Girls do not usually walk big carts. Not blonde-haired blue-eyed girls that speak with more of an old-country accent than any English person I had met. They had tractors and cars for that sort of thing.

"You don't have to come out from behind the cart," I said. "Not until you're comfortable. But I promise I won't hurt you. I just want to ask a few questions."

I smiled at her, and she squeaked like a mouse, darting back behind the cart, but then she said, "Ok."

So she did have more sense than fright. Yet she still possessed too much of the latter

"Where am I?" I asked.

"Where are you?" she echoed back at me, making me realize that despite my needing to know, the question was still odd.

"As I said. I don't remember much. One moment I was-" I hesitated. *I should keep my memories close to the bone, at least until I find out more of how I came to be here.* "One moment I was elsewhere. And now I am here. Tell me, what country are we in?"

"This is the country of Queen Isobel," the cart squeaked.

"The country is *called* Queen Isobel?" I rubbed my back, soothing the ache.

"What? No. It's called Faskar," she exclaimed, all panicky.

We weren't getting there fast enough.

"Will you just come out from there!" I found myself accidentally angry, "If I wanted to hurt you I don't think a cart would hold me back."

"I'm so sorry!" she cried.

While I did feel a tinge of guilt at yelling at the poor girl, I was in far greater need than she was. I had a much higher cause for worry and lost patience with her timidness.

"Come sit," I softened my voice to sound less threatening.

She stood up and appeared over the cart, seeming to deal with direct commands easier than questions.

Upon seeing her fully, my eyebrows shot to the sky.

It *had* been wrong to think of her as a girl. A full-grown woman with the temperament of a mouse is still a woman. The simple servant dress she wore, despite its many layers, attested to that, in the revealing of her ample, yet slender figure.

The only word that seemed appropriate was *pretty*. A girlish word, and yet to call her *sexy* or *hot* was in direct conflict with her clear innocence and temperament—not to mention all those layers she wore.

Never had there been a more obvious possession of maidenhood.

"What is your name?" I asked her.

"Phoebe, sir."

She couldn't meet my eyes, but that didn't stop me from watching her. She daintily stepped over, pulling up her dress so that its length didn't trip her up. Dirt rimmed the edges of it, suggesting she had walked quite the distance. It was a highly inappropriate length for a walking dress. But to wear less must not be appropriate in this world.

World—was I on another planet? The country she mentioned did not exist, not in my memory.

"And what continent are we on?" I asked casually, hiding my own panic.

I looked up at the sky.

The sun was just a regular ol' sun. I would have been fooled into thinking it was the same one back home.

"Umora," she said, lifting her dress to allow herself to sit down.

Her bare ankles and calves became revealed, and she

gasped and sat down, quickly covering them up with her dress.

This was a highly puritan society, like middle-aged Earth.

I suppose I should have been panicked, *even* frightened. Everything I had ever known was gone from me. But this shy, bashful woman made all my leader instincts kick in. *I could be frightened later, right now I had to act befitting my status.*

What status? I had none, I was nobody's boss.

"What lies beyond the continent?" I asked.

"Far away lands, sir," she said, then her lips tightened, but they were no less full and pink.

I frowned. "You don't have to call me sir. Call me Harry."

"Yes, si-Harry."

I sighed. "I'm going to be honest with you, Phoebe." I looked at her blue eyes, her mouth opened slightly. She kept a focus on me, eager to hear what I would say. "I don't know anything about where I am—this society, the roles that befit a man and woman. Technology. *Nothing*. I know that's a lot to lay on you, but I need your help. If I asked you a few questions, would you mind answering them? I'm sure there's some way I could pay you back." *Think chivalry.* "I would happily push that cart for you if you walked by my side and answered my questions. How does that sound? As you can see, I have no weapons. And if it would make you feel safer, you may walk behind me."

Her lips met momentarily, and then her eyes darted to the camera hung around my neck and she asked, "What is that?"

I looked down at the camera. On it would be proof of my life—and yet, how on Earth would I get the pictures off it?

Ha. That saying doesn't even make sense now. *How on Umora...*

"This? This is just a camera, it takes a snapshot of a moment and captures it forever."

Phoebe's mouth opened wide, her already-big eyes grew wider. She screamed 'Witchcraft!' and jumped up out of fright.

Then she stumbled over her ridiculous dress. Her knee held down the material while she tried to get back up. Her dress pulled tightly over her behind. I felt only *mildly* guilty for storing a mental image of her body, filling in the gaps I hadn't seen.

I got hard.

It was a good thing I was sitting down and she was behind the cart, otherwise, who knows how terrified she would be if she had seen my lap.

I thought I was being smart when talking of my camera, I thought I was wowing her, and her curiosity would override her apprehension. I forgot where I was. It was stupid. I should have known better.

"Stay back, Witch!" The cart screamed, "If you touch me, Anja will strike you down!"

AFTERWORD

Every few days I upload a *fully edited* chapter of this story to my **Patreon.** If you want to read it first before it hits Amazon, click the link below! You'll also get to see the more *revealing* cover artwork, as well as some other benefits, like voting on girl types:

https://www.patreon.com/kirkmason

Don't want to join my Patreon? Then come on over to my free **Discord,** where I hang out all the time:

https://discord.gg/GDN7dnwF9p

If you just wanna know when my next book comes out, join my **mailing list:**

shorturl.at/nuGIO

Also, I have a **Facebook** group:

www.facebook.com/groups/kirkmasonland/

ABOUT THE AUTHOR

Thank you so much for reading my story! It was written by a regular guy in his thirties, paying rent by tapping on a keyboard.

When I'm not writing, I enjoy watching tv shows like Firefly, Steins Gate, and Game of Thrones (*most* of the seasons). I jog to keep fit, and then ruin it at night by drinking Guinness.

I fell in love with the harem genre for the way it lets men be men, leaving behind the worries and responsibilities of their life to experience something crazy and out of this world.

But then again, sometimes it's enough just to chill out on the farm with your harem—because real life can be hectic, and you need to get a little cozy.

Whatever the story, a review can make or break its success, especially at the beginning of its launch. That's why I'm asking you, if you enjoyed it, to leave a five-star review so that others can too. *And please try to avoid mentioning spoilers. :)*

Want to report a typo, or just need to reach me?
Kirkmasonbooks@gmail.com